A CONFUSING QUARTET

In the competition for Chloe Rothwell's hand, four contenders had forged out ahead of the pack.

There was Lord Francis Hensley, whose polished manners and high connections almost covered up the vast vacancy of his mind.

There was Thaddeus Invers, whose wit and wisdom were stolen only from the very best authors.

There was Julian Stoddard, famous for his success both at the gaming table and in the boudoir.

And last but hardly least, there was Sir Richard Davanant, who was far too good a friend for Chloe to consider turning into a lover.

All four were in a race against each other to win Chloe—and Chloe was in a race against time to make up her mind . . . and her heart. . . .

The Dutiful Daughter

SIGNET Regency Romances You'll Enjoy

- [ ] **THE LONELY EARL** by Vanessa Gray. (#J7922—$1.75)
- [ ] **THE WICKED GUARDIAN** by Vanessa Gray. (#E8390—$1.75)
- [ ] **THE WAYWARD GOVERNESS** by Vanessa Gray. (#E8696—$1.75)*
- [ ] **THE GOLDEN SONG BIRD** by Sheila Walsh. (#E8155—$1.75)†
- [ ] **LORD GILMORE'S BRIDE** by Sheila Walsh. (#E8600—$1.75)*
- [ ] **THE SERGEANT MAJOR'S DAUGHTER** by Sheila Walsh. (#E8220—$1.75)
- [ ] **THE REBEL BRIDE** by Catherine Coulter. (#E8951—$1.75)*
- [ ] **THE AUTUMN COUNTESS** by Catherine Coulter. (#E8463—$1.75)*
- [ ] **LORD RIVINGTON'S LADY** by Eileen Jackson. (#W7612—$1.50)
- [ ] **BORROWED PLUMES** by Roseleen Milne. (#E8113—$1.75)†
- [ ] **THE SMUGGLER'S DAUGHTER** by Sandra Heath. (#E8816—$1.75)*
- [ ] **THE CORMAC LEGEND** by Dorothy Daniels. (#J8655—$1.95)*
- [ ] **NIGHT SHADOW** by Dorothy Daniels. (#E8763—$1.75)*
- [ ] **THE MONTAGUE SCANDAL** by Judith Harkness. (#E8922—$1.75)*
- [ ] **GWENDOLEN** by Clare Darcy. (#J8847—$1.95)*

* Price slightly higher in Canada

† Not available in Canada

The Dutiful Daughter

Vanessa Gray

A SIGNET BOOK
NEW AMERICAN LIBRARY
TIMES MIRROR

NAL BOOKS ARE ALSO AVAILABLE AT DISCOUNTS IN BULK
QUANTITY FOR INDUSTRIAL OR SALES-PROMOTIONAL USE.
FOR DETAILS, WRITE TO PREMIUM MARKETING DIVISION,
NEW AMERICAN LIBRARY, INC., 1633 BROADWAY,
NEW YORK, NEW YORK 10019.

SIGNET, SIGNET CLASSICS, MENTOR, PLUME AND MERIDIAN BOOKS
are published by The New American Library, Inc.,
1633 Broadway, New York, New York 10019

First Printing, January, 1980

1 2 3 4 5 6 7 8 9

PRINTED IN THE UNITED STATES OF AMERICA

The Dutiful Daughter

1

Lord Edward Rothwell, fifth baron of the honor of Rothwell, sat in his late father's morocco leather chair in the book room, contemplating his immediate prospects with satisfaction, if not pleasure.

He had reached the mature age of twenty only last month. In the five years since he had succeeded to the title he had nearly paid off his father debts, and in two years from now he could underwrite his sister Lydia's Season in London.

He frowned. Lydia was entirely too eager at seventeen for her introduction to London society. He had said, only last month, two years, and he would stick to it. He had all the stubbornness of a weak character. Lydia might weep, cajole, defy—but he was the head of the family, and Lydia must obey him.

His glance stole to the box of books newly arrived from his booksellers in London. Probably more than half would have to be returned as unfit for the eyes of the ladies of his family. If there was another epic poem by that romantic fool Scott . . . !

He looked forward to this afternoon when he would, at his leisure, open the box and delve into its contents. A duty, after all, but a pleasant one.

He reflected upon his family. His mother, Lady Rothwell, was entirely too partial to his youngest sister Sophy. Lydia was often scanted, but it did not occur to Edward to rectify injustice where he saw it. As a matter of instinctive reasoning, from Lydia's slights he turned naturally to Chloe.

A faint smile crossed his plump face. Dear Chloe—his half-sister, more like the Bradfords, her late mother's people, than the Rothwells. Too bad she had never had her chance in London's marriage mart. She had barely arrived in town to stay with Lady Rothwell's sister, five

1

years ago, when their father died unexpectedly. Chloe had, of course, hastened home, and somehow she had never gone back. He could now be grateful that her small income, from the first Lady Rothwell's dowry, had been added to the funds he needed to restore the family income without stinting on necessities. Thank God his mother had not had to suffer.

His thoughts dwelt fondly upon Chloe, a little long in the tooth now for marriage. At twenty-four, she had a year to go before putting on her spinster's cap. She seemed content here. His mother let her have her way in running the house. Edward could congratulate himself on his untroubled life.

Enough self-indulgence, he decided, and turned to his unopened letters. One, addressed to Miss Chloe Rothwell, bore the imprint of a firm of London attorneys, a name he knew only slightly. He opened it, and perused the contents—and his tidy world reeled before his bulging eyes.

Shortly before that fateful moment, the object of Edward's fond thoughts lay upstairs in her bed. Chloe Rothwell opened her eyes reluctantly, and closed them again against the bright June sunlight streaming through the suddenly opened curtains.

"Bess!" she protested.

Bess turned from the windows and approached her mistress's bedside. "Thought you wouldn't like to be late to breakfast, Miss Chloe," said Bess, "seeing that her Ladyship is already down."

Upon that news, Chloe's eyes flew open. With one sweep of her hand she laid the bedclothes back. Accepting a dish of hot tea, she cried, "Oh Bess! What time is it? She will not be pleased with me."

Bess, made brave by her twenty-four years' service to Chloe Rothwell, muttered, "She'd be late too if she'd been up all night with Cook, moaning and groaning with toothache!"

Chloe prudently ignored her maid's words, and asked, "How *is* Cook this morning? She was sleeping when I left her." She set down her empty cup.

"Only a couple of hours since," Bess pointed out, holding out a snowy chemise and deftly dropping it over Chloe's head. "Still dead to the world, so Field says."

In a few minutes, dressed decently if not with great care, Chloe hurried downstairs to the breakfast room. As

Bess had gloomily told her, Lady Rothwell was halfway through her enormous breakfast. When Chloe entered the room, Lady Rothwell lifted her eyes once, and then returned them to her plate.

"There you are, Chloe. I must say I thought you would have more respect for me than to appear so late at breakfast. No regard for my feelings, but then, you young people always think only of yourselves."

Since this was not an original thought with Lady Rothwell, and since Chloe had heard it often enough before, she paid little heed to it. Immediately, Field was at her side with the silver coffee pot. Prevented by the presence of Lady Rothwell, he could express his gratitude to Chloe for her night watch with his wife, the cook, only by assiduous attention to her needs. Her plate was piled high with ham and scrambled eggs and her coffee cup was filled to the brim.

Usually Chloe's perceptions were blunted, from long familiarity with the other members of her family. But lack of sleep, perhaps, had honed her senses to a fine, sharp edge, and she looked at them now as if they were strangers.

Chloe's half-sister Lydia stared into space, and Chloe could guess that her thoughts were entirely upon London. Lydia had the fixed idea that when she arrived in London she would enter a new life, being miraculously transformed into another creature, a gossamer being with fabulous social graces. Her fancy spread itself to encompass balls, routs, and myriads of faceless suitors.

It could not be claimed that printed romances had addled Lydia's brain. Edward's careful scrutiny of the books that entered the house was proof against what he called morbid fancies of romantic writers. Lydia's own imagination was fueled by her dissatisfaction with her life as it was and the belief that London held the pot of gold at the end of her rainbow. She had not even, so she thought, begun to climb the rainbow.

Although Lydia was at an age when most girls were planning the next year to be in London, she was unfortunate in that the Rothwell fortunes had struck a low ebb. While Edward was congratulating himself at this moment in his book room on bringing them all out of the River Tick without disaster, Lydia's prospect of staying at home for two miserable years chafed her unbearably.

Her younger sister, Sophy, sitting opposite at the table, was a replica of Lady Rothwell when young. Sophy at thirteen was already lumpish. For Lady Rothwell, the years had turned her juvenile plumpness into grossness and she now filled the armchair with her bulk. Sophy's pudding face concealed the curiosity and intellect of her father, but she lacked his great charm and kindliness. Sophy was no longer under the care of a governess. Finding her life at Rothwell Manor somewhat confined in scope, she sought with every means at her disposal to augment its liveliness. She was often found listening outside doors, and no drawer was safe from her. Chloe's insight lasted only a few moments, but it was enough to unsettle her. I'm sickening for something, she told herself. Lack of sleep, that was all. These were her family, and she loved them dearly.

"The eggs are hard," complained Lady Rothwell. She ignored the fact that this was her third helping. "Chloe, I wish you will speak to Cook about this. She is getting careless."

"I must tell you, Mama, that Cook is suffering badly from the toothache and is in bed," said Chloe.

"Well," said Lady Rothwell, "I suppose I must not blame her for the eggs. I hope I am too well bred to chide a servant for what is not her fault. But—" she pushed her plate away—"my appetite is totally gone. I cannot abide ill-dressed meals."

Indicating to Field that she wished her cup refilled, Lady Rothwell turned to her mail. "At last, a letter from Sister Hensley. I have been wondering what is going on in London this long time. It has been more than a week since I have heard from her. Such a thick letter. It will probably take me most of the day to read it."

Lady Rothwell's sister, Mrs. Hensley, had welcomed Chloe to London for two weeks, five years ago. She was a kindly woman, yet an inveterate gossip, and managed to gather all the tidbits that rumor cast around the city. The truth of them, as Mrs. Hensley would have been the first to admit, could not always be counted upon, but then, the truth would always come out in the end, wouldn't it?

This letter was full of the doings of her son, Francis. Francis, whose breeding and manners were impeccable, had spent the Wednesday night at Almack's. He had also been one of a party that had played cards at the Prince Regent's—and Mrs. Hensley took this as a feather in her own cap, even though there had been more than a hundred at Clarence House.

Chloe's mind wandered, but was jerked back to earth by Sophy's saying, "Francis isn't very bright, is he?"

Lady Rothwell said, oppressively, "Francis has sufficient intellect for his station. I wish his father had left him a greater fortune." Her voice faded away, and then she picked up the letter again. "Here is something! Sir Richard Davenant—returned from the Continent already."

Chloe felt a queer tightening in her chest. Sir Richard Davenant was their nearest neighbor. In earlier days, Chloe had considered Richard her best friend. An only child, Richard had been a lonely boy and found his companionship in Chloe, only four years younger. Since her brother, Edward, was still in leading strings, Chloe and Richard had been great comrades. But the time had come when Richard's life took a different turn, and he had gone away to further his education. When Chloe had made her brief appearance in London, Richard, in Italy, had not been at hand to help her through difficult days.

It was strange, she thought, that she could now not remember his features. What shape was his nose? What kind of eyebrows? She remembered his eyes were blue, but she could summon recollection no farther.

She had missed him so sorely, when he first left Davenant Hall, that she had deliberately put him out of her mind. It was at about that time that Lady Rothwell turned over the running of Rothwell Manor to Chloe and she had sufficient on her mind to thrust Sir Richard out to the fringes of her consciousness. But here he was in Mrs. Hensley's letter, back in London, and Chloe could not explain her sudden shortness of breath.

Lydia felt no such restriction. Almost bouncing in her chair, she cried, "Do you suppose he'll come home? He hasn't been at Davenant Hall for years! What do you think he's going to do next?"

Sophy said, "What difference will it make to you?"

Lydia said, "Such a deal of entertainment he'll be obliged to make. We certainly will count on invitations, and it will be nearly as good as London!"

Sophy jeered. "Already you're dreaming of becoming Lady Davenant! No chance of that!"

Lydia pouted, "He's not married yet, or we would have

heard about it. So he must not have met anyone yet that he likes."

Then, realizing how much she had given away of her inner thoughts, Lydia blushed furiously and sank into silence.

Lady Rothwell ignored the squabble between her two children. Taking up her sister's letter again, she informed her family, "Davenant is said to be hanging out for a rich wife."

Sophy inserted neatly, "That lets you out, Lydia."

Lady Rothwell looked reprovingly at Sophy. "There is no need to be vulgar, Sophy. Sir Richard has all the money he wants, and he does not need to hang out for a rich wife." She turned back to her letter. "Lady Theale says—you remember, Lady Theale is Sir Richard's cousin—that he is about to offer for Thalassa Morland. No, it's Thalassa Morland or Penelope Salton or Eugenia Folkes. My goodness, he has a choice, doesn't he! I don't believe I know these ladies, although the names are familiar. Thalassa Morland must be old Lord Morland's daughter, and her mother is—"

Lady Rothwell descended into the tangled web of genealogy. Being of only ordinary good breeding herself, she had made it her business to follow the convolutions of marriages and connections throughout the upper stratum of society. Finally Sophy, impatiently, extricated her mother from the morass. "Doesn't Aunt Hensley say which lady he is offering for?"

Lady Rothwell addressed herself once again to the subject. "No, but the betting is high on which of the three he will offer for. The rumor is that he will within the week make his choice known."

Sophy crowed, "Doesn't sound as though he's waiting for you, Lydia. He's not even coming here!"

Lady Rothwell ignored the interruption and read on. "He is coming down to Davenant Hall, according to this. He may even be here already!"

Finally, Lady Rothwell, knowing well where her best interest lay, noticed that Chloe was not eating.

"Chloe, are you ill?"

Chloe shook her head. Lady Rothwell sighed in relief. "With Cook sick, I vow I could not bear it if you were to fall ill, too, for that would be a tragedy. I doubt whether Field could run the household."

Chloe was brought back to earth by her stepmother's injunction. She had been overset at hearing Richard's name. What would he be like now? Was he really coming down to Davenant Hall? She felt that she could not wait to see him, and at the next moment that she could not bear to see him again.

If he were going to offer for one of the ladies of London, then it was quite likely he would not come down to the Hall for any reason except to put it in order for his wife. Somehow, she had never thought of Richard with a wife. He was still, in her mind, the companion with whom she had explored the brook that ran through their lands, ranged forest and meadow, the playmate who had played Crusader with her, the friend who had always understood her childish complaints.

But Richard with a wife! That was something she could not quite believe in. Yet Lady Theale had always been in her cousin's confidence, and if she said he was about to marry, then it had to be the truth.

By this time, in the book room, Edward had had time to compose himself. He had read the letter from the attorneys twice, and then set it aside while he dealt with the other mail. If he ignored the letter, perhaps the news therein might go away. At length, knowing he could delay no longer, he picked up the mail and marched to the door. Unconsciously he stopped and squared his plump shoulders in a vague attempt to fortify himself. And yet, he reflected as he walked across the foyer to the morning room, this was nothing but good news. It might mean a change in his life, but basically Edward was not selfish and—as soon as he got used to the idea—would rejoice at Chloe's good fortune.

When he entered the morning room, his mother hailed him with the news that filled her mind. "Sir Richard is home at last, and Sister Hensley says he may even now be at Davenant Hall. I vow, it will be pleasant to have a man of such high fashion living near to us. I am sure he will fill the house with company—after he marries, of course— and it will do Lydia and Sophy no harm to have a man of such elegance closely identified with their interest!"

Edward dared not trust himself to answer. His own mind was filled with the letter about Chloe's affairs and he parceled out the magazines to the rest of the family with less than his usual comment. "Here's your magazine,

Lydia," he said, omitting for once his strictures on the foolishness of the fashions and the stupidity of women who tried to keep up with them.

He also ignored Lydia's routine response, "I wish I could see the magazine first."

Lady Rothwell took him to task. "Edward, I don't think you heard a word I said. What do you think of Sir Richard's coming home at last? We must go over and call on him at the first opportunity. And congratulate him on his marriage."

Edward roused himself enough to say, "Marriage? Old Davenant marrying? I thought he must have given up the idea."

Sophy, glancing across the table at her sister Lydia, said, with malice, "If you expect to catch Sir Richard, you'll have to be up to the crack of fashion, for he is used to the best, you know."

Edward, roused to the sense of his responsibility, interrupted. "Lydia, I hope you do not consider that every fashion in that magazine is yours for the asking, Sir Richard or no Sir Richard. There is not enough money on hand to indulge your extravagant tastes. We are not poor, but we are far from plump in the pocket. If you had your way, all our income would be on your back. That is poor food for breakfast."

Chloe, rightly ignoring the routine wrangling among the two sisters and Edward's futile attempt at setting them straight, eyed the head of her family with a certain uneasiness. Edward wore an air that she could only describe as one of suppressed excitement. It was hard for her to believe that he was only twenty. He seemed almost old enough to be her father. It was too bad, she reflected, not for the first time, that their father had died so untimely a death. Edward had been elevated to responsibilities he was not ready for. The result had been a sad settling of his character into channels of rectitude and humorless duty. Had her father lived, however, it was possible that Edward would have still become the sober patriarch he now appeared to be. He would have come to it, later rather than sooner.

Edward's air of excitement was now so palpable that Chloe was moved to comment upon it. "What is it, Edward? Have we all been sold to the bailiffs?"

Edward turned. "Strange that you should say that,

Chloe, although I must once again deplore your mischievous sense of humor." He held the letter in his hand, tapping it against his open palm. Waiting until all eyes were on him, and clearly enjoying his sense of importance, he said, "Chloe, here is a letter from some attorneys in London. It is addressed to you."

She reached out her hand for it. He appeared not to see her gesture. "I must say," he added, "it is a surprise to me. I had no idea——"

Chloe took a firm stand. Interrupting him with decisiveness, she said, "Edward, let me have my letter." Obediently he handed it over. She saw the seal was broken, and said, with a near approach to crossness, "Edward, you've read my mail. I do wish you could restrain yourself."

She was immediately sorry, for a wounded look passed across his face. She opened the letter and read its contents. Edward was saying, as she read, "As your trustee, I thought that it was my duty to see what the attorneys had to say."

She finished the letter and started again at the beginning. Edward, unable to wait any longer, informed the rest of the family of her surprise. "Chloe has received a legacy," he said with as much importance as though he himself had been able to gain it for her. "From her great uncle, on her mother's side. Mama, you remember old Bradford."

"Bradford!" exclaimed his mother. "I thought he was dead long ago."

Sophy, fastening upon the one point of interest, cried out, "A legacy? How much?"

"Old Bradford has left Highmoor—his property—to his niece Chloe. No other family left, so it seems. An attractive country residence, I dare say—quite a windfall for her!" he beamed.

In the meantime, Chloe, dropping the letter to the table, stared into space, totally stunned. The one word she could say, and that hardly above a whisper, was "Highmoor." It was like a dream, and she shook her head, thinking she had slept too late and perhaps had even taken some of Cook's laudanum.

She looked pitifully at Edward and said, "Is this real? Is it a cruel hoax?"

Edward smiled benignly, and said as a kindly godfather might, "Highmoor. I remember hearing the house has a pleasant prospect. The old man was something of a miser, wasn't he?"

Chloe shook her head in bewilderment. "I really don't remember him. Once my mother took me to Highmoor to visit. I couldn't have been more than two, and all I remember is a vast beard and a brocade waistcoat." Her voice trailed away and then she abruptly recalled, "And a great white wig!"

Lady Rothwell said, to no one in particular, "I must say, I was glad when powdered wigs went out of fashion. A nasty habit, I always thought, shedding over everything."

Little by little the news sank into the thoughts of each Rothwell. Even Lady Rothwell's ruminations turned inward. While a spectator might have assumed that her thoughts revolved entirely about herself, he would have been wrong. Lady Rothwell had a strong sense of family. To see her children advance upward on the ladder of society was her dearest wish.

While she had long since become accustomed to thinking of Chloe as her daughter, yet the early days, when Chloe was only a pixie-faced child without a mother, still lay strong among Lady Rothwell's secret thoughts. She could remember the pangs she felt when Lord Rothwell enjoyed playing with his daughter, and Lady Rothwell herself had hastened to present him with an heir. But while she would have defended her feeling for Chloe as being all that a maternal feeling should be, her reaction to Chloe's legacy was tinged with certain other less sterling considerations. Foremost among her considerations was that Chloe's legacy must not escape the family coffers to repose in someone else's strongbox.

Chloe cried, "I can't take it in! I don't think I'll really believe that Highmoor is mine until I see it. Edward, when can I go? How far is it? May I have the coach?"

Chloe felt that until she held the legacy in her hands she would not quite believe it. Her fancy allowed her to walk through dimly remembered halls, to gaze upon furnishings that she did not remember, and yet ringing through her mind was the cry, "It's mine! I have a place of my own!"

Edward turned serious. "I am sorry to tell you, sister, that I don't believe it is wise just now."

Hopes dashed, Chloe protested. "Whyever not?"

"Well, for one thing, it is too far away. It would take a

two-day trip, for we could not go and come back in a day. I doubt that the house is habitable just yet, for after all, old Bradford was sick a long time before he stuck his spoon in the wall."

Chloe had to admit the force of all these arguments, but it did not make her happier. This was not the first time that her wishes had been thwarted, nor would it be the last. But yet, this disappointment ranked higher than all the rest. To be kept away from something that was her very own, was outside of enough.

Lady Rothwell was cudgeling her memory, also, and now produced the results. "I remember having heard about Highmoor," she began, "although I never had the privilege of visiting there. Lord Bradford was not what one might call an expansive host. Now that I think about it, I don't remember anyone who ever had been there. But I understood it was a handsome place, with a fine prospect." She turned thoughtful for a moment and then added, "I have always heard it said that it had very fine grapes. Francis is very fond of grapes."

She fell silent, and Edward flashed her a puzzled look. He was not sure what his mother had in mind, and like most men, uncertain of their womenfolk, eyed any deviation from the norm with suspicion.

Lydia jumped up from her chair and cried out, "Chloe, I am so happy! Just fancy! You have your own place now! Too bad it isn't a house in town, for we would all go to London and we would have such a fine time!"

Sophy, averse to being left out, said, "Where is this place, Chloe? Is there pots of money?"

Suddenly Chloe became too overset to answer questions hurled at her head like so many buzzing bees. Later she realized that there was no need to worry about answering the questions, for Lydia and her mother had taken it upon themselves to discuss the fine prospect of traveling to London, if only Chloe's house had been on Belgrave Square.

"But perhaps there is a chance of renting a house," suggested Lady Rothwell. "We could stay with my sister Hensley while we looked about for just what would suit me—I mean Chloe."

Making an excuse, Chloe hurried out of the room. She got as far as the foyer before she could not restrain the tears any longer. Edward came upon her thus, sobbing, and was immediately touched. Patting her shoulder awk-

wardly, he soothed her with words that were wide of the
mark. "Now then, Chloe, it's not that bad. You'll never
have to leave Rothwell Manor. Nobody's sending you
away or even sending you to London. As a matter of fact,
I don't know what you'd do in London now."

Chloe, recognizing his sincere need to help, managed a
watery smile and said, "You mean I'm past enjoying myself in London? Well, Edward, perhaps you're right."

Edward, covered with confusion, attempted to make the
situation better. "You are so much valued at Rothwell,
truly I cannot imagine how we would get along without
you." He continued in this vein for some moments, not realizing that he sounded very much as though he were giving a testimonial to a valued servant.

At last she wiped her eyes and said, "What a fool I am!
Imagine weeping over good news!"

Edward decided the time had come. He needed to make
his own position quite clear, and he said, turning her
gently, "Come into the library with me. We have much to
talk about."

2

Alone in the library, the door closed behind them, Edward
suddenly found himself without words. Chloe sat in a
chair near the desk and thought of small things, for she
could not quite realize yet the big thing.

She noticed the box of books standing in the middle of
the floor, awaiting the pry bar that would open the
wooden crate, the desk where her father had sat so many
times, and the shelves lined with books of a previous age.
Edward was not a collector and felt himself out of step
with the present literary age. Chloe had only pleasant
memories of this room, for her father had rarely scolded
her.

Edward found his voice. "There is no need for me to
tell you how happy I am for you," he began. "It has al-

ways been a source of regret for me that our father left no provision for any of his daughters. Had it not been for your mother's dowry, there would be little enough for you."

"My mother's trust?" Chloe asked.

Edward said, heavily, "Your trust has prospered under my management, and the income has improved. It is a small enough amount, but I don't try to conceal from you, a welcome addition to the family funds, and I appreciate your unselfishness in turning the income over to me. For the family, of course. But now, with this legacy——"

He left the words dangling in the air. Chloe felt herself required to answer, but all she could say was a plaintive, "What shall I do, Edward?"

He smiled approvingly. "I knew you would deal with this good fortune in a sensible, down-to-earth way. I must look into this for you. I hardly know where to start, but first I will write a letter to the attorneys. On your behalf, of course."

Chloe's thoughts circled like a hound trying to pick up the trail and come once again to the point. "Why may I not go to Highmoor?"

Edward allowed a nettled expression to cross his face. "I explained that to you, Chloe," he said. "It would be a most rash proceeding. We do not know what condition the house is in, we do not know what servants would be available, we cannot simply hare across country like a break-neck rider after a fox." He was pleased with this rare flight of fancy. He went on, in a more serious vein. "I shall let you know what is best to be done. I will need, of course, your power of attorney, as you have already given it to me in the matter of your mother's trust."

Surprisingly, Chloe hesitated. "I do not think I am ready——" Then, seeing the look of hurt cross his features, she amended her remark. "Did the lawyers' letter say that Highmoor was entirely mine?"

"Yes," said Edward, "you read it."

"I should like to look into my legacy myself." She was nearly as astonished as Edward to hear such rebellious words issuing from her lips. Like a cautious swimmer testing the water and finding it too cold, she drew back. "All right, Edward, whatever you say. But—why did you open my mail?"

He looked surprised. "I always do," he told her. "I am responsible for everyone under my roof."

Then, possessed of a need to convince her, he pulled from a drawer a fat folio containing the records of the trust account left to Chloe by her mother. More to appease him than because she wished to know, Chloe began to peruse the balance sheets. Her rebellion was already gone, and good riddance, she thought, for it was an uncomfortable feeling. While she was looking over the trust accounts, he was busy with pen and paper making out a power of attorney.

Chloe had no head for figures, but it was clear from following through the simple columns of figures that Edward was telling the truth when he said he had kept her money intact for her. She had not expected otherwise. She said as much to him. With appropriate expressions of gratitude, she succeeded in smoothing his ruffled feathers.

Chloe signed the document. Handing it back to him, she said, "I know this is just a formality, Edward, for you always do what is best for us. I believe I have not thanked you sufficiently for your care of the small amount my mother left me, but you know I am grateful."

The door opened suddenly and Lydia burst into the room. Edward chided, "We are engaged in business matters, Lydia. Have you no sense?"

Lydia, always ready to wrangle with her brother, chose not to this time. Instead, she hurried across to Chloe and cried, "Chloe, I can't wait to talk to you! What are you going to do with your fortune? Won't we have fun spending the money? What will you do first? I know you won't want to go to London until later this summer, but we'll be in good time for the Little Season, and they say London is beautiful in the autumn."

She prattled on, but Edward cut across her chatter with a heavy warning. "We do not know yet how big this fortune is."

Lydia turned and, with supreme disregard for logic, cried, "The attorneys wrote, didn't they? They don't do that for just nothing, do they? Edward, you're so fuddy!"

Turning back to Chloe, she coaxed, "Come on and let's talk about this. I vow, I have nothing else in my mind!"

She tugged at Chloe's wrist and pulled her up. Edward, seeing the conversation getting away from him, began to remonstrate with Lydia. It was not long before the two were engaged in a fruitless wrangle. Chloe, to her own surprise, was conscious of a wish to have her own fortune to herself, for just a little bit. She had never had such great news, and she needed to have time to think what it meant.

Feeling herself greatly daring, she slipped out of the room. Neither one of the two combatants saw her go.

Chloe's attempt to escape proved unsuccessful at first. Lady Rothwell had been lurking in the hall, waiting for Chloe to emerge from Edward's book room. She had quelled Field with a glance, and caused him to remember urgent business elsewhere. Upon catching sight of Chloe, she cried, "Ah, there you are, Chloe! I think I failed to tell you how shocked I am by this news, shocked in a perfectly delightful way, of course! How rare it is that any good fortune comes to us! I vow that in my late husband's time, life was much more exciting. You must excuse us, Chloe, if we make overmuch of this! I am sure that any amount of good fortune will not change your disposition in the least. And you will have me to help you. If I notice that your behavior reflects an immodest sense of gloating, of what I may call an unbecoming attitude of authority, simply because you have fallen heir to a fortune, through no virtue of your own, I shall be glad to point out any lapses on your part. You are my dear daughter, you know, and I feel your interests are so close to my heart that whatever I do will be understood in the best light. Although I do not anticipate that you will for a moment forget your duty."

Chloe, in her turn as speechless as Edward had been, scarcely knew what to say. In the end, Chloe managed to escape by the fortunate recollection that she must inquire about Cook's tooth.

"By all means," encouraged Lady Rothwell. "I cannot understand what has happened to the lower orders. They think nothing of inconveniencing the entire household with an illness of their own. I should not dream of inconveniencing everyone simply because my tooth gave a twinge now and then."

Chloe, her mind recalling Cook's face swollen to twice its normal size, forbore to answer. With a quick excuse, she slipped out of the foyer and disappeared behind the stairs into the kitchen wing.

Cook was in the kitchen, her head tied up in a rag, holding a hot poultice on the offending cheek, and mumbling without moving her jaw. With some difficulty Chloe urged her back to bed and straightened out the upset routine in the kitchen. At length, she slipped up the back stairs to her room.

Emerging from the wooden stairs onto the carpeted hallway on the bedroom floor, she hurried soundlessly to her room. Opening the door, she surprised her younger sister standing at the dresser on the far side of the room. Sophy jumped, startled, when Chloe entered. Turning quickly, she said, "I was waiting for you."

Chloe said, dryly, "Not precisely waiting, I think?"

Sophy was not crestfallen in the least. It was obvious that she had been going through Chloe's possessions, and she did not try to hide her activity. "Well," Sophy said, "at least now you'll be able to have some real jewelry. All you've got is your mother's pearls."

"That's all I need."

"Now you can have grand jewels!" Sophy pointed out.

Chloe said, repressively, "Grand jewels would be most unsuitable for a spinster."

"You won't stay unmarried long. Mama says as soon as the news gets out you'll have offers in plenty."

Chloe, laughing, said, "In that case, I won't need any grand jewels. My fortunate husband can furnish them!"

Sophy, enjoying herself as the bearer of gossip, was not to be diverted. "Well, of course, there's no use in having a legacy unless people know it. And how better than to——"

"Drape it all on myself, around my neck?"

Sophy renewed her attack from a different angle. "Well, of course I don't mean that! But as soon as the news gets out, Mama says, you'll have offers in plenty."

This time Sophy succeeded in shocking Chloe. "You mean that your mother says that I have no charm except for whatever money I might have?"

Sophy, at last, was cowed. She had never seen Chloe's gray eyes with such sparks in them, and she slid off her chair. "Mama didn't say that." In a conciliatory tone, she added, "But you must remember, so Mama says, that in your London Season you didn't *take*."

Chloe said, "That's because I had to come home before I got started, because our father died."

Suddenly Chloe realized that she was wrangling with Sophy on what was after all a problematical question on a juvenile level.

Sophy tendered an olive branch, saying, "I didn't mean to hurt your feelings." She sidled around the room and out the door.

Suddenly Chloe realized that she had had too much. The news of the legacy, and all the conversation about it since then, had the same effect as a duck nibbling at watercress—more than she could stand.

The homely comparison somewhat restored Chloe's good humor. The thought of Sophy and Lydia and Edward all with fat ducks' bills nibbling away at her almost made her laugh aloud. This was the flaw in her character, she thought, among many. She had often been reproved for the mischievous sense of humor that came from her mother's people.

She sat down in the chair recently vacated by Sophy and contemplated her recent behavior. Selfish, that's what she was! She wanted to keep her legacy to herself. To consider that her family's good wishes for her flawed the legacy in some way was totally unworthy. Suppose it had been otherwise? Suppose that they had paid no attention to her legacy, and not even asked her what she would do with it? That would be far worse.

Then, of course, followed the thought—what *would* she do with it? She barely remembered Highmoor. She remembered the great uncle with the powdered wig and brocade waistcoat. She had a dim recollection of hot gingerbread, in a vast room that must have been the kitchen. But she had heard only today that the house had a fine prospect, and presumably she could live there. If she did remove to Highmoor, what would she do there? Her family would stay here, and here she was needed. Needed by all from Lady Rothwell down to Cook, and loved by the people she saw every day. What was there more in life that she could want?

Highmoor, while it was pleasant to think of as her own place, yet right now rattled emptily in her thoughts.

There was no point in going over her ideas like a squirrel in a cage. She snatched up her shawl, conscious only of the need to be alone. She paused near Lady Rothwell's sitting room door with the commendable intention of telling her stepmother where she was going, and paused, forming her words in advance. The door to the sitting room was ajar, and Chloe hesitated too long.

Lady Rothwell's voice floated clearly through the air.

"Sophy," said Lady Rothwell fretfully, "don't bother me now. I am writing a letter to Sister Hensley in London, and I wish to get this off today."

Sophy's voice came through also, curiously adult. "I guess you will probably tell Aunt that we are coming to London in time for the Little Season."

Lady Rothwell said, crisply, "That remains to be seen. No, I am not writing my sister about that."

Chloe was rooted to the floor. She could not interrupt, for it would indicate that she had overheard too much, nor could she pull herself away.

Sophy's voice came clear as a bell. "Well then, you're sending for Francis. Is that right?"

Lady Rothwell laughed, but said no more. Chloe, cheeks burning because she had been eavesdropping, fled from the hallway as though she expected either Sophy or Lady Rothwell to come out upon that instant. She hurried down the stairs and out of the house. She paid no heed to where she was going but crossed the broad lawn, seeking with the instinct of a wounded animal the shelter of the forest. In this case the shelter was only a small copse of birch trees at the foot of the lawn, but she was glad to be out of reach of curious eyes.

Her unalloyed joy at having a house of her own, a legacy from her unknown uncle, was tarnished around the edges by Sophy's remarks about suitors flocking to wed not Chloe, but her legacy.

Not only Sophy's cruel words but Edward's, as well, had cut. They had implied that, no matter whether Chloe had stayed for the entire Season in London or not, she would never have attracted a suitable match.

Her thoughts ran in undisciplined channels, the familiar ruts having been left behind long ago. Since the announcement that she now owned Highmoor, it seemed to her as though she had entered a strange country, in which all landmarks had vanished or unaccountably changed shape.

She reached the end of Rothwell land, where Davenant land began. She looked beyond, where the path disappeared into a hedge, reminding herself that this, at least, was real.

She could not from here see the towers of Davenant Hall. Sir Richard was probably just now a very happy man. If his cousin's information was correct, by now Richard would have offered for one of the three ladies he was reported to be hanging after in London. Chloe had no doubt that if Richard offered marriage he would be immediately accepted. She could not imagine any one refusing Richard.

She shivered, and thought she must turn back before it started to rain. Glancing at the sky, however, she saw that no cloud marred the bright blue heavens over her head. The storm raged only in her emotions.

3

Sir Richard Davenant, at that moment was, if not exactly unhappy, yet far from feeling elated. As a matter of fact, his forthcoming marriage existed at the moment only in Dame Rumor's eye. Although many people envied him his choice among at least three of the leading belles of London, yet he had left them all and turned his back on London. This day, he was spending his first day in five years at Davenant Hall.

His factor, having been in Davenant service for many years, was efficient and honest. Richard had no complaints about the management of his estate in his absence. Glancing over figures, ledgers, and plats of the various farms under his ownership, he found everything in order. He dismissed his factor with praise for his endeavors, and wandered through the house.

The Holland covers had been removed, and now Richard could see signs of absentee ownership. There was nothing really wrong with the house or its furnishings. His staff had taken care that moth had not eaten nor dust corrupted. But it seemed as though a film lay over everything. Richard even ran a finger along the top of a marquetry cabinet to prove to himself that there was dust, but his finger left no trace. All in his mind, he reflected sourly. Richard was ordinarily a cheerful person, tolerant and possessed of maturity arising from self-wisdom. He knew he had a tolerable presence, was not ugly, and possessed certain graces. His fortune was ample, though not spectacular. His experience was wide, having spent five years on the Continent diving into untrodden ways as suited his fancy.

He was not a vain man, but a realistic one. He had very little doubt that had he offered for any of the three ladies whose names had been coupled with his, he would have been readily accepted. None of the three was in her first Season, and in fact had been out for two or three years.

As he walked through the corridors of his own house, peering into rooms, spending time in others, part of his mind made note of items wanting attention. The furnishings seemed sterile, without life. His tastes had been changed by his experience abroad, and while the furniture was good and in fine condition, yet much of it did not please him.

He blamed his *malaise* on his surroundings, at coming home and revisiting the scenes of his youth. But yet there was a deeper reason, and he knew it well.

At length he faced it. He had returned to London with the idea that he was of mature years, and must, for the sake of his family name, contract a matrimonial alliance. He had spent only a short time in London, hardly long enough for Mrs. Hensley to write to her sister, and yet his welcome in the salons of the ladies who made London society what it was, was instantaneous and warm.

The entire field of matrimonial eligibles was laid out for his inspection, and he had been unable to make up his mind.

There were three ladies, at the end, who were clearly open to offers. Richard was fully aware that they expected—indeed, all London expected—that he would offer for one or another of them within the next fortnight. But, at the end, he could not bring himself to choose. He told himself that it was simply a matter of making up his mind—and he needed to get away to think. Hence, he gave swift instructions to make Davenant Hall ready for his arrival, and he followed hard upon the heels of the messenger.

Richard was a man of direct action, and he had given much thought to the qualifications he would require. He had seen marriage as a duty, and a project to be accomplished. Yet there was something missing, and he had, in what could only be considered cowardly fashion, left

London and come down to Kent, on the pretense of needing to arrange his thoughts. He was not getting very far with the task.

Summoning Dall, his butler, he informed him that he was going to pay a courtesy call on Lady Rothwell. With a half quizzical smile, he said, "I suppose Lady Rothwell still lives?"

Dall agreed that Lady Rothwell indeed still lived. Lord Rothwell had been gone these five years. That left Miss Chloe Rothwell and the new Lord Rothwell. Strange it was to think of fat Edward, who had followed Chloe and Richard on their cross-country jaunts up the stream to fish, his fat little legs unable to keep up with the others, as Lord Rothwell.

"You said, Miss Rothwell? Miss Chloe Rothwell?" Richard demanded.

"Yes, Sir Richard."

"Then she has not married?"

The butler agreed. Sir Richard turned his winning smile upon his butler and said he would be back for dinner. He started down the drive. He chose to walk when he could, and had not even thought of riding.

Partway down the drive, memory jogged his elbow. He turned abruptly to the right and dove into a path almost hidden by brambles. The old shortcut had grown over, and he found his way hard going. He would have to send one of the men with clippers to clear the path if he were going to travel this way again. Once out of the thicket, however, the way cleared, and he quickened his pace. By the time Chloe had reached the rustic bridge, still out of sight from Richard's view, he was striding on a path that would lead him directly to the bridge. He breathed deeply of the fresh morning air.

It was good to be home again! By the time he had followed the path where it dipped into a valley and began to rise on the far side, he decided he was a fool to leave Davenant Hall again. At the top of the far rise, a small copse held some fine trees. It did not look quite the same as he remembered, and he stopped, puzzled. The trees had thinned themselves and saplings still stood as dead trunks. These too would have to be cleared out. There was much work to do here!

Beyond the copse at the end of the path was a gate, separating Davenant land from Rothwell land. With the familiarity of an old friend, he unlatched the gate and strode through. There should be, he remembered, a stream flowing right here, and a bridge. . . .

The bridge was where he expected it to be, but it had an added ornament. As he drew near, he could see the slender figure leaning on the wooden rail, almost invisible in her gray morning gown, the color of early mist. He would not have seen her had it not been for her buttercup-yellow shawl.

He stopped for a moment, hesitating, wondering whether he would be welcome on Rothwell land after all these years. He was conscious of being an intruder, and yet something in the abject posture of the damsel at the bridge reached him, and he could see that the lady was in obvious distress of mind. Conscious of a rising tumult in his chest, he strode rapidly toward the bridge. The only thought in his mind was to help. But memory, in its subtle way, whispered things in his ear, and although he did not listen, yet he was aware of a meeting which might be— diverting.

He stopped at the edge of the bridge, not to startle her. He spoke then, saying, "Is there anything I can do?"

She was very close to him, so close he could see the woven threads in her shawl, but her face was still hidden. As he spoke, she turned, startled by his approach, and lifted large gray eyes to his face. The appeal in them, naked and distressed, was sufficient to move him strongly. In fact, he thought later, he was moved as by a thunderclap. He recognized her at once.

Richard, strongly exercised, cried out, "Chloe!"

"Richard?" she quavered, and held out both hands in appealing welcome. She found she could not speak. There were too many things to say, and not enough time—nor the right time—to say them.

For him, the years of absence from Davenant Hall, the years of traveling the highways of Europe, and the byways, had fallen away as though they had never been. Even his recent weeks in London, had you asked him, were erased from the tablets of memory. Chloe stood before him, the trusted, dear friend of his childhood, and he knew the source of his restlessness. He had come home— all unknowing, but following a sure instinct—home to Chloe Rothwell.

His first impulse was to share with her his new understanding, as he had long ago shared all his thoughts and dreams. But being the kind of man he was, thinking of others before himself as a matter of course, he managed to keep a rein on his tongue and hold back the words that first occurred to him.

Chloe stood before him, her hands imprisoned in his. She made no attempt to draw away, nor even to hold back the tears that ran freely down her cheeks. She was the most appealing, the most unhappy, the most——

"Richard," she stammered, "you've come home. They said——"

Restraining his first, nearly overpowering impulse to fold her in his arms and bid her weep on his shoulder, he merely tightened his grip on her fingers and said with concern, "What is the matter? Some tragedy? Has Lady Rothwell . . . ?"

"No," Chloe managed at last to say, "it is only my own foolishness. But you're back! And I'm told I must congratulate you!"

It was a measure of Richard's heightened state of mind that he at once took Chloe's congratulations for his own acuteness of perception in seeing that Chloe was the one woman in the world for him. It did not occur to him that Chloe was speaking of his forthcoming marriage to one of the three in London. They had been wiped from his mind as though they had not existed.

He said, "Chloe, you were never foolish, and I refuse to believe that your tears are caused by your own foolishness now. I wish you could confide in me. Can you not see your way clear to do so?" Seeing that she did not respond, but only hung her head and tried to pull her hands away, he coaxed gently, "The way we used to confide in each other?"

But he let loose of her hands and felt suddenly bereft.

He had been too abrupt, he thought, trying to make her confide in him after an absence of five years. She had no reason to believe that he was the same man he had been when he left, and of course he wasn't. But he was taking his fences too fast. To cover the awkward moment, he teased her gently. "Remember all the times that we had together? You may have forgotten, but I have not. I never betrayed your confidence then."

"Nor I yours," faltered Chloe. She was prey to conflicting emotions. On one hand, she wanted to throw herself upon Richard's sturdy chest and tell him everything she was thinking, but he was not the same man he had been. He had been away for so many years, and now he had given his heart, or at least his hand, to someone else. She had no further claim on him, not even the strong claim of childhood friendship.

Richard too was caught up in the spell of remembered past. He said, "Remember the time we invaded the chicken house, and set the hens to sleeping?"

He waited until her remembered mischievous smile with the dimple high on the left cheek appeared, and, thus encouraged, he continued, "We set the chickens to sleeping, tucked their heads under their wings, I remember now, and set them rocking back and forth asleep, when they should have been laying eggs for your father's breakfast."

"It was my idea," she said, gurgling in remembered amusement.

He continued in this vein until he saw that she was quite restored to good humor, and then, losing his taste for a formal call on Lady Rothwell, said, "I think I shall wait to make myself known at Rothwell Manor for a short while, unless you wish me to go back with you now?"

"No!" she said, and then cushioned her sharpness with a smile. "No, I don't."

"Then that's settled," he said. "You need not think I will relate our meeting to anyone else." She thanked him with a glance, and turned to go back to the house. He stayed on the bridge, watching her until she disappeared at the edge of the birches. He was rewarded by seeing her turn just before she vanished from sight, and wave at him.

Thus satisfied, he turned and strolled leisurely back to Davenant Hall. She had not only routed his uneasiness, his dissatisfaction with the world as he saw it, but she had also worked a miracle, so it seemed. For the first time in many days, he began to whistle as he strode through the small woods and across the valley. His mood was unaccountably cheerful, and this time he knew what he wanted.

4

Back at Rothwell Manor, the day was moving forward in its appointed rounds. Cook's tooth was steadily improving, and whether the remedy might have been the oil of cloves that Chloe had applied during the night, or whether it was the threat of a painful trip to the tooth drawer, really made no difference. Cook was in the kitchen, the pastry for dinner that night had its usual lightness, and her husband Field had lost his worried frown.

The day passed, the evening tea tray was brought in, and the Rothwells eventually trooped up to their various bedrooms in good humor. Chloe herself could not have remembered a word that was said.

Her thoughts were, for the first time in years, totally absorbed in herself. She could remember every detail of the flowered waistcoat that Richard wore at their meeting that morning—how elegant he looked, his graceful ways, his careful dress. His figure was stocky, and she knew that Fashion declared a tall, willowy stature was most to be desired. Chloe thought, quite simply, that Fashion was wrong—the ideal would certainly be a square, sturdy pair of shoulders, an air of total competence.

She was sure, in some recess of her heart that, had she told Richard all that was in her heart, he would have remedied all in some way. But, remembering that he was planning to marry someone else, her tongue was tied.

She slept soundly that night, and although she had hoped to dream of Richard, to bring him once more close to her, she did not.

Again, breakfast at Rothwell Manor proceeded without her. Lady Rothwell announced with satisfaction that she expected that her nephew Francis would shortly arrive for a visit. "For you must know that I have sent for him. I am

25

sure he could have no plans that would prevent him from coming—only the ordinary fribbles of entertainment."

Edward said, with a touch of sourness, "We'll have a few days' grace before he arrives, that's a blessing."

Lady Rothwell lifted her eyebrows. "I expect him here tonight, tomorrow at the latest."

Edward protested, "But it takes two days from here to London by post, and I'm sure he's not going to drop every-thing——"

His mother interrupted. "But I sent my letter yesterday morning by messenger. I hope I know that it takes two days, and I did not wish to rely on the mail. I sent a letter to my sister Hensley by special messenger, and I'm sure she would have had it last night."

Lydia said bluntly, "What is *he* coming for? He just stands around and never says anything. He is so dull!"

Lady Rothwell chided her, "Francis is a very elegant man. He can tell you a great many things about how to go on in London. His breeding and his manners are impecca-ble——"

Edward interrupted. "She's right. He is a deadly bore. Besides, Mama, I hope I know my own duty in speaking to you, but I cannot like this. You may be able to fool Lydia, or even Chloe, but you can't fool me. You have a scheme afoot."

Lady Rothwell was indignant. "Scheming! What a de-spicable word to use to your mother, Edward!" Edward looked at her steadily, and she dropped her glance to her plate. "But I cannot reconcile myself to the prospect of Chloe's fortune going out of the family. Chloe is, after all, the daughter of my own dear husband, and her welfare is above all things my great concern. I don't know what I would do without her."

Every one around the table knew that, without Chloe, Lady Rothwell herself would be forced to take over the running of the house. Each had a personal interest in keeping Chloe at hand, but none of them would have put their reason so baldly as Lady Rothwell.

She continued, "I have always said that family money should stay in the family. Francis, my sister's son, has only our interest at heart. I should certainly be pleased to see Chloe and Francis starting out in life together."

Sophy, irrepressible as always, said, "Chloe and Francis and Highmoor."

Lady Rothwell quelled her with a glance. "That's quite enough, young lady."

Edward, protesting, pointed out that Chloe's fortune was not Rothwell money. "She inherited from Bradford, you know, no relation of the Rothwells at all."

Lady Rothwell sidestepped that neatly. "Chloe is a Rothwell, and what is hers is ours, always has been. And of course, what is ours is hers!"

It would have been better, thought Edward silently, if the Rothwells had had more to give Chloe. At the moment it all seemed to be going the other way.

Lydia, under cover of the conversation, turned to her sister Sophy, taking the occasion to point out Sophy's most recent fault. "You're a snoop," whispered Lydia savagely. "I've told you before—stay out of my room!"

Sophy countered with a simple denial. "I never."

Lydia hissed, "You sneaked in and went through my desk. I told you I didn't ever want to see you in my room again. I'm going to ask Mama for a key."

Sophy murmured, "I wonder what you have that is so secret? Something that you wouldn't want Mama to see?"

The conversation, acrimonious as it appeared, did not go unnoticed by their elders. Lydia said, "You read my diary!"

But Sophy was unfortunate enough not to heed the sudden silence, so that her words, though decently muffled, yet rang out like a clarion. "You shouldn't leave your diary open so that I could get at it!"

Lady Rothwell said, "Now, girls! Sophy, do I understand that you've been reading Lydia's diary again? I vow I thought that you knew better than to do such a despicable thing."

The force of her disapproval was lost when she added to Lydia, "I trust you do not write anything in there that your sister may not read. I believe you have been taught not to entertain undesirable thoughts?"

Edward complained, "Can't you two get along?"

Lady Rothwell said, "Lydia, pray assure me that there is nothing in your diary that I may not read."

Sophy interrupted, "There is, Mama. She tells about——"

Edward broke in. He was the head of the family after all, and if his mother could not quell this unseemly wrangling, then he would have to take it upon himself to do so.

It was distasteful, but a duty was clearly set before him, and he did not flinch.

"I always said," he began, "that Miss Addis could not handle girls. She knew nothing of discipline, and I see the sad result in both Lydia and Sophy." Both girls stared round-eyed at him. It was unlike Edward, so Lydia said later, to interest himself in anything but his own affairs.

"I cannot help but feel that your daughters, Mama, show a great lack of conduct. If I had been consulted earlier, as I think I should have been, we would not now see such a want of training. But I must say, now that my attention is brought to this lack of training, I must do what I can to try to redeem my fault. Lydia, I wish you will tell me why you do not wish your diary read?" Lydia flushed to the roots of her hair. "On second thought, I don't think I wish to know. But I trust that from now on you will take advantage of this lesson. Sophy, you are not entirely free from fault. To go into your sister's room and read her personal affairs is outside of enough. I do not wish to hear of this again."

His criticism of Lady Rothwell was not lost. She, not used to any kind of defiance within her family, protested. "I am perfectly capable of knowing what is best for girls, and I do not accept your interference, Edward."

It was quite possible that Chloe's legacy had rocked not only the recipient, but Edward himself. At any rate, Edward, though civilly enough, pointed out, "It is my responsibility now. I am, after all, the head of the family, and their deportment reflects upon the family as a whole. I shall not like to see Lydia, in two years, traveling to London with such want of conduct. And, Sophy, unless I see a great deal of improvement in your manner, I doubt that you will go to London at all."

Even with this threat hanging over Sophy's head, she seemed unconcerned. It was a long time before she would be eligible to travel to London, and anything might happen to change the current state of affairs. More from a desire to stir things up than to divert attention from herself, with an appearance of innocence, she asked Lydia, "If Francis marries Chloe, then who is going to show you around London, Lydia? You're counting on Francis. Best be nice to him when he comes."

Sophy's precocity did not escape unnoticed. Edward quelled her with a heavy glance. "Lydia will go to London in two years. It is beyond the bounds of possibility that Francis would not be married by that time. Besides, we may all find that London has changed. The old King, I understand, is not well, and by then the country may be plunged into mourning. I recommend to you both, first, a salutary glance at your own behavior, and second, a postponement of all thoughts of London, or indeed of leaving Rothwell Manor for any reason."

Lydia's protest came loud and from the heart. "Not for two years! I'll die!"

Lady Rothwell, having agreed because she was confident remarks this morning, said, "Don't worry, Lydia. Two years is out of the question."

Edward said, "It is decided, ma'am. Lydia will not enter society for two years. I believe you agreed?"

Lady Rothwell, having agreed because she was confident of her ability to overrule her son, said, "Lydia will be nearly nineteen in two years. She must not wait that long. I know you have said that we cannot afford to send Lydia to London before then. But I believe that now we can manage."

Edward, shocked, said, "But it's not the money particularly. That is a factor, to be scrupulous about it. We do not have sufficient funds forward for any kind of display. But I must tell you, not to put too fine a point on it, that Lydia's behavior does not give me confidence at the prospect of seeing her in London. Her head is too giddy. She thinks of nothing but fashion. I should like to see her more settled before I agree to letting her go."

Lady Rothwell, believing she held all the winning cards, said, "But now all has changed, since Chloe is an heiress. It seems to me that Chloe's duty is to see that her sister receives something that means so much to her."

Sophy, without caution, pointed out, "Chloe won't be an heiress if she marries Francis."

Lady Rothwell glanced her way, and said, "If Francis fixes his interest with her, that is all I ask for now."

Edward, his plump cheeks quivering with shock and the force of his indignation, said, "Ma'am, I am adamant. Lydia will not go to London. Not for two years."

Lydia moaned, a small, broken sound. Lady Rothwell, with what she considered ineffable logic, said, "But what good is an inheritance, if one doesn't use it?"

Edward opened his mouth to speak, but what he had in

mind to say was never uttered. For at that moment, a shadow darkened the opened door into the hall. Chloe stood in the doorway, slim and looking somehow vulnerable. All fell into embarrassed silence. Chloe hardly noticed. She was accustomed to being on the fringe of the family, and of listening to a majority of conversations which did not include her except as an afterthought. But suddenly, to her surprise, she found that she was the center of attention.

Edward leaped to his feet and with heavy jocularity pulled out her chair. "How pretty you look this morning!" he cried.

For one horrified moment, Chloe thought he must be drunk. Acutely embarrassed, she murmured a protest that was lost in Edward's bustling about to get her settled. Furtively, Chloe glanced around the table. The others seemed to see nothing unusual in Edward's performance, but Lydia looked more sulky than usual. She and Sophy must have had another quarrel.

The tag end of Edward's conversation, that had come to her ears as she approached the morning room, now presented itself to her recollection. "No trip to London, for two years." This was undoubtedly the reason for Lydia's sullenness. Chloe spared a thought to Lydia's coming disappointment, not at the two years' delay in getting to London, but in London after she arrived. Chloe herself had very few fond memories of the city where she had spent two weeks.

Lady Rothwell informed Chloe, as impressively as though she were announcing an invasion of England, that Sir Richard had arrived at the hall.

Chloe's eyes flew to her stepmother's face and she said, "Has he come here?"

When he left her at the bridge he had said he would wait for another time. She was torn between regret that she had missed him here and a deep shyness over meeting him again.

Lady Rothwell shook her head. "I wonder why Sir Richard has not come. One would think that his first duty was to call on his neighbors. But perhaps he is too busy planning to be married. I have not heard whom he has offered for."

Chloe, her meeting with Sir Richard heavy on her thoughts, prepared to explain her meeting, by chance, with

Richard yesterday. She was conscious of a lurking desire to keep that meeting secret, but since secrecy was not part of her makeup, she opened her mouth to speak.

Sophy, however, forestalled her. Looking across the table at Lydia, she cried out, "Forget Sir Richard. He will have no time for you."

Lydia, fully conscious that she had written certain hidden thoughts in her diary and informed now of how deeply Sophy had delved into that secret volume, blushed furiously. The betrayal of her secret dreams, in such an unromantic setting as over broken scrambled eggs and coffee, moved her to speak.

"You snoop! You did read my diary! How dared you pry!" Her distress became incoherence, and Sophy let the flood stream over her. If an acute spectator had been present, he would have noticed that her smile bore no trace of guilt. Breakfast bade fair to become the usual uproar, and Chloe thought nostalgically of the days before Sophy had been released from the school room. Ordinarily Chloe could have let the wrangling sweep past her, leaving her unmoved. Now she was conscious of a lurking thought—at Highmoor I will insist upon quiet mealtimes. But her second thought was—At Highmoor I would be totally alone.

That afternoon, Sir Richard paid his awaited call on Lady Rothwell. He had not looked forward to this meeting, for the second Lady Rothwell had never been one of his favorites. It was a duty call, no less and no more.

Sir Richard had experienced a revelation on the footpath yesterday, and while his thoughts were all in a muddle, yet one thing came clear to him—he wanted Chloe.

London was forgotten, and his own future was assured. He would settle down at Davenant Hall, as a country squire, with his long-time childhood friend Chloe by his side. He thought no farther ahead, nor did he expect any obstacles to be put in his way. Without vanity, he knew himself to be an eligible suitor, for London had shown him that.

Lady Rothwell's butler showed him into the Green Salon. There he found Lady Rothwell engaged on what looked to be a mammoth embroidery project, something on the order of the Bayeux tapestry. A young girl sat near by, sorting out embroidery silks by colors, and both looked up on his arrival. Lady Rothwell's welcome was almost embarrassing. She was arch and sly by turns. She welcomed him back, saying he had been away too long.

"But I suppose we shall see much of you now, Sir Richard, after your forthcoming marriage." Sir Richard was startled, for he had not declared himself to Chloe, and he was sure she had not leaped to any conclusions. But Lady Rothwell had something else in mind. Sir Richard, about whose prospects gossip whirled like a dervish, was not in London, but here in Kent. If Lady Rothwell were able to penetrate his reserve and inform her sister of his choice, it would show Mrs. Hensley that they were not such dullards as Londoners thought!

He was rocked, but recovered himself shortly and murmured a few noncommittal words. He glanced at the door, hoping for rescue. It was not long in coming. Edward entered and advanced toward him with outstretched hands. His welcome was more subdued than Lady Rothwell's and was far less personal. Over Edward's shoulder, Richard saw what he had hoped to see—Chloe, slipping into the room, like a shadow. He met her eyes, and spoke a word or two to her, but she merely stammered and looked away.

Edward, believing that Richard had come to see him particularly, was full of questions.

"I understand that the Regent is making enemies right and left—is that true?"

"I have heard much about politics, but since I have been out of the country I've paid the governmental vagaries little heed, I fear."

Edward's remarks then moved on to crime on the Continent, making a strong statement on the subject of Grand Tours, when England was sufficient for any man of taste. Richard shrewdly translated the latter into a lament that Edward himself had not been able to take a Grand Tour.

Enjoying himself, Edward seemed most satisfied with the conversation, and announced that he would give himself the pleasure of anticipating many future constructive exchanges with his near neighbor.

Richard, with a bland expression, agreed, but mentally he vowed to avoid Edward's conversations at all costs. He looked up and caught Chloe's eye, and perceived the mischievous twinkle that he remembered well. Suddenly, he felt much better.

As in many a drama on the stage, Richard longed for

some interruption to release him from the toils of Lady Rothwell and her son Edward. A kindly Providence provided such a diversion. The sound of wheels came clearly through the open windows, heralding the approach of a carriage on the gravel drive.

Sophy, less burdened by manners than the others, ran to the window to look. As though under a spell, everyone watched the drive. Richard thought it was hard to tell what they were waiting for, but he did not expect the apparition that drove in. Sophy cried out, "It is Cousin Francis!"

Richard recognized him then. Lady Rothwell exclaimed, "Already? I had not expected him so soon." Francis entered, drawing off his driving gloves, and crossed to greet his aunt. He shied perceptibly when he caught sight of Sir Richard. Richard was reminded of a skittish, untrained colt, but that was a false impression, he knew, for Hensley, while stupid and inarticulate, was no Bartholomew baby. Indeed, Richard reflected, if rumor were right, Hensley knew more about the inside of gambling houses than many another young man. Richard had never heard that Hensley was under the hatches, so there was some common sense in that addled head.

Edward greeted his cousin civilly, but not warmly. Watching Hensley speaking to Chloe, apparently unable to muster a full sentence, Richard was conscious of a strong feeling of relief that Hensley was not related to Chloe. He was Lady Rothwell's nephew, and Chloe's family was not burdened with such an idiot.

But Francis, although he could not make himself understood clearly, was able to congratulate Chloe, in obscure terms, on something that sounded very much like Highmoor.

Richard, searching his recollection for a clue to the meaning of this, was at a loss. But he resolved to look further, for Edward was clearly embarrassed and Chloe looked ready to sink through the floor.

Richard took a pleasant leave of Lady Rothwell, gave Chloe a speaking look of sympathy and conspiracy, and left the manor, walking down the gravel drive where Francis Hensley's curricle had just driven up. He had many things to think about. Lady Rothwell's incursions into his private affairs he was not prepared to countenance. Nor was he taken by Edward. Richard searched his memory.

Edward certainly could not be more than twenty or twenty-one at the most. A young man who had succeeded far too soon to his father's honors and responsibilities, he was old before his time. Richard knew many a man past forty who was no more pompous than Edward appeared to be. There was much to contemplate, but yet he knew one thing—Chloe was the hub around which all the spokes of the wheel revolved.

It was the wrong setting for Chloe. She was an alien in that family, since all of them seemed to resemble Lady Rothwell. How could Chloe endure such a life?

Richard, conscious of his own plans, began to look ahead to removing Chloe from Rothwell Manor, and as his step quickened, he began to whistle.

5

At the first opportunity, which meant as soon as Sir Richard was out of sight down the drive, Lady Rothwell took Francis into her private sitting room. Closing the door behind them, she faced him. "I had not expected you so soon."

Francis mumbled something that sounded like, "My mother, you know . . ."

Lady Rothwell paid lip service. "How is your mother?"

Francis nodded. Lady Rothwell assumed that her sister Hensley was in good health.

Drawing Francis down to a chair beside her, she said, "You know that my dearest thought is to see you settled in life."

Francis shied. "Settled? I don't see any need——"

Lady Rothwell said, "But you must think of your future. These long weeks I have expected to hear that you had offered for someone and planned to be married."

A horrified expression crept across his features. "No, Aunt, I had no such thing in my mind. Not at all."

Lady Rothwell regarded him sternly. "Well, it's time

you did. What are you going to do? Your future has to be settled." Francis did not reply. In fact, his breathing grew more labored, and she doubted whether he could speak. "What about your future? What are you going to do?"

Francis looked up, his eyes clear and innocent, and he said, "I'm going to Brighton."

She allowed an expression of disgust to escape her, and added with the candor of a near relative, "You're a fool, Francis. Are you going to end up an aging rake? Without kith or kin, no children to carry on the Hensley name? Francis, you have to think of this! Don't fidget! Why did you come down so quickly?"

Francis said, without guile, "It wasn't my idea. My mother sent me."

Lady Rothwell rose to her feet and began to pace the room, wringing her hands. Francis watched her with a mixture of apprehension and interest. He'd never seen any one literally wring their hands before, unless it was on the stage. His thoughts skittered on to the most recent play he had seen.

A memorable event it had been, all things considered, for Covent Garden had produced an extravagant Allegorical Festival, called *The Grand Alliance*, in honor of Emperor Alexander, who was in London. *Richard Coeur de Lion*, Richard played by Mr. Sinclair himself, a *pas de deux* by Monsieur Soissons and Mrs. Parker—a grand evening indeed! And then, to top it all, the unexpected appearance of Princess Caroline, wife of the Regent, and—it was clear to everyone—the bane of his existence, appeared at the Gala just after the Regent and his guest were seated. It could have been embarrassing all around. . . .

Francis was brought back to the present with a jerk. Lady Rothwell, taking firm hold of herself, realized that Francis must be forcefully handled. She was essentially a lazy person, yet she hoped that she would always rise to the occasion when it was a question of what her family needed. And just now, she was intent upon keeping Chloe's money in the family.

She met the issue forthrightly. "Francis, you know that Chloe has inherited Highmoor?" Francis nodded dumbly. "And Chloe's fortune would go to her husband. It might as well be you."

Francis looked at her with the patient resignation of an ox, and objected, "But that's Chloe's money."

Lady Rothwell glared at him. "We are nearing the end of June, Francis. By August, I expect to hear that you and Chloe are betrothed. Then she can go with you to stay at your mother's, and Lydia will have her Season in London."

Francis, always a stickler, protested, "But Lydia is too young. She has no business in London."

Lady Rothwell eyed him with disgust. "She wants to go, Francis. I will see that she gets there. Chloe knows her duty, and I hope you know yours, too."

Francis squirmed in his seat. He had no idea that his duty would ever bring him to offer marriage, at least not for another fifteen years.

But Lady Rothwell as always overbore him. "Chloe's money will stay in the family. I'm determined on that. You must marry sometime. Why not Chloe? Certainly no other heiress is apt to come your way."

Her scorn did not leave him unmoved. He stared at his hands and moved them restlessly on his knee.

Lady Rothwell, sensing her advantage, came to stand over him. "You are in sole possession of the field. There is no other suitor here, and I must say that is fortunate."

Francis thought for a long time before he said, "I always liked Chloe." Then, catching sight of his aunt in the last stages of exasperation, he said, humbly, "But will she like me?"

Lady Rothwell exploded. "It is up to you to make her like you. Make yourself agreeable. I'm sure you can do that much to assure your own future."

Francis appeared not to have heard her, for he repeated, "I always liked Chloe." Then, he added, unwittingly tossing a bombshell at his aunt's feet, "So does Julian Stoddard."

Testily, Lady Rothwell inquired. "Where does Julian Stoddard come into this?"

Francis said, "Well, you know, I just mentioned——"

"You mean you mentioned Chloe's legacy to Julian Stoddard? I can't believe it!" Francis's silence spoke for him, and Lady Rothwell was left in no doubt. "You did." Her features settled into grim lines, and Francis knew he had made a mistake. Lady Rothwell, in her agitation, resumed pacing the floor.

Francis, in an effort to remove guilt from himself, said, "Mother didn't tell me not to."

Lady Rothwell, quite properly, ignored this. She had thought that a leisurely courtship and betrothal, before the Little Season, would keep Chloe occupied. Certainly, with the announcement of the betrothal in the *Gazette*, Chloe would be safe from all fortune hunters. She did not consider Francis in that category.

Then, perhaps next year, with Chloe safely married to Francis, they could take a house in London, and could launch both Lydia and, at the proper time, Sophy as well. She reviewed what she knew about Julian Stoddard—none of it good. Stoddard's breeding was good enough, if not spectacular, but his habits left much to be desired. An inveterate gambler, as were many of his peers, yet even Lady Rothwell had heard that Julian Stoddard was more than ordinarily anxious to win. There had been a time when he had left London abruptly, and did not return until certain ugly whispers died down. Perhaps Stoddard would feel that Chloe's legacy was not worth his attention. She demanded of Francis, "Was Stoddard winning when you talked to him?"

Misery in his eyes, Francis responded, "Yes, Aunt, he was."

With only a final exhortation to pay more attention to Chloe than was his usual habit, Lady Rothwell dismissed Francis and they did not meet again until teatime.

Edward did his best with Francis. But upon one subject after another, trade, politics, the state of health of the King, or whatever else, he received only monosyllables. It was Lydia who obtained more than ordinary attention from Francis. Francis seemed overcome by shyness every time he looked at Chloe, and welcomed Lydia's questions about the fashionable world as though she were approaching across the desert with a glass of water in her hand. Finally Lydia came to a subject that even Chloe listened to.

"Which lady did Sir Richard finally offer for? He was here this morning, but we got nothing out of him."

Francis answered, "Don't know. None, I think, at least now."

Chloe was cast down at the mention of Richard's prospective bride, but there was a ray of light in Francis's answer. If he hadn't so far offered, then Chloe could still call him friend without presuming too much.

Sophy interrupted, saying, "If he can't make up his mind, there must not be much difference between them."

Shrewd beyond her years, yet not mature enough to hold her tongue, Sophy was at once in trouble with both her mother and Edward. Chloe busied herself, as was her habit, with the mechanics of tea. Pouring, passing small plates of tiny cakes, refilling cups, she hardly heard the conversation going on around her. She caught a phrase now and then that gave her the gist of the conversation. The vicar had discovered, so he had told Edward, a crypt beneath the small church of St. Stephen's. He wished to look into its contents, for he thought perhaps there might be a Crusader grave, but he was waiting permission from his bishop to conduct the investigation. Edward, to Francis's horror, thought that a visit to the church would be of benefit to his sisters.

"What good would that do!" cried Francis. He was stirred beyond his usual monosyllables. "To go and look into a hole in the floor? That strikes me as ridiculous. I'd think it was best to keep the ladies from even knowing about such a thing."

Edward said, "I am always seeking educational experiences for my sisters. Books are well and good, but there is nothing to take the place of real experience."

"Experience!" exploded Francis. "To go and look at a moldy cellar is one I don't need!"

Edward, however, proceeded on his own way, making his own plans. "I think we might have a picnic, visit the church, and make a day of it."

He turned to his mother. "What do you think, Mama? I think we owe ourselves a day of enjoyment. We have not had time to celebrate Chloe's good news."

Lady Rothwell, drawing herself up on her dignity, said, "You claim it is educational. I suppose it is, and I must—so I am told—bow to your *superior knowledge* of what is the best education for young ladies. I myself would believe that a child, particularly of Sophy's sensibilities, would have nightmares for months after looking into a moldy grave."

Edward was indignant. "It is not a moldy grave, from what the vicar tells me. It is a crypt, well lined with bricks . . ."

So intent had they been on their conversation that they had not noticed the arrival of a visitor. Not until

Field ushered Sir Richard into the salon were they aware that Richard had come to call. He had heard the last few phrases of Edward's prosy discussion of the educational value of a crypt beneath the church. It did not appeal to him.

His eyes flew at once to Chloe, and he was unpleasantly surprised. Chloe was presiding at the tea table, but what disturbed him more than anything else was the withdrawn expression on her face. Yet those around her were her nearest family. Her stepmother, her half-brother and two half-sisters, and a cousin. What was there in this family group that was so distasteful to Chloe that she must retreat into herself and, so to speak, close the door after her?

He told himself, soothingly, that it was no doubt simply the mention of a crypt below the chapel that had distressed her. He glanced at Edward as he crossed the room to pay his respects to Lady Rothwell, and, not for the first time, wondered what kind of machinery moved inside the man's head.

Lady Rothwell, twittering, said, "Chloe, give Sir Richard a dish of tea, and perhaps one of those small cakes. They are not up to our usual standard, Sir Richard, for Cook has decided she had a deadly toothache and so we must put up with the inconvenience, but I wish she had taught one of the kitchen helpers to make cakes the way she does."

Richard moved across to the tea table, his eyes fixed upon Chloe. He was not a man of extraordinary sensibility, but there was clearly some unease in this room. Chloe rang for more tea, and he waited beside her. Edward was moving along, planning the details of his expedition to the crypt. "We have something to celebrate, after all," he said to Sir Richard. "Perhaps you don't know about Chloe's good fortune."

Chloe did not seem, to Richard's eyes, to be the recipient of a great deal of good fortune, but he said politely, "I wish I may know what it is?"

Lady Rothwell, coming down heavily, said, "It is a legacy. An elderly relative whom she did not know at all, which makes it all the better, you see, for there is no grief connected with it, has left her a small fortune. But then, Sir Richard, you have only a slight interest in this part of the country, for I should imagine your life in the future will lie more in London."

Richard raised an eyebrow. "I had not thought it would."

Lady Rothwell, intent upon repelling Sir Richard's possible claim to the fortune that she already envisioned in Francis's hand, said, "But when you marry, then I should be surprised if the new Lady Davenant would wish to spend any time at all in this rural backwater."

Richard, vulnerable to Chloe's pure look of misery, was becoming nettled with her stepmother. "On the contrary," he said. "I wish Miss Rothwell happy with her good fortune."

She did not look up until the new pot of tea arrived. With dignity, she filled his cup. She lifted her eyes, involuntarily, and caught his smile warm upon her, reassuring and altogether comfortable. Suddenly she felt much better. She heard the subject of the expedition to the crypt being renewed, but the discussion went by as though she were behind a wall.

She scarcely heard Richard inviting himself on the expedition. Sophy, always pert, said, "Well then, we'll have to go soon before you go back to London."

Sir Richard, with courtliness, said, "I won't be returning to London for some time."

The response to his statement was all that he could have desired, and much that he would not have wished.

Lady Rothwell, prey to uncertain alarms, cried out, "But why?"

Edward said, civilly, "What good news, Davenant! I have been sorry to think that we would not enjoy the constructive interchanges that we spoke of when you called yesterday. I shall certainly look forward to learning much from your conversation."

Sir Richard managed not to wince, and turned to Chloe. To his delight, the dimple high on her left cheek, which he had forgotten over the years, revealed itself, and he knew of a certainty that she was hiding her amusement.

He did not understand Lady Rothwell's reaction, for why should she be ruffled if her neighbor decided to live in his own house for a few months?

After the least interval required by civility, he took his leave.

He turned at the door to find Chloe's eyes fixed on him, and in them he read a clear message of appeal. He smiled at her reassuringly, and was out of the house and down the gravel drive before he tried to sort out his thoughts. Indignation rose as a spring tide. He was aware of a strong feeling that Chloe's position in that household was not what one might expect of the oldest daughter of the house. Now that he looked back, he could not remember that Chloe had said a word. She had sat at that abominable tea table, served tea, and in all ways acted much like an upper servant-companion. To serve without fuss, to be present without participating—he did not like it.

He reflected on Chloe's legacy. It had not made a splash in London, for he would have heard of it. Society in England was a tightly knit group. There were only a handful of great families, a double handful of families of importance, and hardly above a hundred more who might lay claim to serious consideration. These families, fewer than two hundred in total, kept a watchful eye on each other. A legacy in this closely knit group would be common knowledge in a very short time.

Chloe's fortune, had it been as rich as a nabob's, might have ruffled him, but in the ordinary way his own wealth was more than ample for his needs and whatever domestic responsibilities he might take upon himself.

As evidence of the knowledge shared among these families, all at Rothwell Manor clearly believed him to be on the verge of offering himself in marriage. How surprised Lady Rothwell would be, he thought with a smile, to know that London, in the last few days, had receded to a vast distance and he could hardly remember the three women he had been considering.

But that idiot Hensley! What was he doing here?

Then the thought struck him—Hensley had come down to offer for Chloe, the heiress. Could this be? By the time he strolled into his own entrance hall, he believed that Hensley's attentions to Chloe were with purpose. The surge of indignation, bordering on fury, that swept over him was enough to shake him. He knew now the wife he wanted. He remembered what he believed to be her look of appeal as he had left her. Surely she shared his feelings!

Tomorrow he would offer for her and set everything in order. The only thought in his mind was that by tomorrow at this time his future and Chloe's would be bound together, and settled.

6

It rained in the night and spoiled prospects for the outing. Chloe sighed with relief. She had no wish to visit a moldy crypt. But she knew that she would be accompanying Lydia and Sophy, if Edward thought it was their duty to receive whatever education could be borne on dank air.

Although the outing itself did not appeal to her, yet Richard's expected presence on the expedition both delighted and worried her. It was a chance to see Richard again, and she was beginning to realize that a glimpse of Richard was all that was required to make her day a happy one. And yet, if he were going to marry someone else——

Her thoughts reversed themselves. He was going to stay down in Kent for some time, he said, and surely that did not mean he was in a headlong rush to return to London to his love. But then, her pendulum thoughts told her, he is getting the house ready for his bride.

While Richard, at Davenant Hall, was waking with a whistle on his lips, Chloe's mind moved lower and lower, until her mood matched the leaden skies.

She was not sure why she felt so miserable. The household staff, predictably, was more upset than ever. Francis's valet, Grimsby, conscious of his superior standing in the social scale, had nourished a strong feud with Edward's valet and the butler. By the time that Chloe descended to the kitchen, Grimsby had joined open battle with Field, and she could hear the words of the butler. "And what's more, that fancy wax of yours is standing in the way of my silver polish, and it would be just too bad if you made a mistake—and I would not be responsible for it."

Upon Chloe's entrance, both fell silent. Chloe made a mild inquiry about Mrs. Field's tooth.

Field, grateful for the interruption, said, "I fear it's the

42

tooth drawer for her, Miss Chloe. All night she moaned, and I got not a wink of sleep."

Chloe said, "You should have called me."

Field, raising his eyes to heaven in a martyr's gesture, said, "I'd cut off my hand before I'd disturb you again, Miss Chloe."

Promising to go upstairs and take a look at Mrs. Field, Chloe turned and came face to face with Miss Sinclair, the village dressmaker, who was brought in at times to help with the mending. Mending was beneath Miss Sinclair's dignity, as a rule, but she wished to keep her hand in, in a household where two eligible young ladies would be going to London within the foreseeable future. There would be a great many gowns to make for Lydia, and probably for Sophy, and surely Miss Sinclair would be the first person they would turn to. A present tedium would result in a future windfall. Thus ran her reasoning.

Chloe, after a deadly session with Cook, who moaned, would not agree to go to the tooth drawer, and indeed refused to consider any reasonable means of alleviating her great pain, came down the back stairs from the attic to find a summons from Edward.

Edward, a well-meaning young man, was fond of his half-sister, and ingratitude was a word that he did not recognize. Possessed of less ambition than his father, Edward wished only to see those around him in good health and prosperity and untroubled of mind.

When Chloe came into his reading room, she glanced at the box of books. They had arrived only a few days ago, and already they were boxed and roped, ready for the carter. To Chloe's question, Edward said with scorn, "None of those books is fit to read."

Chloe, gently, said, "How do you know if you did not read them?"

Edward said, "I glanced at them. The romances, from that foolish Minerva Press, are not fit to read."

Once that subject was taken care of, Edward found himself at a loss for words. He hemmed and hawed until Chloe, in resignation, allowed her mind to drift back to Cook's tooth. But finally Edward came to the point. "I should like this conversation not to go any farther."

Chloe nodded agreement, and tried to assume a position of attention.

"This inheritance of yours! I had no idea it would give

me so much trouble. I could almost wish—but then, that's not kind. I want you to have everything you deserve. But I will admit it's a problem."

Chloe lifted her eyebrows and said, "What is the trouble? I gave you my power of attorney. Wasn't that what you called it?"

Edward said, "Yes, yes. But there's more to it than that. I haven't even seen the figures on it, I don't know how much there is, and already the bees are clustering around the hive."

The flight of fancy was so unlike Edward that she scarcely knew what he meant. Finally, he blurted, "I want to warn you about fortune hunters."

A slow blush crept up from his collar and suffused his cheeks.

Hardly able to speak from sheer surprise, she faltered in an unbelieving voice, "You mean Francis?" Edward nodded. "How ridiculous!"

Edward said, "I assure you I am not being ridiculous."

She recalled certain words that she had overheard in the hall that day when Lady Rothwell wrote quickly to her sister in town. Sophy had accused her mother of sending for Francis. And then, surprisingly, Francis had arrived on the heels of the message. Perhaps there was something in it after all, she reflected.

"There is no way I will marry Francis," she said.

Edward, not realizing how strange it sounded, said, "My mother is most persuasive when she wishes to be."

Chloe said, quizzically, "You mean Francis isn't? I do not argue with that. But you must remember, Edward, that I was in London for part of a Season, until the death of our father called me home. Besides, at my age I am no longer a green girl."

She spoke with humor. If there were an underlying wistfulness, it was not apparent.

Edward, disregarding the fact that he was only fifteen at the time, said, "I'm sorry I didn't send you back the next year. There just was not enough money then. Father had more debts than you would believe."

Chloe agreed. "I am sure he did not expect to die so suddenly."

Edward continued, "By careful management, I am dealing with the debts. And in two years I'll see it through.

Lydia can go to London then, but I must get the estate clear first."

"It's no matter. I would not enjoy London now."

She spared a thought to the pleasant world outside Rothwell Manor, of which she had caught only a tantalizing glimpse, but she told herself she was happy at Rothwell Manor, happy enough to spend the rest of her days here. Then, surprising herself even more than she surprised her brother, she said, "I wish to go to Highmoor to live."

Edward was stunned. When he could speak, he murmured, "Totally ineligible. You have only a small amount of money, not nearly enough——"

Chloe pointed out, with unsurpassed logic, "But you said you had no idea about the details of my legacy. How do you know there isn't enough money to live there?"

Fairly caught out, Edward said, "It is totally ineligible. What would people think? That your family had turned you out?"

He continued in that vein, but only after she left did he face the unwelcome truth. Her two hundred pounds a year had been considered part of the household's income for so long that they had learned to adjust their scale of living to include this amount. If she were to claim it and move to Highmoor, two years would not be enough to get the estate out of debt.

Chloe left the library behind her, gratefully, and hurried up to her own room. Her mood had been lowered rather than cheered by Edward, and she needed solitude to talk herself back into good humor. There was nothing in her room even to read. She had grown out of the habit but, as she put it, in her younger days she had enjoyed reading.

Her own room was comfortable, but far from luxurious. She sank into a chair before the dark grate not ambitious enough to light a fire in the grate or even to pull the bell for Bess. Rain streamed down the windows. The wind, fitfully rising, banged the shutters and Chloe shivered.

Lydia hurried in with only a token knock. Never one for beating about the bush, she sank into a chair opposite Chloe and came to the point.

"I'm bored."

Chloe said, "There is a great deal to do. . . ."

She had in mind getting Cook's tooth taken care of, calming the disturbances in the kitchen caused by Francis's valet, teaching the kitchen maids to make gingerbread while giving up on trying to give them a light hand with the pastry, and——

"You could help Miss Sinclair with the mending," pointed out Chloe.

Lydia lifted one hand and dropped it. "I don't know how. If only I could get away to London! Stuffy Edward says *two years*. I'll die before then!"

Chloe said wryly, "I doubt it."

Lydia ignored her. "Edward is so old," she exclaimed. "He has no idea what it is to be young."

Chloe said mildly, "I'm older than Edward, you know."

Lydia said, "But you don't understand! I want to see London while I'm still young enough to enjoy it. Think of all the balls, the routs—and the Tower of London and the lions—" she continued in her panegyric about the details of London which, to her, must surpass anything that Heaven had to offer.

Chloe said, "There'll be time enough to enjoy all that."

"When I get too old! But, dear Chloe, you could help me. If you went to London—or sent me to London——"

"Sent you?" said Chloe.

Lydia nodded impatiently. "Of course you probably wouldn't enjoy all of the parties, you're so—so *settled*."

Chloe was amused rather than hurt by Lydia's thoughtlessness. Lydia was simply expressing the inconsideration of youth. But the hurt rankled, and suddenly Chloe felt very old. Soon she would have to order her spinster caps. The prospect was dismaying, but she saw no help for it. It did not occur to her that Lydia overlooked the possibility that Chloe herself might want to escape from Rothwell Manor. If Lydia were bored, then it followed that Chloe herself might be bored, and Chloe had the means of escape. Lydia quite simply never thought of it.

Chloe moved to the window and watched the rain streaming down the pane. Movement below caught her eye and she mentioned, "There go the books."

Lydia, wrenched back to the present, said, "Books?"

Chloe said, "Yes, Edward sent all the books back."

Lydia said, in a kind of triumph, "Too late!"

Chloe questioned her. "How is this? The books have been downstairs in Edward's book room for three days."

Lydia laughed. "Not all the time! Sophy goes down after Edward has gone to bed and brings the books back upstairs." Chloe allowed her jaw to drop in surprise. Lydia laughed. "I know it's sneaky, but you expect Sophy to be devious. And Sophy reads the books and puts them back before Edward knows they're gone."

Chloe said, energetically, "But if you read the books, then you're as bad as Sophy."

Lydia laughed again. "I have to pay Sophy, so that makes it more honest."

"Pay?"

"Yes. Sophy lets me read the books she borrows, but I have to give her a third of my allowance."

Chloe was shocked. Sophy's character left much to be desired in the way of rectitude, but Chloe had not dreamed she was so blatant as to sneak books out of the book room, knowing that Edward did not want her to read them. Beyond all, then, to charge her sister for the privilege of reading them also! Chloe shook her head.

"By the way," said Lydia, "I want to borrow your new bonnet. For the expedition to the church, you know."

"I haven't worn it yet myself."

Lydia coaxed, "You can buy lots more, now that you're rich."

Chloe gave in, not because she was rich, but because over the years she had formed the habit of yielding before any kind of opposition.

While Chloe was being despoiled of her bonnet and Lydia was retreating in triumph to her own room, Richard arrived at Rothwell Manor. Lady Rothwell had not yet made ready to receive guests. Richard, quite properly asking for Lady Rothwell first and being denied, asked then for Chloe. Field had put Richard into the Green Salon, a chamber of some handsomeness with a fine view of the drive. Chloe hurried down the stairs and patted her hair automatically. She was obscurely glad that she had not yet ordered her spinster caps.

While he was waiting for Chloe, Richard framed his proposal. He was following his original plan to offer for Chloe this very morning. Presuming upon long acquaintance, he did not feel it necessary to ask Edward for his approval. Time enough for the formalities. Richard would have said, if asked, that he simply wanted to straighten things out with Chloe first, to wipe the woebegone look from her eyes. The truth of the matter was that Richard could not wait to throw himself at Chloe's small feet.

Richard was not overweeningly conceited, but he felt justified in believing, from Chloe's greeting on the path that first day and her quiet sharing of amusement with him since then, and especially her look of appeal across the tea table, that she would welcome his offer.

He had a strong suspicion that her position in this household was unhappy, that she would leap at the chance of leaving Rothwell Manor behind her.

Her fortune, whatever it was, meant nothing to Richard. He was marrying now, contrary to all his expectations when he left the Continent and came home to London, where his heart lay. Chloe's legacy meant only one more reason for haste in offering marriage to her, so that the idiot Hensley would be forestalled and Chloe would be spared much distress. There was no thought of rejection in his mind.

The door opened and Chloe entered, and his heart turned over. With new insight on his feelings, he recognized that all these years she had occupied a very special place in his thoughts.

Chloe, suddenly feeling out of breath, apologized for Lady Rothwell and Edward, and stammered some remark about the weather. "There is, of course, no question of an outing today to the vicar's find in the church. I suppose that is why you are here?"

"No, surprisingly enough, I had forgotten it."

The mischievous dimple showed on her cheek, but she did not smile. Instead she said, "How could you have forgotten? Edward was so set on it."

Richard said, "That expedition is the farthest thing from my mind. I came to talk to you."

Her hands fluttered and she swallowed hard. She apologized for her manners, bade him sit in a chair near her, and said, with an attempt at brightness, "What shall we talk about? If it is books, I am sadly out of touch."

Why on earth did she mention books? She scolded herself and then remembered that Lydia's indiscretion about Sophy's purloining of Edward's box of books still lay heavy on her mind.

Richard was diverted by the introduction of the subject of books. It opened a vista that he had not time to explore, and yet he was fascinated by the way her mind worked. Why on earth would she think that he came to make a morning call to talk about books?

She hastened to explain. "Edward received a box of books from the booksellers in London," she told Richard, "three days ago, and he sent them all back this morning. You may have met the carter."

Richard echoed, "Sent them all back?"

"Yes," said Chloe in a matter-of-fact voice. "He felt that none of the books was suitable for us to read."

She could not help but smile at the irony of it—the two younger girls, whose morals and education he was protecting, had read the books, while his older sister Chloe, of what she could only call mature years, was denied the privilege.

Richard, with the beginnings of anger, said crisply, "He is your guardian?"

Chloe, taking his question literally, said, "No, I am too old for that. But it is easier——"

Chloe's explanation was artless, but Richard's astuteness told him much. Chloe was a gentle, yielding person, needing a strong protector. It was clear that in this household she was giving far more than she received. He, Richard Davenant, had the means in his hands of rectifying that situation. He was more than anxious now to get her away from this family that he could only consider selfish. He had chosen the right moment—he was sure of it. She would in only moments see a new vista opening before her.

7

Richard crossed to stand closer to Chloe. Now that the time had come, he was not quite sure what to say. He was not helped by Chloe's eyes fixed on him. He tried to read in their depths something of her thoughts, but his vision turned back on himself. If the truth were told, he rather fancied his role as knight-errant. His regard for Chloe was deeply sincere, but he was in the habit of self-discipline, which included an eye to his own behavior and appearance.

"Chloe," he began, "we've known each other for a long time——"

With a sprightly air, she agreed. Animation crossed her features, as she cast her mind back. "Do you remember," she began, "the time we went fishing—the time you thought you could catch more fish with your hands than I could with my line?"

Richard interrupted. "We would have no surprises for each other. . . ."

He stopped short. It was not going the way he planned. He had lost the fine phrases he had practiced to use—and then he remembered that those phrases he had rehearsed for someone else. No wonder they didn't fit here.

How could he backtrack and start over? Chloe prevented him from the necessity of working his way out of it. "No," she agreed, "we would have no surprises for each other."

She was aware of Richard's uneasiness. The only reason she could think of to account for her old playfellow's nervous clenching of his hands and regrettable tendency to pace the floor was that he had something unpleasant to tell her.

The most unpleasant thing she could think of, at this moment, was that he was about to tell her of his approaching marriage. She smoothed the fabric of her muslin gown across her knees with nervous fingers. She must not give vent to her feelings, especially since she was not quite sure what they were. Richard was to marry, everyone said so. It was only a matter of question as to which of the candidates—there was really no other kind way of putting it—he would choose. Chloe, perhaps prejudiced, could not believe that Richard's suit could ever be refused. Not by any girl of sense, at least.

On the contrary, while Richard's mind dwelt on matrimony, to be sure, his vision was entirely different from Chloe's. Even though Lady Rothwell had raised an eyebrow, in coy questioning, he still did not realize how firmly the impression of the certainty of a London wife was imprinted on the household at Rothwell Manor.

His immediate worry was his unaccustomed lack of fluency. Before he could blurt out his true intentions—and it looked as though that was the only way he could put his thoughts into words—he saw tears welling in Chloe's speaking gray eyes. He was totally unmanned. He could not have said a word had his life depended on it. His impulse was to gather her into his arms, and then his imagination faltered.

Chloe herself was on the verge of leaping to her feet and fleeing out of the Green Salon. She could not bear this painful interview any longer. And yet her training, more rigid than that of either of her sisters', held her civilly seated, with a bright air of expectation on her face.

Richard took his courage and his scattering wits in both hands and opened his mouth.

Through the open window came the sound of a four-wheeled carriage, coming fast on the gravel drive. Chloe leaped to her feet, seizing upon this heaven-sent excuse, and ran to the window to look out. Richard, conscious of a vast relief, and yet thwarted, followed her to the window. The green damask draperies were pulled back and fastened, and their view was unobstructed. The carriage came around the curve before the house, a fashionable curricle driven by a pair of blacks.

While the two of them watched through the window, standing companionably side by side, they watched the driver descend from his curricle.

Chloe breathed, "What a dandy!"

"The latest crack," agreed Richard. But then, he thought, there was something not quite sharp, else perhaps too sharp, about the man.

Richard thought how out of place the man looked. He was not dressed for the country—he would look better driving his rig across Hyde Park. At the moment that Richard recognized him, Chloe cried out. "What on earth is he doing here? I had thought Julian Stoddard a dyed-in-the-wool city man."

Richard exclaimed also. "I agree. I heard he was having a run of luck for a change. What on earth does he want with Rothwell?"

Richard, in his surprise at seeing Julian Stoddard, was jolted out of discretion. He had no very high opinion of Edward Rothwell, but he did feel he was honest, and he was not so sure about Julian Stoddard.

Stoddard alit and looked up at the façade of the house. Chloe pulled back quickly from the window with a muffled exclamation, and her expression changed. Richard, newly alert, noticed the change in her features and said, quietly, "What's the trouble?"

She looked at her hands and with an obvious effort of will kept them from trembling. She said, with wistful resignation, avoiding Richard's glance, "I believe he does not come to see Edward. I believe he comes to see me."

Richard, shocked, grew stern. "To see you? It's not possible."

"I know it's hard to believe, but you see——"

He said, "Stoddard is a gambler—a man of very little account. Why?"

He realized there was no easy way to say what was on his mind. Why would Julian Stoddard, an habitué of some of the lower forms of London entertainment, a notorious gambler, come to see this quiet lady, of great charm, discernable only to the few who could appreciate such a refined treasure. But Chloe seemed not to mind his sudden silence. "I know it seems impossible," she said earnestly, "but you see I am an heiress now."

Richard, still struggling to make sense of all the ideas that presented themselves to his unwilling scrutiny, said, "I believe your stepmother mentioned something of the sort. I confess, I paid her little heed."

Chloe explained. "I have inherited a legacy from my great uncle, but I should not wish you to think I am overweeningly vain about it. It is only that Francis has come down from London, and I have been told he seeks to marry me. Believe me, it is a surprise to me, but Edward told me as much. And now, Mr. Stoddard has arrived, and truly I see no other explanation. Especially since Francis and Julian Stoddard have become quite good friends of late, you know."

To Richard's sympathetic eye, she looked beset. She was clearly not able to deal with her sudden popularity, if that was what it could be called. Suddenly, she turned to him and dumbfounded him. "How grateful I am to you, Richard!" she exclaimed. "You are the one person I know who cares nothing for my inheritance. You, and believe me I do appreciate it, did not mention marriage at all. You have proven to me how worthy you are of trust. I am so grateful to you! I am so fortunate in my one Great Friend."

In an impulse, she grasped his hands and he lifted them

to his lips, while the shards of his proposal of marriage lay around his Hoby-shod feet.

Richard was in a situation that puzzled him. While he had not thought it clearly through, yet he was obscurely aware that he had not met with many defeats in his life. Blessed with fortune, a pleasing countenance, and an amiable disposition, he had found his way smooth before him. His first impulse, at the unaccountable behavior of Chloe, was to blame her for what was, after all, a slight.

He found that he was not annoyed with her for refusing his offer of marriage, for after all it had not escaped his lips. Nor would it, under her strong representations that it would be unwelcome to her. No, the slight that Chloe had put upon him was entirely unwitting on her part. It was simply that he disliked being put in the same category as that idiot Hensley and the gambler Stoddard. He was not a fortune hunter, and there was no reason why Chloe should think he was. But it was a blemish on his character if he did not stand apart from those two that she held in such loathing.

So, she had put him fairly out of the running for her hand in marriage. He should have been cast down, for she had, after all, talked his future into a cocked hat. But yet he was conscious more of anger than of resignation. Striving to be impersonally analytical, and stemming the rising tide of emotion, he tried to tell himself that if Chloe didn't want him—there were those who did.

His vigorous stride down the gravel drive, hurrying away from the site of his defeat, had the effect of vanquishing his indignation. He could think now only about Chloe's unhappy face tilted up to his. Her air of wistful resignation wrung at his heart, and he remembered then her surprisingly strong hold on his hands. The sight of Julian Stoddard had certainly unnerved her. Grasping Richard's hands, she had clung to them in a strong grip, reminiscent of a drowning person. By the time he reached the foot of the drive, his strong intellect had provided him with an eminently logical solution. He could not drop Chloe from his thoughts, nor did he want to, until he was possessed of a greater understanding of her than he now had. He had not thought her capable of strong emotion, envisioning his marriage to her as a pleasant shallow stream with amusing ripples, and a certain understanding. Now, however, his ideas were subtly changing. The legacy did not matter, to him at least. But what did matter was that he believed Chloe was too kind, too soft-hearted, even too inexperienced to deal with what looked very much like fortune hunters. Try as he might, he could not conceive of Chloe married to either of the two who were filling the stage at the moment.

Nor, to be honest, could he envision himself married to anyone else. The fleeting thought that had come to him, at the moment of indignation when she turned him down—that his life had not been permanently shattered for there were certain ladies in London who could mend it easily—that thought was gone. He had not even noticed when the possibility of marrying someone else had left him. All the London diamonds of the first water were now as nothing to him. He did not even trouble to decide why each of them would not suit him.

Now, after she had turned him down, he realized that Chloe was filling his thoughts as never before. He had not envisioned a refusal. But now, he knew that he had been stirred to his depths. All he wanted in his future was Chloe, her speaking gray eyes, the mischievous dimple that flickered high on her left cheek when she was amused.

But Chloe, he told himself sternly, wanted him only as a Great Friend. She had said so, in no uncertain terms. She had stressed her gratitude that he had not mentioned marriage. Faced with a challenge that he had never before faced, Richard felt stirring in him an emotion that he did not quite recognize. He hoped he was not so ill-bred as to deal with Chloe only on the basis of a challenge. That would be shabby indeed. In essence, he wanted Chloe as his wife, and before he was through, he would have her.

"Great Friend" was a promising beginning for wedded bliss, he told himself quite rightly. Friendship lasts a lifetime, whereas any grander emotion flares and dies. If he were to be her Great Friend, he would certainly bend his efforts in that direction. What would a Great Friend do?

He gave a thought to his providential luck. He had nearly ruined everything, back there in the Green Room. He had almost thrown himself at her feet, with the probable result that she would have scorned him then and forever. Stoddard fortunately had arrived before Richard had spoiled his chances.

It was clear that Stoddard came for the fortune he had heard of. Stoddard and Rothwell had nothing in common, and, in fact, Richard was surprised that they had even met. Hensley, being kin to Lady Rothwell, was more understandable.

Richard, considering these new developments, fixed upon Chloe's basic trials. Her agonized words, as she had clung to his hands, threw a bright light upon the situation at Rothwell Manor. Her family was clearly not protecting her against these circling jackals. Any family, no matter how disaffectionate one with the other, would have built up the campfire for mutual protection. But the Rothwells, he thought—mixing his metaphors with abandon—had opened the door and let in the wolves.

The anger that Richard had felt upon quitting Rothwell Manor was now transferred against the Rothwells *en masse*. He entered his own front door, still bemused by his strenuous thinking. If he were to be Chloe's Great Friend, he would protect her against these others, wouldn't he?

A few lines of poetry entered his head—was it Lochinvar who "staid not for brake, and stopped not for stone," in his pursuit of fair Ellen? Richard stood, arrested, in his foyer. A smile glimmered and then spread over his features. Now he knew the best way to outflank his rivals. It was only one way, but it was a start. He moved into his book room, sat down at his desk, and began a letter of instructions to his man in London.

8

Meanwhile, at Rothwell Manor, Julian Stoddard was interviewing Lord Rothwell. Edward, hastily summoned to receive the unexpected guest, sat behind his desk in the book room, his fingers playing on the empty desk top.

Stoddard, bending his considerable charm upon Lord Rothwell, whom he had begun to despise, was explaining his visit.

"I was passing through on my way to Brighton. The Prince Regent has gone down, you know, to escape the fatigues of his court, and he's asked a few of us—and I'm proud to say I am one—to keep him company. I had a few things to take care of in town, so I was not able to travel with Prinny."

"If you're late," said Edward, "then I do not see why you made this detour to Rothwell."

"I remembered meeting Miss Rothwell several years ago," said Stoddard, wearing an expression of innocence, "and at that time she had spoken so much about her home that I vowed then to make your acquaintance as soon as I could. But I have been traveling, and the years have just gone by."

"Abroad?" questioned Edward. "I should like to hear of your travels. You must stay to dinner!"

Meeting Chloe at dinner, Stoddard paid her flattering attention. She scarcely lifted her eyes from her plate. It was going to be uphill work, he decided. He had thought that he could fix his interest in a short time, but it looked like a long siege. Curse Hensley, anyway!

Francis Hensley was, in fact, not overjoyed to see him. Stoddard gave him a meaningful glance and then turned his attention to his hostess. Lady Rothwell, never one to conceal her emotions, was very nearly rude.

"I wonder that you can tear yourself away from your companions," she said, "for I had not expected that anyone from London knew where we lived."

Julian replied gracefully, and Lydia, fastening her eyes upon him, began to ask questions. Stoddard began his practiced series of anecdotes, tempering them to the young ears of his audience. Before long, he was gratified to notice that Chloe too was watching him, and he allowed himself without caution to embroider the tales of adventures on the continent, in most of which he played a leading, if unrealistic role.

At length, judging the moment nicely, he tore himself away from the Rothwells. Edward, having enjoyed his company and congratulating himself that for one meal at least he did not have to listen to his idiot cousin, told Julian Stoddard that if he could see his way clear to coming back, at a future time, Rothwell Manor would welcome him. The invitation was not seconded by Lady Rothwell, nor did Chloe do more than bid Stoddard a civil farewell.

The door had scarcely closed behind Julian Stoddard

when Lady Rothwell rounded on her son. "What is that man doing here? Why did he come?"

Edward, trying to mollify her, said, "I found him good company. At least for once we didn't sit around the table chewing over the same conversation."

Lady Rothwell, anger rising, cried, "So, our discourse bores you. It is better than whatever lies that rake put out!"

Edward, wounded, said, "I found him interesting. And I hope I may invite whom I wish to my table?"

Lady Rothwell, ignoring the signs of trouble, continued. "I do not like my daughters to be exposed to such false tinsel values as held by that man. Coming in on a family he had never met! That is outside of enough."

Edward, trying to stem the tide, said, "He said he had met Chloe in London. And of course he must know Francis."

"Francis is not the host here," pointed out Lady Rothwell with more accuracy than tact. "If Francis had invited him. . . ." Her voice trailed away and she fixed her nephew with a smoldering eye.

Then, aware that she was being indiscreet, she looked around quickly. "Where is Chloe?"

Sophy said, "She said she had a headache and went to bed."

Her helpfulness was unfortunate, for it brought Lady Rothwell's attention to her. "What are you doing down here? You should have been in your bed long ago. Off with you at once."

At that moment the tea cart was brought in. Surprisingly meekly, Sophy took three small cakes and made her way out of the room. After Field had left, Lady Rothwell's complaints continued. Turning to her nephew, she said, "You brought him here."

Francis exclaimed indignantly. "You think that I can pull Julian Stoddard around on leading strings?"

"You told Stoddard about Chloe!" Lady Rothwell, piling her plate high with dainty cookies, continued. "You didn't know enough to keep your mouth shut about Chloe's legacy. Surely you must have expected all the fortune hunters in the capital to come down to try to fix their interest with her."

Francis, although inarticulate, was not entirely stupid. He knew that he was as much a fortune hunter as any of them, but he salved his conscience by telling himself that at least he liked Chloe, which was more than the rest of them did.

"I wish you may not have ruined your chances," Lady Rothwell pointed out.

Francis, struggling for words, finally found them. "What's a man supposed to tell his friends," he asked with reason, "when a man's mother tells him to leave town?" He labored under a sense of real injury, and wished with all his heart that he had never come down to Rothwell.

Lady Rothwell said, "You could have made up some story that would have been better than this!"

Francis, shocked, said, "That's lying!"

Edward, feeling it time to intervene, said, "I must commend you, cousin, on your moral stand. It is not often that one finds such honesty. I entirely approve of telling the truth. If Stoddard came because you told him about Chloe's good fortune, you have your own good conscience to justify you."

Francis looked at Edward much like a small dog that was unused to praise, and hardly knew what to think of the hand stroking his head. But then, he spoiled it. "It's not honesty," he said painfully, "it's only that I can't remember what I say, and I get all tangled up. Best to tell the truth, and then I don't have to worry."

With an exclamation of disgust, Edward turned to the tea table and pointed out to his mother that she had eaten the last of the cakes.

Sophy, licking crumbs from her fingertips, straightened up from her position outside the door and decided it was time to make her retreat. Far from ascending to her bedroom, as she had been bidden, she had lingered outside the door of the salon. The discussion within, while not exciting, was the best there was in the house. Thoughtfully, she climbed the stairs. At the door of her bedroom she hesitated, and then, changing her mind, hurried down the corridor to Chloe's room.

She had entirely forgotten that Chloe had given the excuse of a splitting headache when she had left the assembly downstairs. But to give Sophy her due, even had she remembered, it would have made no difference. Now, without knocking, she slipped into Chloe's room. Pausing a moment to let her eyes get accustomed to the darkness, she could hear Chloe's heavy breathing and knew she was already asleep. What a nuisance!

She crossed to the bed. She shook Chloe's shoulder under the comforter to rouse her. Chloe did not awaken at once, and Sophy wondered whether she had taken a sleeping draught. But at last her efforts were rewarded and Chloe murmured, "Go away."

Sophy whispered urgently, "Wake up, Chloe. Come on, wake up!"

At length Chloe rose from the depths of her sleep, and with a huge sigh said, "Oh, it's you, Sophy. What do you want? What's wrong?"

"There's a great row going on downstairs."

"And they sent you upstairs to tell me?"

"No, they don't know I heard it."

"I wish you hadn't. Why aren't you in bed? What time is it?"

Sophy, quite rightly, ignored her and launched on her narrative. "Mother is totally angry with Francis! She says that he brought Stoddard here, but I don't really mind because he was so interesting."

"How do you know all this?"

"Well, I *listened*. How else? And don't tell me that I shouldn't listen. I've heard *that* before. But nobody ever tells me anything, so how can I learn if I don't listen?"

Her logic was impeccable, to her. "And Francis says he didn't tell Stoddard or at least didn't tell him much. And Edward says Stoddard can come back, and Mama says Francis is a fool. I thought everybody knew that, but Mama had to tell him again."

Chloe sat up in bed and pushed the pillows behind her. She pulled the comforter up around her shoulders, against the night chill, and said, "Sophy, what difference does all this make?"

"How exciting is must be to be sought after! It's a new experience for you, isn't it, Chloe? Imagine having two men waiting to marry you!"

Chloe's response was inarticulate. "Don't get married, don't even get betrothed, until after you take Lydia to London," Sophy begged. "It would spoil everything if she didn't go."

Chloe said, faintly, "I'm not going to London."

Sophy told her, comfortingly, "Just because your head

aches. You'll feel better in the morning, after a good night's sleep."

Sophy, having carried the day, removed herself. The rest of the night, Chloe was wakeful. She fought her headache, refusing to take the drops of laudanum that would have sent her to blessed sleep because she knew there were only a few drops left in the bottle. But even the laudanum would not have helped her low spirits.

There were three choices left to her. One was to marry Francis. Her stepmother would be delighted, but Chloe was not sure about Francis. She was sure that if she said the word Francis would live up to her expectations of marriage, but she herself was not overjoyed at the prospect. She liked Francis well enough, but a lifetime of listening to his struggling for words, his inarticulate expressions, would drive her to the brink of insanity. She had stayed after dinner long enough to hear her stepmother's assessment of Julian Stoddard's visit. It was inconceivable that Stoddard would come after her on the basis of her legacy. She remembered that she had told Richard that in the morning, but now she remembered that as though it had happened a week ago.

Stoddard as a husband was out of the question also, but she could refuse both and stay at Rothwell Manor, her own home, where she had been born.

In the cold gray light of morning, the thought came to her that Rothwell Manor could not be her home for the rest of her life. When Edward married, as he would, being a dutiful head of his family, what then?

Surely she could not stay in a house with a new mistress. In the ordinary way, the ladies of the house would remove to the dower house. Lady Rothwell would quite likely protest, for it was much smaller than the manor. But there would be no choice, and Chloe dreaded to move into smaller quarters with her stepmother and her two sisters.

There was a third alternative—to remove to her new home at Highmoor and live there.

But in the unfriendly dawn, living alone had very little allure. Notwithstanding her frequent impatience with her stepmother, with Lydia and Sophy, and the myriad of small nettling incidents of the day, yet she shrank at the thought of living alone. Chloe had become conditioned to all the inconsequential incidents of a retired country life, and though her existence was not exciting, yet it was familiar and therefore comforting in a way.

Memory took her back over Stoddard's adventures related over dinner, and if he had thought to lure her interest by his tales of derring-do in various unlikely incidents, the effect on her had been just the opposite.

She could not look with any favor upon a life beset by bandits, thieving landlords, and uncomfortable coaches driving over impossible mountain passes. As a matter of fact, Stoddard's warmed-over escapades gave rise only to a certain doubt of the narrator's veracity.

While Chloe's knowledge of the more lurid novels of the day was nonexistent, yet logic told her that this kind of incident, where one routed bandits with the sword and traveled in deadly peril of losing one's life, was not reasonable, and in fact probably had not happened at all.

Restless, unable to stay longer in bed, she dragged the eiderdown over to a chair from which she could watch the sun rise. No doubt Richard could tell her what would be best to do. She longed to lean on his sturdy common sense and find in it the support for her own decisions. When she saw Richard again she might even broach the subject of removing to Highmoor, to see whether his thought, being based on broader experience, would be the same as Edward's.

But there was no hurry, she thought comfortably. Stoddard was already out of her life, having dropped in only on his way to Brighton to bear the Prince Regent company. Chloe could be sure that Edward would stand on her side against Francis, so that she was far from being beset by two suitors.

She was surprised to find that her headache had all but vanished. She laid her head back on the chair and thought with great comfort that Richard was home now and would advise her truly. She fell asleep, at last, and woke only when Bess brought her morning tea, and Sophy came in on her heels to sit with Chloe.

Sophy was full of news again this morning. She made perfunctory inquiry about Chloe's headache and did not wait for the answer.

"Cook's tooth is worse, you know," she said. "She thinks she is going to die of it. Her face is all swollen, out to here—" Sophy demonstrated, holding her hand exaggeratedly away from her cheek—"and they had to get a bigger rag to tie up her head with."

Chloe said, "Oh dear, I have to go to her. Where's the bottle of laudanum?"

Bess said oppressively, "First with your tea, Miss Chloe. Cook's tooth been bad all night, and another ten minutes isn't going to make a difference."

Sophy pursued her own line of thought, and said, "Field couldn't sleep either. He couldn't clear away until late. There was so much wrangling in the parlor that he dared not enter to take out the tea cart."

Chloe drank tea and began to hunt for the bottle of laudanum. Sophy crossed to the windows, where Bess had drawn the curtains open. "It's a fine day," Sophy pointed out. "Francis is still in bed. Maybe we can go on our picnic today."

Chloe said, her voice muffled as she bent over a small cabinet, "I must get cook to the tooth drawer today."

Sophy said, "She's such a coward! She'll never go."

"It won't be easy."

"But what about our outing?"

Chloe said, "Not today, not for me."

Sophy said, with scorn, "Spoilsport! Always with your nose to the grindstone."

Chloe thought, How else are we to manage? Mama does nothing, and somebody has to see to these things.

Sophy, finding she could not budge Chloe, left. In moments she was back, her eyes wide with suppressed excitement. "Julian Stoddard is coming up the drive!"

Chloe, stunned, gazed at her half-sister, aghast. "But he's gone!"

"That may be, but he's back."

Chloe objected. "But he said he was going to Brighton. What's he doing here?"

Sophy said, ghoulishly, "Maybe he's going to fight a duel with Francis! Over your hand! Isn't that exciting?"

Rightly, Chloe ignored Sophy's fancy. She hastily gulped down the last of the cold tea and sent Bess away. She searched through her wardrobe until she found a gown that was suitable for town wear. Hurriedly she dressed herself and swept her hair up and anchored it with pins in a style more convenient than fashionable. Sophy, watching her, cried out, "What are you doing?"

Chloe answered, matter-of-factly, "I am taking Cook to the tooth drawer."

With great common sense, Sophy pointed out, "You'll never get her to go. She'll just want more laudanum to ease the pain, and then she'll say the tooth doesn't hurt any more and no need to have it out."

Chloe waved the bottle aloft. "But there is no more laudanum, see? Only a couple of drops in the bottom. That much will serve to get her to town, but I must get a new supply."

Sophy said promptly, "I'll go with you. If you can get Cook to go to town to the tooth drawer, that's something I don't want to miss."

Chloe said, "No, there's no need for you to go." But Sophy hurried out of the room on her way to change her clothes, and Chloe, with a sigh of resignation, picked up her shawl and empty bottle of laudanum, and descended the back stairs to deal with Cook, a notorious coward.

9

A strenuous quarter hour later, Chloe emerged from the kitchen wing and came face to face with Francis. Her cousin, laboring under a sense of injustice, caught sight of Chloe and burst into speech.

"Very bad form," he said. Having expressed himself, he stood blinking at Chloe, waiting for her comment.

On her own mental track, Chloe said, "But nobody else will do it. Cook needs to be taken care of, and I am on my way——"

Francis said, "What has Cook to do with it?"

Chloe looked at him, bewildered. "I really could not say, Francis. But Mrs. Field is truly the only person I'm concerned with just now."

Francis was impervious to hints. "Making a morning call," he exclaimed, "as though he were intimate, and besides he's supposed to be in Brighton."

Chloe, filling in correctly the gaps in Francis's exposition, made a guess. "You are talking about Julian Stoddard!"

Francis, aggrieved, agreed. "Who else?" he asked simply.

"Truly, Francis, I have no time for Julian Stoddard now. Cook is totally miserable, and I finally got her to agree to go and have her tooth extracted. I must hurry before she changes her mind. I was on my way to Edward——"

It occurred to her finally that Francis looked more than ordinarily upset. "What is the trouble?" she asked.

Francis said, in a voice that would not have been inappropriate had it heralded doomsday. "He's still here."

His information brought Chloe up short. "You mean he's still here?"

"That's what I've been telling you," said Francis.

"Oh dear," she cried. "I was on my way to tell Edward where I was going. I dare not wait longer, for Cook is just now on the verge of refusing to go at all." She took hold of Francis's sleeve. "I'm so grateful to you for telling me. I do not like to take the chance of meeting Stoddard on the way. I will go out the service drive, if you would do me the greatest of favors. Would you tell Edward where I have gone with Cook? I'm taking the chaise, but——"

She thought again. "I suppose you wouldn't go with me?"

Francis shuddered. "I certainly would not. I have a horror of tooth drawers."

Chloe said, impatiently, "So do we all, but it must be done."

Francis said, "No, I can't go."

"You do not even need to see the man."

Francis, for once, was adamant. He sent his tongue exploring a tender tooth of his own, and, that done, claimed he was afraid the tooth drawer would see right through his cheek.

Chloe said, with resignation, "Then if you won't go with me, at least you can tell Edward where I have gone. I don't know when we will be back, and you all must do as well as you can for lunch, for Cook will be in no way able to deal with it when she comes back."

Francis vanished, and Chloe turned back to the kitchen. Summoning help from Field and two footmen, and bending an imperative glance on Bess, Chloe managed to get Mrs. Field, moaning as though in her death throes, as far as the light carriage. It took the combined efforts of all of them to hoist her ample figure into the chaise. Chloe climbed in beside her and Bess followed, sitting on the opposite seat, and they were ready to set off down the back drive. Young Franklin, an assistant groom, was allowed to take the reins. Just before he whipped up the horses, Sophy ran out the back door. She joined them without ceremony, saying only, "I was waiting for you in the front hall. Were you trying to get away without me?"

Chloe said, repressively, "No, only to avoid Edward's caller."

Sophy nodded wisely, and, to Chloe's great gratitude, maintained silence for the next few minutes. Young Franklin, full of his own importance at driving Miss Rothwell to town in sole charge of the light carriage, drove his horses rather too fast down the service drive. Chloe was too distraught to protest, and Sophy watched the trees go by at a dizzying speed with excited anticipation. This was going to be a drive she would remember, she thought.

Franklin negotiated his first turn and emerged on the well-traveled road to town without incident. Things were going very well, he thought, and allowed his fancy full rein, an attitude that reflected itself inevitably in lax hands on the reins of the pair he was driving.

If he did well this time, and he had no doubt that he would, and won Miss Rothwell's approbation, there was a clear road to the top. As clear as the road ahead of him, he thought, and envisioned himself as second coachman. Even, his fevered ambition whispered in his ear, when old Coachman himself got beyond it, Franklin would be right in line for the position. First coachman—it was a dizzying height.

His imagination ran riot, and since his eyes were fixed upon the vision in his thoughts, he failed to see the milepost hidden in the roadside grass. Driving, as he thought, to a peg, the wheel of the carriage caught the milepost. There was a grinding crunch, and Chloe knew that disaster had come upon them.

The carriage tilted toward the damaged wheel, and cook's ample figure was thrown over on Chloe. Bess and Sophy were jumbled together in the opposite seat, hands flailing to catch hold of something. The moment was quickly gone, for the horses, hearing an ominous sound behind, shied. The carriage was pulled along reeling like a drunken vehicle on the grass, and, overcome by gravity, landed on its side in the grass. Brought up short by the heavy weight of the coach, now immobile, the horses were brought to a shuddering halt. The disaster was of sufficient magnitude that no one noticed a hired outfit coming down the road behind them.

Its driver was Julian Stoddard. He was near enough to see the accident as it happened, and his heart bounded within his chest. Julian had been making heavy weather of a conversation with Edward when Francis Hensley had arrived with Chloe's message. Without tact or even discretion, Francis had blurted out Chloe's message to Edward. Stoddard, always a man to take advantage of whatever came his way, pricked up his ears at this new development.

Francis, holding Stoddard in justified dislike, took a certain pleasure in informing Edward that Chloe had left the house. He shot a glance sideways at Stoddard, as though to say, You'll not see her this day.

Edward frowned. "Chloe is right. The tooth must come out. We have had enough upset on account of it already. And you say they took the chaise? I wish they had taken the carriage."

Stoddard, intent on his own goals, leaped to the conclusion that Chloe was suffering toothache. He took his leave, trying not to be suspiciously hasty, and hurried down the driveway. Certainly Chloe, suffering as she must be, would look with favor on a stalwart companion. Stoddard did not give more than passing attention to the circumstance that might be considered strange—Chloe's brother's and cousin's giving no thought to accompanying her on what must be after all a very painful errand.

Stoddard turned at the gatepost and headed toward town. There was no vehicle in sight, and he whipped up his horse in order to catch up with Chloe. He formed no very clear plan as to what he would do when he overtook her. He supposed she must have a maid with her, and he possessed enough compassion to think that she was receiving very shabby treatment. He turned a corner in the road and faced the same straightaway that Chloe's groom had come a cropper on. He congratulated himself, for down the road he could see what looked very much like an over-turned chaise.

Approaching the accident, he was gratified to see Chloe, apparently none the worse for the spill, standing in the middle of the road. He leaped down from his curricle, tied the reins, and came to her.

"I come at a timely season, it seems," he began.

She looked at him without favor, and then, aware that she was being almost rude, told him, "I am too distracted to be civil. How are you, Mr. Stoddard?" Without waiting for an answer, she turned to Franklin. "If you're not too hurt, get up and see to the horses. You will be fortunate if you have not barked their legs, for I don't know what Edward would say to you."

The groom, flushed with embarrassment and dismay, limped toward the horses and grabbed their bridles.

Sophy, completing her survey of the chaise, said, "The wheels look all right, and I see no broken axle. What on earth possessed him to turn us over on a straight road?"

Chloe ignored Sophy, shot a discerning glance toward Cook, sitting on a grassy bank, moaning, and turned again to the hapless groom. She helped him unhitch the horses, all the while her thoughts mulling about what to do next.

Julian, remarking with a corner of his mind that Chloe did not seem to be suffering too badly from the toothache, offered his help.

"Do you help Franklin set the carriage up, for I cannot leave the horses," she suggested.

The next few minutes were filled with activity for all—holding the horses, trying to set the chaise on its wheels, all to the antiphonal moaning of the ample figure on the bank. They were all too busy to notice another chaise in the distance approaching. With Chloe giving crisp orders, the chaise was soon on its own four wheels again. Julian then, for the first time, was able to look directly at Chloe, and noticed with some surprise that her face showed no signs of swelling.

But Chloe turned to Stoddard, her face glowing, and thanked him profusely. "I don't know what we would have done had you not come along, Mr. Stoddard. I really must get to town at once, and I don't believe I should risk the chaise any further."

Julian, bowing handsomely, said, "My vehicle and I myself are at your service, Miss Rothwell."

"Oh, excellent," cried Chloe. "Cook, did you hear that? Mr. Stoddard is going to take you to town to the tooth drawer. You will feel fine presently."

With Bess, who had been staring into space in a state of minor shock, Chloe managed to get Cook to her feet and propelled toward Mr. Stoddard's curricle. If Chloe noticed the look of total dismay on Stoddard's face as he realized that Cook was the victim of toothache, and not his prey, she gave no sign of it. She helped get Mrs. Field into the curricle, and told Bess to climb up, too. "For you will not like to have the sole charge of the patient," Chloe told Stoddard brightly. "If you would be good enough to set both the cook and Bess down in front of the tooth drawer, I will try to find a way to get there."

Cook, half unconscious with the last drops of laudanum, hardly knew one chaise from another. She knew that she was in total misery and saw no reason to hold back the moans that gave her some comfort. She gave every sign of moaning constantly the six miles to town.

Julian Stoddard, seeing no way out, climbed grimly into the curricle. He had been fairly caught. Miss Rothwell, far from being the helpless maiden in distress, had made a fool of him. Between tight lips, he said, "How will you get to town?"

Chloe said, "We are not far from home, and we can walk back. When you get to the tooth drawer, there is no need for you to wait, Mr. Stoddard. I would not put that much burden on you."

She smiled brightly at him, and Julian Stoddard made ready to pick up the reins. Chloe's approval was glowing, and in spite of himself, Julian had to acknowledge that he was beaten this time. He was seething, beneath his bland exterior, and whipped his horses up into a strong trot.

Chloe watched him go down the road, and said to Sophy, "How fortunate it is that he came along. And I must say, I am not sorry to be relieved of Cook's moaning all the way."

Sophy said, brightly, "What shall we do now?"

A lazy voice drawled from over their heads, "Perhaps I can be of service."

The two girls looked up to see Sir Richard, controlling his pair of grays with one hand and looking down at Chloe with a smile. Sir Richard was fully appreciative of the situation. He took note of Stoddard's chaise, the three figures in it crowded together, leaving at a fast pace. It was amusing to see Julian Stoddard, the well-known rake and gambler, saddled with a cook and a maid, when Richard was quite sure his trap had been set for Chloe. There was much to be explained, but now was not the time.

Richard said, "Don't worry, all will be well." He dropped his groom to help Chloe, giving him instructions about getting the chaise back to Rothwell Manor. "Let me take you to town," said Richard. "You really should be there, Chloe."

He reached his hand down to Sophy, and then to Chloe, and they set out in Stoddard's wake.

Stoddard set a fast pace, in mingled anger and resentment. He had looked back once and seen another gentleman picking up the girl that he himself had stopped to help. How had she done it? He had no way of getting rid of the wretched woman except by depositing her at her destination. And the sooner the better.

Behind him, the occupants of the other vehicle were enjoying themselves. Sophy, full of excitement at the accident and their rescue, was hard to silence. Her audience could not easily escape, and she proceeded to explain to Sir Richard about her good friend Emma Partridge. "Her mother—you know, Lady Partridge—plans to go to Bath. She says it is not as fashionable as Brighton, but on the other hand she says it is more distinguished. Lady Partridge and Emma will be gone for a month or two. I think I'll die while they're gone, for you must know that Emma is my great friend."

Richard said, "I agree with Lady Partridge. The Regent's vicinity is apt to be a little stimulating."

Sophy said, "Do you think so? I should like above all things to see the Prince Regent. I understand he is so gross that he can't walk without help. Is that right?"

Richard, somewhat absently, agreed that the Prince Regent's weight was indeed a problem.

Sophy continued to prattle about Emma and her plans for her trip, and Lady Partridge's plan to take all her own linen, as well as everything else she would need, as though she were removing forever.

With Sophy's artless prattle, and Richard's pleasure at knowing that Chloe was with him, the time passed swiftly.

They pulled up at last before the tooth drawer, and found Julian Stoddard with his hands full.

Julian had made the trip in a short time, but Mrs. Field had not had sufficient motive so far to get down from the chaise and up the stairs to the rooms over the drapery shop. Chloe jumped lightly down from Richard's chaise and ran to where Cook and Mr. Stoddard seemed bound together forever. Standing on the sidewalk, she looked up at Bess, whose woebegone face gave mute evidence of the ordeal she had just passed. Not one to like a fast ride, in the open curricle the ground had passed far too swiftly beneath her half-closed eyes.

By dint of sheer authority, Chloe got the sufferer to the sidewalk and then bent her efforts to thanking Julian Stoddard. Richard, silently, came to stand unobtrusively beside Chloe. Julian received Chloe's thanks grimly, and hardly replied. He left quickly, and Chloe turned to Richard.

"Are you all right?" said Richard.

"Yes, I am fine, but I do wonder how I will get Cook back to the manor. I cannot impose further on Mr. Stoddard."

"Especially since he will take care not to be close enough to be imposed upon," Richard pointed out. He smiled then, in a conspiratorial fashion, and suddenly Chloe smiled back. The mischievous dimple appeared on her left cheekbone, and she said, "He truly didn't like it much, did he?"

Richard said, "The best thing is to have Rothwell send the coach, and I will see to that."

"But you have no groom?"

"No, but I will send a messenger from the inn."

Chloe looked doubtful, and Richard told her, "Don't worry. I will not leave you alone in town."

Thus reassured, Chloe and Sophy dealt with the patient. For the time being her hands were full, but she thought how grateful she was to Richard. When he came along, it seemed as though all trouble smoothed out, all obstacles were removed from her path.

Later, Chloe tried to forget the next hour. Cook was miserable, stubborn, and in severe pain. But the tooth drawer, a mincing little man, was possessed of surprising strength, and was more than a match for Cook. Sophy, avoiding the inner office at all costs, stood at the window and favored her audience with a running commentary on the sights she saw below. Finally Chloe bade her to be silent, and Sophy subsided. Sophy commented, "I suppose you'd rather hear Cook moan than hear me talk." But her grumbling quieted, and there was an ominous silence from the inner room.

It was perhaps half an hour later when Mr. Tully came out, wiping his hands. "I've given her an opiate, which will keep her quiet until you can get her home. Do you have more laudanum?"

Chloe and Mr. Tully discussed the opiate, and the small vial was refilled. Tucking it carefully away, Chloe said, "I wonder if we could wait here until the coach from Rothwell Manor comes." Sophy, with a tight little smile, said, "The coach is waiting downstairs."

Chloe said, "For how long? You didn't tell me?"

Sophy said, "You bade me be silent."

Chloe said, "You wretched child. Here I've been worrying how we would go on."

Cook was more dead weight than cooperative. Richard's message had been comprehensive enough so that not only did the coachman come, but two footmen to help with Cook. Once stowed inside the coach, with Bess and Sophy beside her, Chloe looked up to see Richard beside her. "I came to see you on your way."

Chloe said, "I can't thank you enough. I do not know what I would do without you."

Richard thought, it is my hope you never will have to, but he only smiled. He saw them off trundling down the street and turning on the road that would take them back to Rothwell Manor. Richard, with much to think about, decided to look up Julian Stoddard. He had a few things to say to him, but he did not readily find him, and soon dismissed him from his mind. If Stoddard was a man of any sensibility, he would have left town already.

10

That fine weather was the last for some time. The rains set in, and bade fair to stay. Chloe gave Julian Stoddard no more than a passing thought. He had come along when she needed him, but no man of humanitarian impulses could have left Cook moaning on the grassy bank. Chloe felt no unusual obligation to him.

As a matter of fact, the household demands filled her days. Her legacy seemed very far off, and since life was proceeding in its accustomed channels, she was content to let it be.

Julian Stoddard, however, was still in Kent, and he had not forgotten Chloe's fortune. He congratulated himself that he was one of the very few who knew that Chloe was now an heiress. But he was still sulking at what he considered Chloe's malicious scheming. How had it come about that, instead of helping Chloe in her suffering, he had been saddled with a fat, moaning cook?

He could not quite put his finger on Chloe's fault, but he believed that she made a fool of him. Only the knowledge that he, more often than not, had pockets to let kept him here. Besides, the tab at the inn here was far cheaper than his lodgings in London. Another advantage was that the bailiffs did not know where he was.

While Julian worked off his sulks, life at Rothwell Manor continued. In spite of the teeming rain, Sir Richard was able to ride over to Rothwell Manor at least for short periods. Even though he did not always see Chloe, he could not stay away. Sometimes Chloe appeared, and his day turned into sunshine. But more often than not Lady Rothwell received him, sitting on a small divan and not bothering to rise when he came in.

She claimed to be working on an embroidered screen. Richard could see no progress on it. The same half-finished fish swam in fragmentary waves, and although his interest in the screen was cursory, yet he found it hard to find another subject in which both he and Lady Rothwell had the same degree of interest. On his third visit, when the weather was still lowering and rain fell at times from the leaden sky, Lady Rothwell beamed at him, saying, "How glad we are that you are back in the neighborhood. I vow it would be a dreary day without your visit."

She turned to Lydia and complained, "I wonder whether Chloe could make an effort to keep my cup of chocolate filled. I hate to bother the servants, but Chloe could certainly do me this small kindness."

Lydia, ignoring their visitor, said fretfully, "Chloe might hire another servant or two. She has enough money now to make things easier for all of us."

Edward, entering to greet Richard, objected. "I will hire all the servants necessary. I'm sure Chloe does more than her share at keeping the household running smoothly."

Lydia said, fretfully, "You said we can't afford a London Season, so I thought we were poor."

Edward, horrified, shot an apologetical glance at Richard and frowned at Lydia. Richard, amused, knew that Edward wished for his absence, but he was enjoying himself, and there was always the chance that Chloe might come in.

Edward, mortified at Lydia's want of conduct, said so. "I have become more and more appalled," said Edward heavily, "at your behavior. You must gain a little more decorum before I ever agree to let you go to London. You would be a disgrace to us all."

Lydia, her cheeks flushed, rose awkwardly to her feet, spilling Lady Rothwell's embroidery silks all over the floor. Lady Rothwell cried out, but Lydia fled the room. She did not bother to bid farewell to Richard, but only muttered broken little phrases, and Richard was quite sure he had heard the words "getting even."

What a household! His dear Chloe must have a harder time than he had thought. Yet there was no complaint from her.

Lady Rothwell said, comfortably, to Richard, "You see, Sir Richard, we do not stand on ceremony with you. You are such an old friend, it is as though you were part of the family."

Richard was conscious of a wish that they did stand on more ceremony with him.

She turned the subject neatly. Coyly, she began to tease him. "Soon we will have a new lady at Davenant Hall, I suppose?"

Appalled, Richard's wits left him. He was considering the unpleasantness of Chloe's existence in a household of people with whom she had so little in common. His wishes overleaped his circumstances, so that he was thinking of Chloe away from Rothwell Manor and safely installed at Davenant Hall. Richard agreed absently. "Yes, and soon!"

Chloe led a life here of some strictness, and Richard knew that there were few, if any, books for her to read. She had the burden of the household, while her stepmother did nothing. She was at the beck and call of Lady Rothwell, and was exposed to Francis Hensley and Julian Stoddard, as well, as suitors.

Eventually, still bemused, and without regard for the cat he had inadvertently let out among the pigeons, Richard took his leave. He had satisfied Lady Rothwell's question about a new lady at Davenant Hall, and did not realize that Lady Rothwell's thoughts ran along entirely different channels from his. Lady Rothwell was considering the exact wording of her letter to her sister, in London. For once, Lady Rothwell would have the latest gossip. Sir Richard was certainly going to offer for someone, and in a very short time.

While Richard would not have bothered about the gossip passed on to Mrs. Hensley, he would have been dismayed to realize that his words, spoken absently, would have been relayed to Chloe before he was down the drive. "So you see," said Lady Rothwell, "that Sir Richard will not be with us very long. He is, after all, a man of some elegance, and London is his proper habitat."

Chloe, taken aback by the reminder that Richard's marriage would be arranged soon when she had been almost able to forget it, told herself once more that he was only her Great Friend. She tried to bolster her own spirits without success. It was the weather—the gloomy miserable leaden weather!

The next day the weather turned fine, in that clear freshness that comes after heavy rain. But Chloe was still in the mopes, and this time she could not blame it on the weather.

Lady Rothwell, finally stirring herself, called Francis. Closing the door behind him, she told him pointblank her concern. "I do not see any signs of a betrothal between you and Chloe," she said at once. "Have you come to an understanding?"

Francis, his worst fears realized, found that his tongue would not obey him. Instead, he was forced to shake his head.

"I had hoped to see more signs of progress by now, Francis." Francis, at a loss, cast his eyes wildly around looking for escape. While all the world might see Lady Rothwell as an indolent, selfish woman, calling her servants or her family to do the slightest task for her, and moreover not overburdened with intellect, Francis, who had known her since his childhood, saw her as a fire-breathing dragon.

He had strong and vivid memories of Lady Rothwell descending upon him when all he wanted was to be left alone—and forcing him against his will to do one thing or another. While his method of existing with his mother was simply to move out and take rooms of his own, yet he felt his bones turn to jelly when Lady Rothwell spoke to him. It was beyond reason, he knew, and yet there it was. He had no defense against his aunt.

She, dimly aware of this, pursued her advantage. "I shall plan an outing," she announced, "for you and Chloe. I think a day in the open air, to take advantage of this beautiful weather, will be the thing. I shall send Edward along, to preserve the proprieties, you know, but I shall expect you to remember your duty to your family and to yourself. That inheritance, I've told you before, must on no account leave the family. There is no reason why Chloe's money should go to enrich some total stranger."

Francis stared dumbly at his hands. But Lady Rothwell was not finished. "And what possessed you to tell Julian Stoddard about Chloe's fortune? I am in half a mind to refuse him admittance to the house."

Francis stammered in dismay. "You can't do that! Not the thing!"

"Well, perhaps we've seen the last of him anyway. But I expect tomorrow to have some news to write to your mother."

While Lady Rothwell's strenuous representations to Francis were designed to fill his backbone with starch and impel him to ardent wooing, her efforts fell short of the mark. She was not working with malleable material. Although Francis, in the ordinary way, rushed to do her bidding, yet she had pressed him too far. Instead of making Francis more determined to press his suit upon Chloe, the result of Lady Rothwell's remarks was simply to make Francis more distressed, more inarticulate than ever.

He had the strong feeling that he was akin to a rabbit caught in a trap, and even a rabbit has a wish to escape, he told himself. Francis toyed with the idea of escaping back to London, but the same paralysis that kept him from offering for Chloe also kept him from summoning his chaise and his valet and removing himself from his aunt's vicinity.

Lady Rothwell, stirring herself unusually, planned the outing. There was a particularly fine view over the Vale of Kent—"not that horrid crypt the vicar discovered!"—and Lydia and Sophy were enthusiastic, for their lives were so uneventful that even a carriage ride and picnic stood out as a high point of pleasure. But Lady Rothwell also insisted that Edward leave his books and accounts and go along. For she said, in the privacy of the book room, "You know that if Francis and Chloe go on an outing, someone must go along to preserve the proprieties."

Edward protested. "They've been playfellows since the cradle. What folly do you think Francis could come up with now?"

Lady Rothwell, smirking, said, "Chloe may consider Francis her playfellow, but his status has changed. He is a suitor, and therefore you must go along."

Edward, from long experience, realized that when his mother was set, the easiest course was to accede to her demands.

Midway through the next morning, the picnic outing started down the drive. Never were participants on what was, after all, supposed to be a gay sight-seeing occasion, more glum. The chaise, now fully repaired, held Chloe and her two sisters. Edward rode beside them, and Francis on the other flank. A dog cart with the picnic supplies had gone on ahead.

Edward's mouth was drawn, reflecting the recent report of his farm manager, who wished to cull out certain sheep and replace them with a new strain. Edward disliked innovation, and his interview with his agent had become somewhat heated.

Now he was thinking of the problem, weighing advantages and disadvantages in his thorough, painstaking way. On the other side of the carriage rode Francis Hensley. It would be hard for anyone to read Francis's thoughts, and it was quite likely that there were none. He liked Chloe well enough, but he was not ready to be leg-shackled. Yet he saw that dire fate approaching, and there was nothing he could do about it. If his Aunt Rothwell told him to jump off a cliff, he feared that he would oblige her.

They reached the end of the drive and were turning away from town when Edward caught sight of Richard riding toward them.

Greetings exchanged, Edward said, "Why don't you come along with us? There is plenty of food, and the weather is fine, for a change."

Edward wanted company in his enforced attendance at the picnic. Edward often spoke of Richard's elevated conversation, and faced with the prospect of Francis all afternoon, hailed Richard as one might, on hands and knees on the desert, greet an oasis.

Richard, holding such an outing in aversion, stopped to speak to Chloe. To his surprise, Chloe did not meet his eyes. Instead, she focused on a point somewhere beyond his left ear and spoke civilly, but not warmly.

Richard was daunted. What's happened now? he thought, and sensibly dismissing speculation until he knew more, he changed his mind instantly and accepted Edward's invitation.

The picnic spot was not more than an hour's leisurely drive away. The prospect from the elevation was indeed fine, and the servants, having arrived before, were already laying out the cloths and cushions and unpacking the picnic hampers.

Richard coaxed Chloe to stroll with him to a vantage point somewhat apart, and said, very kindly, "What has happened to put you in the mopes? Don't tell me Cook has another toothache?"

Chloe smiled slightly, and said, "No, she's quite well."

Richard forebore to ask her any more, for he sensed her distress. He said, simply, "You must know, Chloe, that I am at your service. Whatever I can do to help you, I will do."

Chloe thanked him, but bit back the sharp retort that would have explained all to him. She could not take advantage of his kind offer when he was all but betrothed to somebody else. He was her good friend, but she must not lean on him. She must learn to stand on her own feet, even though, since Richard had come back, she was more and more conscious of a strong temptation to throw herself upon his chest and unburden herself of all her troubles.

And yet, she had no troubles to speak of. She was possessed of a house, Highmoor, and she could remove there at any time. But she feared loneliness more than she feared her present unhappiness. "Shall we go back?" she said. They strolled back to the picnic site, and Chloe wished she had an appetite for the fare. There was cold chicken, rolled in a special herb-flavored batter of Cook's own concoction. There were peaches and grapes, and wine. There was ratafia for Chloe and Sophy and Lydia.

Sophy cried out, "I am sharp-set! That fresh air has certainly given me an appetite."

After everyone was full, Lydia watched the gentlemen drinking wine, "Please, I'd like to taste it. Francis, pour a little out for me. Here's my glass."

Francis, recoiling in indignation, refused. "You're far too young for wine. It's not the thing."

Lydia pouted, "I am grown up enough for that. Everybody treats me like a child."

Edward, tearing himself away from a discussion with Richard, was shocked. "Lydia! What are you thinking of? Even Chloe doesn't drink wine!"

Francis contented himself with one remark, "Unseemly!"

Lydia gave every sign of imminent tears. Sophy, watching her out of the corner of her eye, hid a malicious smile. Lydia appealed to the arbiter of elegance. "Sir Richard," she cried, "tell them that I'm old enough to drink wine. You think I am, don't you?"

All eyes were on Richard. Any man of sense would have agreed with the other men, so thought Edward. But to his great surprise and startled disapproval, Richard said, "Yes, I think you are old enough. This is port, and you will probably like the taste of it. It's quite sweet."

In a stunned silence, Lydia reached her glass out. No hand moved to the wine bottle. Richard finally lifted the bottle by the neck. Then, he added, with a deceptive air of casualness, "Many women in London choose to drink lemon squash, for instance, or ratafia. But you are old enough to know what pleases you." Pouring wine slowly from the bottle, he added, "I know of one young lady who was turned down by Almack's because Lady Jersey had seen her drinking wine. It wasn't even port, which of course is more ineligible."

Lydia cried, unbelieving, "And they snubbed her for *that*?"

Richard said, "I agree it is totally unreasonable. But there it is. The poor girl left London the next week, for without a voucher at Almack's nobody invited her anywhere."

Lydia's glass was half full. And Richard was pouring even more slowly. She gave a long, shuddering sigh and said finally, "I don't think I want any after all."

It had been a near thing, thought Sir Richard, conscious of great relief. He had half expected the girl to drink the wine in sheer defiance of her brother. But Lydia, having a modicum of sense, had come down on the right side and Richard's reputation was saved.

As though by accident, he glanced at Chloe and caught her eye. He saw, to his satisfaction, glowing approval in her glance. Her gray eyes spoke warmly to him, and he felt cheered by her approval.

Her earlier mood was banished, and he decided not to ask any more about the cause of it.

The day wore to an end, and the party returned to Rothwell Manor. Richard left them at the gates of his own estate. They were weary, after a day in the open air. Francis, especially, had been overtaken by lassitude, and begged a place in the coach. Silence fell upon them. Each was wrapped in thought, and basked in the mild air of contentment.

Lydia, half asleep, had visions of Sir Richard watching over her when she went to London, even Sir Richard at her feet imploring her to *have Mercy on him*.

Edward, finding his thoughts clear after a discussion with Richard about sheep, knew what he would say to his factor. The culls would go, and Edward would purchase the new stock to upgrade his flock. It was a hard decision, but Sir Richard's thoughts on the subject were well taken, and Edward was gratified.

Sophy was wondering, with an eye to her own good, whether Edward's mood was genial enough to mention again the journey that she wished to take with Emma Partridge.

Francis, quite simply, was sound asleep and snoring.

Chloe's thoughts were jumbled. She tried to put Sir Richard out of her mind, for she knew the trap that lay there when Richard would bring his bride home to the Hall. She had no intention of falling so deeply in love with him that she would be miserable the rest of her life, but now, every time she closed her eyes, she could see his features. His nose was strong, his jaw was firm and would have given rise to speculation that he was a hard man to deal with had it not been for his sweet smile—the smile that could turn her heart over—and his kind, laughing eyes. It was no use. She could not banish Richard from her mind, nor in the long run did she want to.

They turned into the drive and the wheels crunched on the gravel. They rode up to the front entrance, past the stable wall. Edward, his proprietary glance noticing everything about his domain, jolted them all awake. He cried out, "Whose phaeton is that in the stable yard?"

11

The seat of a high-perch phaeton was visible, rising above the wall.

Edward said, wondering, "Nobody in this neighborhood has one. I myself consider them totally unsuitable for country driving."

Francis, at last aroused by the confusion around him, took one glance at it, and mumbled, "Good God! Did I wake up in Hyde Park?"

Lydia, predictably, was much pleased. She cried out, "Look at all the visitors we've had! More than in the whole past year put together." She reached out to touch Chloe's hand. "It's all thanks to you and your legacy!"

Chloe managed to say, "Nonsense." Lydia bounced a little on the seat and said, "This is only the beginning of

how it will be, Chloe, when you take your house in town."
Edward was too far away to hear Lydia's remarks, but
Chloe thought, with a sinking heart, I do not look forward
to London!

Her own stay in London was far too vivid in her mind
for her to remember it with pleasure. She had been there
only briefly, but no matter how kind Lady Rothwell's sister, Mrs. Hensley, had been, Chloe herself was not pretty
enough, nor well enough dowered, to cut much of a
swathe. She was shy, and did not show well in company,
and although the circumstance of her recall—her father's
sudden death—was overwhelmingly sad, yet she was conscious of a small amount of relief. She knew she would
not "take."

She still bore the scars of what she had fancied as rejection. She did not know that her own charm was sufficient,
after one grew acquainted with it, to bring her friends
who, while not numerous, would yet be appreciative and
steady. She had only the recollection of rejection, and here
in her own home, with her own family around her, she felt
secure. The legacy that had come to her, while gratifying,
yet was unsettling.

No matter what Lydia hoped, Chloe herself would not
enjoy the whirl of a London Season five years late. Chloe
had a fearful feeling, akin, if she only knew it, to one who
hears the distant roar of a cataract downstream.

She was not left in peace to dwell on her sinking feeling
about London, for Lydia was climbing over her, the better
to see the fashionable rig in the stable yard before the carriage moved on to the front door. Edward, troubled in his
own way, said, "A man's a fool to trust himself to the
roads in that!"

Once within doors, they found that Lady Rothwell was
entertaining the owner of the vehicle. If Chloe had been
troubled before, at the sight of the visitor her heart sank
to her toes. She remembered him, without pleasure, from a
party in London where she had been on the sidelines and
Thaddeus Invers had given her one glance and then forgotten her. Chloe, puzzled, wondered why he had wandered so far from London. Lady Rothwell, glaring at her
guest in a most uncivilized way, seemed to share Chloe's
doubts. But Edward, and Francis as well, recognized the
purpose that shone from their visitor's eyes when he
caught sight of Chloe.

They had apparently interrupted the newcomer in a rec-
itation of his genealogical attributes. Long known as one
of the most voluble of the men one might chance to meet
in London, he was now demonstrating the accuracy of his
reputation.

He was well connected, and possessed of a competence.
Clearly he was not a man of conservative tastes, as
demonstrated by the high-perch phaeton outside, and one
might well question his common sense. To ride in a vehicle of such extreme design from London into Kent was
not only uncomfortable but perilous.

For his part, Thaddeus Invers was in Kent only from
necessity. His family wished for him to marry. There were
no immediate heirs to his uncle's title, and his own branch
of the family was anxious to succeed to the honor. Invers,
to do him credit, was possessed of no such ambition, but
he was easily swayed, being not of strong will but of a certain shrewdness. His bent was intellectual, but his mind
was more mirror than wellspring, reflecting current
thought.

He had been on the London scene for some years, and
by now had worn out or been refused all avenues of eligible marriage. The news was now beginning to circulate
among London salons about an heiress in Kent. Thaddeus,
recognizing the desperation of his family and knowing that
duty called him, had come down to investigate.

Being essentially a bore, Thaddeus had developed a
thick shell of insensitivity that was his sole protection. He
took delight in knowing people and dropping their names
casually into the most trivial conversation. It was by dint of
his imperviousness to insult that he was able to say with
all the accuracy of an eyewitness, that the Prince Regent—for example—was fond of a certain gold brocade
waistcoat.

In many circles this kind of hobnobbing with the elite
gave him entry, and a certain welcome. However, Lady
Rothwell, seeing in him a rival for the claims of her
nephew Francis, was less than cordial.

He turned toward the newcomers with a look of great
relief. Edward, however, disappointed him, for his welcome was no warmer than his mother's. Thaddeus crossed
quickly to Chloe and bowed over her hand. He murmured
that he remembered her well from the occasions when he

had seen her before, and Chloe barely restrained an exclamation of "Fustian!"

He was passing through on his way to Brighton following the Prince Regent, for Prinny had expressly summoned him to attend him—so he said.

The attitude of his hearers gave no sign that they believed him. He waited hopefully for an invitation to dinner. Since none was forthcoming and he had sufficient perception to realize that they were all exhausted, their cheeks unbecomingly flushed with their exposure to the fresh air, he took his leave. He lingered again over Chloe's hand, and left gracefully.

Edward said, "I suppose he can't help it."

It was a cryptic remark, but Chloe, who had caught Thaddeus's words as he bent over her hand just before he left, was not so sure. He had told Chloe, with assurance, that he would call on her tomorrow. She was distressed, and said, "Oh, pray——" and could not finish.

He was convinced of his own tact and acceptability, and took her reluctance to be merely maidenly embarrassment. She was merely playing coy, and he rather liked that in a woman.

By the next day, Rothwell Manor was a-buzz with speculation about Miss Rothwell's legacy. Although it had been rumored, there was little said about it after the first surprise. But now the unexpected advent of suitors for her hand and fortune let down the barriers and the servants' hall was rife with speculation.

Cook said, flatly, "There isn't a one of them that's good enough for Miss Chloe. Why, I could tell you of the times that she has gone out of her way to be kind to us all, and I say there isn't another mistress like her in the world."

Cook's husband, Field the butler, automatically taking the opposite view from his wife, said, "She'll be happier with young Hensley, for he dotes on her. I can't say the same about the others."

Cook snorted. "I suppose you know all there is to know about it, Mr. Field," she exclaimed. "Now what I think is——"

What Cook thought was that Miss should go to her own new home and get away from this family. For they were all leeches, according to Cook, whose recollection of Chloe's kind hand when she was ill was still vivid. Bess, Chloe's maid, declared at length her own wish to go with her mistress when she went to Highmoor. But outside the door of the servants' dining room, two of the footmen were surreptitiously gambling on which of the three suitors would win out.

The gambling fever, no less strong in Rothwell Manor than it was at certain well-known gambling haunts in London, spread from the servants at Rothwell Manor, seeking a wider scope, to the Davenant Hall staff.

Richard, quite by accident, learned of the wagers. His butler, not knowing that Richard had entered the hall, was chastising the footmen for gambling on such an event. Richard moved into the morning room, and Dall served him with his breakfast. Richard passed a remark or two about the weather and then, without changing the tone of his voice, said, "What is it the men are gambling on?"

The butler said, "I am sorry it came to your notice, Sir Richard, for I should keep a firmer hand on the footmen. They are just boys, and need to be taught a great deal."

Richard said, "I quite agree. But what was the subject?" Dall did not answer at once, and Sir Richard raised an inquiring eyebrow. The butler, having known Sir Richard since he was a boy, recognized that this was no time to evade the truth.

In halting words, he apprised his master of the question, Which of Miss Rothwell's three suitors had the inside track?"

Richard, conscious of an anger that was suddenly on the boil, said, "*Three* suitors?"

It was thus that he learned of Thaddeus Invers' arrival.

The butler had expected Sir Richard to be irritated by the gambling. But Sir Richard was nearly white with anger. There was a telltale flicker of the muscle of his jaw, and the butler's heart sank. He knew Sir Richard in this mood, and he wished with all his heart to be elsewhere, instantly. But to his gratification the moment was gone, and Sir Richard smiled again somewhat easily. The butler, thus encouraged, and not averse to picking up some inside information, allowed himself to probe delicately, seeking Sir Richard's opinion as gently as one's tongue explores the vicinity of a sore tooth. His own information was that Hensley and Stoddard had not much to recommend them, but Invers was considered quite certainly a dark horse.

Richard, dismissing Dall without real information, gave himself over to reverie. He had much to think about. Apparently the matter was getting more serious than he thought. He had been able to dismiss that idiot Hensley, for no woman in her right mind would marry him. Julian Stoddard, a gambler himself, was merely testing the throw of the dice. Richard could not believe that Stoddard was at bottom serious about offering to marry Chloe. But Thaddeus Invers—that was another question entirely.

He reviewed mentally what he knew about Thaddeus Invers—a snob, a shallow intellectual, very fond of his own voice, and altogether a lightweight. Some people called him, behind his back, and mockingly, a Puritan preacher. They did not know how close they came to the mark.

Richard knew what most people did not know—that Invers was a son of a Puritan divine and was ashamed of it. He was well connected, and his connection with his uncle's family was genuine. The uncle, a very minor baronet, did not recognize all members qf his family, and his cousin, who had married a clergyman, and not Church of England at that, had been cast out of his life. But still the Puritan preacher, his wife, and their thirteen children clung to the relationship, a one-sided affair.

Thaddeus, coming to London to make his fortune, was at once made aware that chapel goers, as his father was, were not accepted in the best society. But it was clear to Richard and to the few who knew his family that Thaddeus Invers came rightly by his ardent wish to impart information to all and sundry. Richard thought, Once again, heredity tells.

But to think of his Chloe subjected to this kind of rampant fortune hunting—Hensley and Stoddard and especially this newcomer, Invers—caused Richard's indignation to simmer and then to boil.

This kind of footling procrastination could not be allowed to continue. If Chloe's half-brother could not scatter the suitors, then he himself would. He was reminded strongly of Homer's tale of Penelope and the suitors who importuned her while waiting for Ulysses to return. Richard himself was no Ulysses, he thanked the Creator, but he could scatter suitors.

He dressed with great care, purposely avoiding any dandyish aspect, for he would not compete with Stoddard. Dressed in buckskins suitable for the country, he set out from his front door and headed toward Rothwell Manor.

He was cheerful, for he had yesterday felt that he and Chloe understood each other. She had smiled on him then, and he was encouraged. He thought that, when she had held off that first day, telling him she considered him only her Great Friend—she must have been impulsive. Now, on further acquaintance, he was convinced that she regarded him with more than ordinary kindness.

At the Manor, he found Chloe beset, not by suitors, as he half expected, but by a family row. It was not the first row that Richard had been privileged to see, but he devoutly hoped it would be the last.

Hardly conscious of his arrival, Lydia and her mother were talking to Chloe. Lydia and her mother for once were on good terms, with a common goal. They were seeking Chloe's support, now backed by her inheritance, against Edward.

Edward's face was becoming alarmingly red, and Richard wondered if there was a tendency to apoplexy in the family. Edward's father had died suddenly, but Richard, not at home at the time, could not remember the cause.

"Chloe," said Lady Rothwell, "it is a simple thing. I wish to give a dinner and ball for all our friends and neighbors. It is an entertainment long overdue, and I feel that the time has come to go out in society a bit more."

Chloe, looking beset, said, "It is not my decision to make. It is yours, Mama, and Edward's."

Lydia said, "Well, you can say you're in favor of it, can't you?"

Lady Rothwell said, "Of course, Chloe, you must say what you think."

Her attitude gave rise to little doubt that Chloe's opinion was to be in favor of the ball.

But Edward, almost pounding his fist on his knees, said, "I refuse to allow it. It is too pretentious, too out-of-place. We should keep more to ourselves, lest our neighbors think we are vaunting ourselves simply because Chloe has had a bit of good fortune."

Lydia for once was silent, letting her mother lead the attack. Lady Rothwell was nothing loath. "It is time that our girls got some experience at being in society," said Lady Rothwell. "You tell them they are not at ease, which I doubt, but so you say. Then you deny them the opportunity to get the very experience you chide them for not having. I declare, Edward, your reasoning baffles me entirely."

It was clear to Richard that this was not the first time the subject had been mentioned. Edward was heated. He said, unequivocally, "Lydia is too young for London, and she is too young for Kent. She is certainly not old enough to come out at what would be after all a ball that appears to be in her honor. Unless you had in mind to present Chloe to the entire county?"

Lady Rothwell was taken aback. "Certainly not. Chloe needs no introduction to our friends and neighbors." Lady Rothwell was having second thoughts. If she did in fact invite the entire county, as it seemed her plan was, then all would have a chance to meet Chloe, knowing full well that she had received a legacy. Since it was her heartfelt wish to bring Chloe and Francis together, she could see that her plan for a large entertainment would defeat her own purpose. Unless Chloe could be persuaded not to join? Lady Rothwell dismissed the idea as soon as it came.

Richard stood in the doorway, his stomach turning in disgust. He glanced at Sophy, whose bright little eyes, like a chipmunk's, were watching her mother and her brother. It was clear to Richard, who had no illusions about Sophy and her malicious nature, that the child was assessing the relative merits of each side. And when the outcome was clear, on that side Sophy would be. Ever one to range herself on the side of victory, with its attendant advantages, Sophy had only to bide her time.

Edward, with a start, noticed Richard. Chloe had not yet said what she thought about the ball, but her cheeks were flushed. Richard was not sure whether it was the prospect of all the arrangements, which he knew would unfailingly fall upon her slender shoulders, or whether she shrank from appearing in public with her stepmother's doubtful protection.

The family row broke up. It was not over, but was merely postponed to a later time, when the combatants would have gathered further ammunition and start anew.

Richard and Chloe were left alone. She exclaimed, "How fortunate I am in having a friend!"

"Is it something you can talk to me about?"

"Yes, I feel so guilty. I sometimes wish I were not here. It must be wrong of me not to love my family more than I do. I want to go and live at Highmoor, but Edward says it is totally out of the question."

Richard was ready to lay his heart at her feet. She wanted to leave Rothwell—he would provide the means. Highmoor was inappropriate, he agreed with Edward on that, but he was too wise to say so. He had opened his mouth to say what was in his heart, when she broke out.

Vehemently, she cried out, "I wish I had never heard of the legacy! I cannot help but feel that people are more conscious of it than I am. I do think of Highmoor, to be honest, as though it were a dream. But I keep seeing in people's eyes the idea that here's Chloe Rothwell, *nothing* without the fortune that she has inherited!"

Richard said, "I'm sure you are mistaken."

She ignored his protest. "It is an ugly feeling, and I wish I could wash it away as one washes dirty hands, but I can't. I begin not to trust people."

Richard said calmly, "No one?"

A great deal hung on her answer, he thought, and yet he made no effort to sway her mind. She turned to him, with that glowing smile that wrenched something inside of him. "Only you, Richard, for you want nothing of me. I cannot tell you how grateful I am to you that you have asked me for nothing. I don't see that ugly look in your eye, the look I see in that disgusting Mr. Invers', for instance." She took Richard's hands, and he felt hers cold and shivering within his fingers. "I pray you, Richard, do not change. I should be lost indeed without my Great Friend!"

The words he had planned to say to her stuck in his throat, and he could not speak over the lump they made. But he must say something, for there was too much in his eyes, and he feared she would read it. Swallowing hard, he said, to his own great surprise, "I'm going up to London tomorrow."

"To London?" she queried. "I had hoped you would stay. . . ." and then, blushing, her voice trailed away.

He said, "I do not wish to tell you why, but I will be gone only a couple of days." Then he added. "I will trust you not to say anything about my trip to anyone."

She nodded, her heart too full to speak. Without a doubt Richard was going to London to see someone who claimed his devotion, and he would come back and tell her which one he had chosen. She was at least grateful that he did not now confide his hopes to her.

Richard saw that she was troubled and took it as a sign that she missed him and was glad of his presence. He had no way of knowing what was in her thoughts, and therefore it did not occur to him, naturally, to deny her supposition.

In due course Richard took his leave, kissing her hand as he left. He did not look back. He was low in his mind, the reverse of his cheerful mood when he had come up the drive. Then he had thought that like Lochinvar, he would come out of the wilds and carry her off, not stopping for brake or for stone. But the bride, contrary to Lochinvar's, was unwilling.

Chloe, watching him go down the drive, saw her one main support in her trying life going to marry someone else. If Richard's mood was low, which she could not know, her own was at the nadir.

In London the next day, Richard sat across from his attorney, Mr. Aston. His mood was no lighter than it had been when he left Chloe the day before. Several thoughts had come to Richard's mind overnight. There were several inquiries he wished Aston to make. "Edward's reputation, Mr. Aston?" he asked. "He has in his hands a trust. I wonder whether he has played false with it?" Mr. Aston, a wisp of a man, dry as his own briefs and full of repetition, but as shrewd as any man in London, said, "Oh no, tut tut tut tut, Sir Richard. Lord Rothwell is totally honest. Following the hint contained in your letter last week, I have made inquiry. The trust is in fine shape, has even been augmented. The interest is paid out regularly into the trustee's hands, Sir Richard, and what happens to it then I cannot know. But the capital is in fine shape."

Richard mused. "Then that's not the trouble." Then, making a decision, Richard said, "Now here's what I'd like you to do." He gave him certain instructions, and finished, "Be ready to act."

Mr. Aston, eyeing him shrewdly, said, "In what direction?"

But Richard could not tell him. "I don't know yet, but I am uneasy."

Mr. Aston, as Sir Richard was one of his best clients, escorted him downstairs to his town phaeton. In an arch fashion, totally at variance with his normal manner, Mr. Aston said, "Are congratulations in order, Sir Richard?"

Richard his mind totally on Chloe, said, "Soon, I hope."

Richard would have been more circumspect, even with his man of affairs, had he foreseen the next couple of hours. He was walking down Mount Street, and turned into Oxford Street. In a landau, coming his way, was Penelope Salton. She had caught sight of him, and there was no escape. Her mother, Lady Salton, was with her, and they were, so she told Richard, on their way to the fashionable shops, for, she said, "You know there are two parties coming up at Vauxhall and I certainly want to look my best. Are you coming back to town for them?"

Richard made a noncommital answer and would have moved on, but they had stopped before their destination, and Richard in pure civility escorted Miss Salton and her mother into the shop.

It was unfortunate that Richard did not glance around him, for he might have seen Lady Rothwell's sister emerging from a nearby milliner's. Mrs. Hensley, whose bright little eyes missed nothing, saw Miss Salton and Lady Salton, escorted by Sir Richard Davenant. It was settled then! He had chosen Penelope, and Miss Morland and Miss Folkes must be ready to tear her eyes out! In high glee, planning as she rode home in her barouche the exact words she would use, she hurried to her desk and sat down to write her sister, Lady Rothwell.

12

Toward the end of the week, when Richard had returned to Davenant Hall, he took the next step in his campaign.

Edward, a smile of satisfaction creeping across his plump face, announced to the family that they had received an invitation to visit Davenant Hall. Lady Rothwell crowed. "I shall be glad of a chance to see the residence again, for I have not seen it since old Lady Davenant was gone. It is a fine house, and the prospect is delightful. It will be a pleasure for us to have such close contact with

Sir Richard, and his wife, and I look forward to a great deal of entertainment."

The invitation, though addressed to Lady Rothwell, included Chloe and the two girls.

Chloe, as always, was torn between anxiousness to see Richard again and dread of what he might tell her. Lady Rothwell was no help, for she insisted that this was a neighborly way to announce his engagement to the Rothwells. "For you must know," she said, "that we have always been on intimate terms with the Davenants, and this is a sign that nothing will change."

Nothing except her own relation with Richard, Chloe thought dismally. Edward said, "I care nothing for the house, of course, but I understand that he is going to have additional barns erected and I should like to talk to him about the new sheep I've ordered."

Chloe was unusually difficult to please that day. She put on a light yellow muslin, which she discarded in favor of a turquoise round gown with a taffeta sash, and then discarded them both in favor of a moss green with a shawl to match. She was, surprisingly, the last to arrive in the hall.

Sophy said, "You are so flushed, Chloe. Don't you feel well?"

"I'm perfectly fine!"

They set off down the drive for Davenant Hall. While much older than Rothwell Manor, the Hall was a more attractive residence. Chloe had often been in it when she was a child, but rarely had she arrived at the front entry in a carriage.

Richard stood on the doorstep to welcome them. Suddenly shy, Chloe hesitated until Richard smiled winningly at her, and she hastily stepped inside. The house was sunny and pleasant. Richard showed them one or two of the rooms on the ground floor, which were much lighter in aspect than those corresponding rooms at Rothwell Manor. It was hard to tell why, Chloe thought, except that Richard's mother had made every effort to bring daylight into the house, and provided cheerful, bright furnishings.

Dall served tea, and Lady Rothwell could find no fault with the service. The silver pot and its appurtenances bore a high degree of polish. The cups had been fashioned early in Josiah Wedgwood's career, and bore a distinctive appearance that was most charming.

Lady Rothwell remembered Richard's mother in detail.

She spoke approvingly of Lady Davenant's taste, and Richard's conversation was reduced to murmured words such as, "I remember when she did that."

Eventually, Richard broke away from the grasping conversational tentacles of Lady Rothwell and remarked in a voice that included the entire party, "The house needs a woman's touch again, I fear. My housekeeper tells me of many areas that need attention, although I confess I would not notice them myself."

Lady Rothwell beamed upon him, and it was clear that she expected him to say more. Since Richard's mind was traveling on a different road, he did not understand her meaning. She was forced to put it into words. Archly, she queried, "I suppose we will soon hear about a new Lady Davenant."

Richard, in the grip of his obsession about Chloe, was startled. Had he been so transparent? Was it possible that Chloe had changed her mind about receiving his offer? He glanced sidelong at Chloe, but she was steadily regarding her fingers, joined in her lap. For a very short time, Richard was at a loss for words. Then he caught Chloe's movement and looked at her directly. She was turning toward him with a startled expression, and her eyes were miserable.

His interpretation, not knowing that Rothwell Manor was agog at the thought of his marrying someone from London, was that Chloe was begging him silently to deny his interest in her. On the surface, Richard recovered quickly and said gallantly to Lady Rothwell, "When the right time comes, believe me, you will be among the first to know."

She smiled, accepting this promise as only her just due, and sank back in her chair.

Richard, casting about in his mind for an escape from this embarrassing conversation, hit upon the one thing that would turn the trick. He turned to Edward. "Rothwell, would you like to take a look at the stables? I've got a new animal that came over from my cousin's stable, and I'd like your opinion of it. Theale is a good judge of horseflesh, I think, but I'd like to show the horse to you."

Edward expressed his delight at the invitation, and the two men went to the door, and stopped. Richard turned back and looked at Chloe, and said, "Would you like to come along?" Without ceremony, and with the general aspect of one fleeing from an invader, Chloe leaped to her feet and hurried to the door. She turned back and spoke civilly to Lady Rothwell—"We'll only be a few minutes"—and left, walking between Richard and Edward.

At the back of the house they paused, and Chloe looked out across the slope down to the stables and beyond, to the woods. From here even the turrets at Rothwell Manor were hidden by the tall trees, and Davenant Hall gave her a feeling of being isolated from the world. Smiling brightly at Richard, she followed him down the slope to the stable. They walked past neglected gardens. Richard pointed out, with mild regret, "There are so many things that need to be done, and I can't find the time."

Evans, Richard's head groom, emerged from the stables and watched them come. Chloe listened with half her mind to Richard and Edward and the lilting cadence of Evans. Evans still kept a bit of Welsh in his speech, pleasant to hear.

But Chloe, while she was interested in horseflesh, was diverted by the stable boy, who watched her curiously from a side door. She smiled at him, and he bobbed his head. He was clearly bothered by something just beyond the door, for he kept looking back and down, and Chloe moved toward him. The door opened, and out came the most enchanting puppy Chloe had ever seen. He was a combination of white and brown, a spaniel of impeccable breeding except for one lop ear. His littermates, all six of them, staggered out of the stable darkness behind him. They hesitated in the light, but it was the lop-ear who perceived Chloe and staggered to her on his weak little legs.

She moved closer and exclaimed over them. Lop-ear, aware of her approbation, reached out a tentative paw and touched her slipper. Without thought, she was down on her knees and lifting the small dog. Richard spoke over her head to the stable boy. "They're really growing, aren't they?"

Stiff with the consciousness of his low position, the stable boy could not find words, but Richard said, "You're taking good care of them, I can see."

Expanding under Richard's praise, the boy said, "Aye, they're all fine, except that one."

Edward's pompous voice came in. "Too bad that one's got a bad ear, for he looks more alert than the rest. Chloe, put him down and look at this one," Edward continued, anxious to show Richard his knowledge of dogs.

Chloe, suddenly aware of her lack of dignity in kneeling on the dirt playing with the puppy, got to her feet, but the little puppy pawed at her slipper again, clearly telling her that he did not like her desertion.

She stooped and picked him up, and stroked his head, fondling the drooping ear, while the puppy licked her hand, then struggled to apply his tongue to her cheek.

The mother of the puppies watched solicitously from the door, as her seven progeny gamboled in the sunlight. She eyed Chloe with some jealousy, for Chloe was clearly taken with the one flawed puppy.

Richard said, "I have an idea, Chloe. Why don't I give you one of these puppies?"

She turned to him, her eyes alight. "Oh, Richard, how good of you! I should love to have one."

Edward said heavily, "That's very generous of you, Davenant, and I'll see that the stable boy takes good care of him. Which one will you give her?"

Richard said, calmly, "Any one she wants."

Chloe gave the others a cursory glance. Edward picked up one after another pointing out the good points. "You see, this one's ears hang down as they should, but I confess that brown spot across his nose gives him an awkward appearance. Now this one——" Edward's voice continued, while Chloe scarcely heard. She turned to Richard, and said, "May I really have one?"

Richard said, "It's your choice. Take the one you want."

Edward, in high gig, chose one that while dull, standing closest to the door without much curiosity, yet had the perfect markings that Edward set store by. He picked him up, holding him outstretched away from his body, and said to Chloe, "Here's the one you should have, if Richard will let it go."

Chloe gave every indication of listening to Edward and taking his advice, but she still clung to Lop-ear. "I want this one, Edward."

Edward protested, but Richard, seeing that Chloe and the lop-eared dog were totally engrossed in each other, said, "Chloe has made her choice, and I would not for the world part them now."

At length, Chloe was persuaded to return the puppy to

his mother, upon Richard's promise that as soon as he could, the puppy would be on its way to his new owner.

Chloe walked beside Richard up the slope toward the house. She said, shyly, "I've never had a puppy of my own before." Her eyes glowed when she thanked Richard once again.

Edward was not satisfied, and murmured to Chloe that Davenant would have no opinion of her judgment. Richard interrupted, and said, "It was a clear affinity. It will take a better man than I am to separate them." Chloe paused, looked back toward the stables, but the pups were all inside again in the straw. She sighed and turned again toward the house.

The three of them entered the salon to find Lady Rothwell and Sophy in an amicable discussion about Lady Partridge's journey. Lady Partridge was going to Bath, and Sophy could think of nothing else. Sophy's voice came clearly through the door as the three approached from the stable to the hall. "Lady Partridge knows all about what's going on in London——"

Lady Rothwell interrupted her. "My sister Hensley keeps us informed, and I must tell you that there is much my sister could tell us if she only would. She has sworn me to secrecy on some things, but——" The three entered the room, and put a stop to the conversation by their entrance.

Lydia, judging by her enraptured face, was lost in her own dreams of cutting a wide swathe in London within a few months. She had never been quite reconciled to Edward's dictum that London would be hers two years hence.

She felt perfectly able to take on all the fashionable world, if she only had the right clothes, and the right introductions to society. Aunt Hensley would furnish the latter, and Chloe's generosity would have to provide the former. Lydia just now was picturing herself in a gown fashioned of the new, nearly transparent muslin, carrying a swan's-down muff, flirting with faceless and innumerable lords. One, of exalted status and unfathomed wealth, had just sworn eternal devotion to her, and she was loftily refusing him. . . .

Edward said, "Lydia, are you all right? Have you got the headache? Your face is screwed up! Are you in pain?"

Lydia descended from her cloud-landau with a sickening thud, with a strong resentment toward her brother. Edward would always spoil things if he could, even if he did not know, as just now, that he was thwarting her dreams.

At length the Rothwell carriage stood at the door ready to carry its passengers back to the manor. Richard, handing Chloe up into the carriage, promised he would bring her the puppy in a few days. "Have you thought of a name for him?" he asked.

She had not given it much thought, but she said, "Perhaps Nelson would be a good name, for he too had a handicap that he overcame."

Richard considered seriously for a few moments, and then said, "Perhaps Nelson would be a good name except it would always call attention to the flaw."

"I quite agree. It is best for the puppy's peace of mind that we ignore his lop ear."

Richard said, quirking an eyebrow, "Wellington? That is much too heavy a responsibility to bear. Very few heroes could walk in Wellington's boots."

Lady Rothwell said, "What's all this about a puppy? Chloe, you're never going to have a puppy? I cannot think that I will like it."

Chloe, for once, did not heed her stepmother. Richard, with a slight smile, said, "How about Nimrod, the mighty hunter?"

Chloe, remembering the tiny dog that was far more affectionate than heroic, chuckled. She rarely laughed aloud, usually expressing her mischievous amusement by a smile, or even a twinkle in her eyes and the appearance of the dimple on her left cheek. Both Edward and Lady Rothwell were startled to hear her peal of laughter.

The carriage was set in motion then, and trundled down the drive out of sight. Richard was pleased with his afternoon. He had seen Chloe in Davenant Hall, which opened up gratifying vistas for the future.

He had fathomed her private wish, unknowingly touched the spring that opened up her heart in his direction. The puppy was an inspired gift, and would provide many an opportunity to keep close to Chloe. She would need to ask him questions about the puppy's upbringing, and he would certainly have to make daily inquiry as to the health of the small dog.

He could still see in his mind's eye the glowing happiness warming her expression, shining from her speaking eyes, as though he had reached to the sky and brought down a star for her to hold.

He turned and walked up the steps into his house, past Dall, holding the door for him. Chloe's extraordinary happiness over the small gift opened up a certain amount of insight into the life she lived at home. If a puppy meant so much to her, it spoke volumes about an arid existence. He was angry and pleased at once. How dared they keep her from the rich life that should be hers? By the time he reached his book room and closed the door behind him, he realized something else.

He stopped dead still on the carpet, and felt the shock of recognition. For the first time in years, he was in love. He had regarded Chloe these last few days with affection, with indignation on her behalf, and with a determination to make her his bride. It was a suitable match, especially since she trusted him and he knew her well. It was a match born of disgust at the shallowness of London, of the knowledge that his true life was to be spent here on his estates and not in the city, and based upon a praiseworthy desire to rescue Chloe from her abominable relatives.

But there was more to it now, and he groaned mentally. He had not expected such a grand passion to hit him, as he was nearing the age of thirty. This time, this love bore no resemblance to the love of his green years, nor to the feelings he had experienced toward various Cyprians of his close acquaintance. He was in love, head over heels, for the rest of his life. Now all that remained was to convince Chloe that he had no designs on her money. He knew her well enough to know that he must tread softly with her, approach her gently, and persuade her gradually. If she once took against him, he would have the devil's own time in bringing her back into his arms.

But, knowing for the first time his true feelings about her, his reflections turned rosy.

His dreams would have been rent in shreds could he have heard Lady Rothwell on the way home. She knew for a fact, she told her family, that Sir Richard went to London to offer for Penelope Salton. Her sister had with her own eyes seen the two of them going into a fashionable shop on Oxford Street, with Penelope's mother Lady Salton beaming upon her daughter's suitor.

"The die has been cast," announced Lady Rothwell, "and we'll have a new Lady Davenant before long!"

13

The residents at Rothwell Manor, having returned from their outing to Davenant Hall, pursued their own interests. Each of them was unaware of the depth of feeling hidden behind the impassive features of their recent host. It was as though Richard's deportment served in some way as a reflecting mirror.

Edward felt that he had found a fellow spirit, interested in the same things he was—good horseflesh, conservative management of the estates, and a certain right-thinking political bent.

Lady Rothwell found him an attentive gentleman, with an open hand for hospitality and a recognition of her as his nearest neighbor, one to whom much attention was due.

Lydia's mind, beset by the swirling temptations of the world, was prey to all the imaginings of her romantic and quite shallow nature. She was not overly influenced by the novels that Sophy had purloined from Edward's box, for she was not so foolish as to think that wicked noblemen and damp grottoes were apt to come her way in the ordinary event. But Lydia believed firmly in her own magnetism, and in the philosophy of love at first sight. Her dreams were shapeless, and her rosy thoughts swirled in chaos. The result was that Lydia felt she had moved a step closer to her dream of conquering all London. She had made a good start with Sir Richard, so she told herself.

Chloe remembered the sunshine, the warmth of Sir Richard's welcome, and the comfort that she felt on her visit to Davenant Hall. She remembered the total devotion of the puppy. Richard's smile came into her musings more than once, and she reflected that she was in grave danger of feeling more for Richard than he was willing to accept. She recognized Richard as a solid rock to which she could cling if need be.

But Lady Rothwell had ruined the entire visit, cast a shadow over her satisfaction with the outing, and in fact thrown her into a blue-deviled mood. If Richard had in fact decided to marry, and that quite soon, then Chloe's acceptance of Richard's attention had to stop almost before it started. Her mood was dark and gloomy, and she emerged with difficulty from it in order to respond to the endless demands of running a house of the size of Rothwell Manor.

Waylaid in the hall by Miss Sinclair, the seamstress who had come from town to help with the mending, Chloe was presented with the problems of ruined bed linens. There had been none bought for some time, and they were now showing the signs of wear. Miss Sinclair lifted her hands helplessly and let them fall. "I can't do anything with this, at least to make it usable as a sheet. I can cut it up into pillow casings, and perhaps that would be suitable for the servants, but what do you want me to do?"

Chloe, with some difficulty, brought her mind to bear on the ragged sheets. There was no question but what she must seek Lady Rothwell's instructions on this. Bidding Miss Sinclair wait, she searched out her stepmother. Lady Rothwell was in no mood to consider sheets. She told Chloe, with an unjust air of reproval, "You must not spend your time on such small housekeeping chores, but let Miss Sinclair do what she wants to. Although I think it's time we found a new seamstress to do the linen, for Miss Sinclair will be busy enough with our new gowns for our journey. I feel that Miss Sinclair is not as good a seamstress as we would find in London, but we must make do with what we have."

Chloe, with a feeling that she had strayed into an alien country, echoed blankly, "Journey?"

Lady Rothwell was impatient. "You know that we are going to London in the fall. This was all arranged. My sister Hensley is looking about for a suitable house for you to take, roomy enough and with a good address, that will be available in time for the Little Season." Chloe, with a cold feeling somewhere in the region of her stomach, said, "So soon?". Then she recollected a word that Lady Rothwell had used, and the whole scheme opened up before her. She herself was to take the house in London. This was part of the new plan that Lady Rothwell had laid out, designed to put Chloe's legacy to the best use.

"I do not wish to go to London," she said, hoping she sounded more firm in her voice than she felt in her mind.

Lady Rothwell's reaction could have been predicted. "Not wish to go? I would think that you would enjoy London, but then perhaps you see it as a stage for your own endeavors. I really don't know how I can break the news to Lydia. If there's one thing she has her heart set on, it's going to London in September. I certainly thought that this was all settled."

Lady Rothwell's raised eyebrows emphasized her remarks.

Chloe said, in confused, broken phrases, "I didn't know—I don't remember—I don't remember—I——"

"I was about to tell you, Chloe, that my sister has found just the house for us. I believe she has already begun the negotiations. It will be very embarrassing for her to have to break them off. I certainly thought you knew what you owed your family."

Chloe faltered. "I could not take a house in London. . . ." Her voice trailed away. She had the unsettled feeling that the ground was sinking beneath her feet and there was no place secure to step.

Lady Rothwell said, "I can well imagine that you would not wish to go much in society, but you certainly would not be so mean-spirited as to prevent Lydia's having her Season."

Chloe fixed her eyes upon a flower in the patterned rug. She dared not look at Lady Rothwell, for she did not want her stepmother to see the tears that had sprung to her eyes. Lady Rothwell, on the theory that hammering home one nail is not nearly as good as five nails in the same spot, continued, "Think about it, Chloe. You owe a great deal to me and my family. To think of all the sacrifices we have made, and taken you in as though you were one of us—now you can repay me. For the first time you have it in your power to do something for me and you balk. I had thought you more generous." Chloe began to tremble inwardly, and the tears overflowed.

Murmuring some word of excuse, she turned and fled, tears blinding her as she raced down the hall. Miss Sinclair called to her, but Chloe dashed up the stairs and sought the refuge of her own room. She closed the door behind her, and for the first time in a long time she turned the key in the lock. She had no wish to undergo the scrutiny of either Sophy or Lydia at this moment. She stood in the middle of her room, not seeing her surroundings, and gave vent to the strongest language she knew. "I wish I had never heard of Highmoor!" She threw herself on the bed and gave way to wracking sobs.

In the meantime, Francis Hensley, having gone to London for a couple of days, returned. He had no wish to return to Rothwell Manor, but his fear of both his mother and his aunt guided his actions. However, somewhere he had found sufficient stiffening in his spine to enable him to stand up to Lady Rothwell. Before she had the chance to greet him, he said point-blank, "I do not wish to marry Chloe."

There, he thought, *I've said it.* His knees were shaking, and he hoped that was the end of it, for he could not endure more. Lady Rothwell, for her part well pleased with the impression she had made on Chloe, and dismissing Chloe's tearful distress as being temporary only, turned her talents to instructing Francis in his duty.

Lady Rothwell was not a hypocrite. She believed what she said, and although sometimes it took some convincing for her to be persuaded of the truth of her position, once convinced, she had no backward glance.

She had told Chloe what she considered only the truth, that she, Lady Rothwell, had spread her benign influence over Chloe as though it were an umbrella. She did not give full thought to the fact that Chloe as a Rothwell daughter had every right to live there. Lady Rothwell had not been overly jealous, but her late husband had held a special place in his heart for Chloe and Lady Rothwell had been forced to treat Chloe as one of her own, and this was still a barrier in her mind. Lady Rothwell considered her three children as true Rothwells, and Chloe, who was entirely biddable and of a sweet nature, had been unable to stand up to Lady Rothwell's ambitious family feeling.

Now Lady Rothwell bent her severe glance on her nephew.

"I seem beset by ungrateful persons," she began in a matter-of-fact voice. "I have put you in the way of financial security for the rest of your life, and you balk at the fence. I had thought you had more bottom than this. Chloe is already in a susceptible state, and I wish you now to go and seek her out. I will expect to hear of your engagement before dinner tonight. Your mother has arranged for a house in town, and I should like to see you settled before September."

Francis, opening and closing his mouth without a word, looking unhappily like a fish, all but backed out of the room, as though leaving the presence of royalty.

An unhappy and inarticulate man, he was conscious of a great struggle within his breast. He was torn between his formidable aunt, who was asking the impossible of him, and certain troubles of his own. Francis had no wish to marry Chloe, and he was as sure that she did not want to marry him as he was sure of anything. He was a realist, and knew that many a marriage was founded on financial considerations, but he was able to manage well enough on the small income left to him. He had no need to be leg-shackled, and he was in no danger on his own of falling into Parson's mousetrap. But his circumstances, ordinarily comfortable, had changed in the last month. Normally a moderate man, and one alive to all the pitfalls of the darker side of London, last month he was inveigled into a game of chance, where his ordinary caution had not played him true. The game was in a private house, and his luck ran against him. He thought, it could have been a crooked game, but he wasn't able to prove it against his host. He had played for deep stakes and was at this moment under the hatches. He had hoped to get out of his debts, and given time he certainly could have. But Julian Stoddard held his vowels, and Stoddard himself had other plans.

Stoddard, in a position to enforce his demands on Francis, promised to forgive half of Francis's debts if Francis were to get him access to Rothwell Manor, where Julian Stoddard, with Francis's help, would pursue the heiress Chloe.

Francis, every fiber repelled at the idea of Stoddard and Chloe, had very little choice.

While Stoddard was a very real peril, Lady Rothwell was closest at hand, and Francis, his aunt's injunction still ringing in his ears, went to find Chloe.

With the frankness of old acquaintance, Francis sympathized with Chloe's tears. His own woes were similar to hers, and Lady Rothwell loomed like a specter over the two of them.

At length, Francis, the words forced from him by his rising misery, said, "We could run away."

Chloe, with a rueful little laugh, said "I wish we could. Where shall we go? To Gretna Green?"

Francis paled.

Chloe instantly regretted her playfulness. Putting a hand on his, she said, "I did not mean it, Francis." But Francis, still laboring under Lady Rothwell's injunctions, managed to stutter out a proposal. Chloe, recognizing that Francis was a pawn, as she herself was, turned sweetly to him and said, "We wouldn't suit."

Francis allowed a look of unbounded relief to cross his undistinguished features. Half of his unwieldly burden was lifted, and he could certainly do no more.

Perhaps Stoddard would reconsider. It was a forlorn hope, as Francis could have understood on reflection. The last day or two in London, he had run into Stoddard, who had put the situation before him in unvarnished terms. But Stoddard himself had called previously, received a very frosty welcome, and retreated. Surely even Stoddard would know that his alliance with Chloe was out of the question.

Francis moved the rest of the day in a growing, and quite unreasonable, euphoria. Chloe had refused him, and Lady Rothwell must see he could do no more. If the lady was not willing, then nothing Francis could do would change her mind. She did not want to marry him any more than he wished to get married himself.

Stoddard, in London yesterday, had accused Francis of not paving the way well enough for him, but now there was still no sign of Stoddard, and grasping at a hint that Stoddard had given, Francis with unreasonable optimism decided that Stoddard had changed his mind.

And somehow, he brooded, he would get the money to pay off Stoddard. He would also, beyond any doubt, stay well away from any of Stoddard's friends, for Francis clung to his lesson learned as a limpet to a rock.

But Stoddard, in London, was unaware that he had given Francis any loophole. Stoddard's own affairs were not prospering, and he had the gambler's fear that Lady Luck would leave him. Perhaps she had already begun her withdrawal, but had given him one last chance. Stoddard, aflame with the idea of an innocent heiress in the wilds of Kent, had grasped his last chance of avoiding financial disaster as a braver man had once plucked the nettle Danger.

He had by the most propitious circumstances found that Hensley was in his debt. The amount was not great, certainly not enough to settle Stoddard's future, but by great good chance he had learned of Chloe's inheritance.

Stoddard, never a modest man, was inordinately pleased with his machinations, overlooking the fact that when Hensley fell into his grasp he had not known about Chloe's inheritance. Stoddard was sure, following his last encounter with Francis, that the way to Chloe's heart, and purse, would be paved this time.

Stoddard arrived at Rothwell Manor, expecting all to be ready for his benefit. He had not heard of any change in Francis's own luck, and he was certain that Francis, being a man of self-preserving qualities, would have made all ready for Julian's descent upon Rothwell Manor.

However, Lady Luck played Julian Stoddard false. He returned to find that he was not the only man in possession of the information about Chloe's inheritance. He was unaware that Thaddeus Invers was already on the scene, with a determination for his own benefit quite as strong as Julian's. At the moment when Stoddard was turning into the drive, Thaddeus Invers was already at the house. He had planned an outing, riding out from the inn at town to invite the Rothwells to a nearby ruined abbey. Edward, possibly feeling there was safety in numbers, was encouraging Invers, as opposed to Francis Hensley.

Lady Rothwell, constitutionally averse to jolting her bones over rough roads, as she was prone to say, yet felt that she dared not allow Chloe to be in sole company of Thaddeus Invers, and decided to accompany the picnic party. She had the strong feeling that Hensley needed to be prodded into doing his duty, and if he didn't know what was best for him, she did, and would have to see that it happened.

Julian Stoddard rode up the gravel drive, whistling in optimistic anticipation, and arrived at the front of the house to survey an astonishing and daunting scene.

The Rothwell carriage was drawn up before the door. Lady Rothwell, moving her bulk slowly, flanked by Chloe and Bess, the maid, was ready to mount into the plush interior. A footman stood on either side of the door, ready to hand her up. Behind this little group, Lydia, a pout settling on her face, and Sophy stood with Edward near the gig in which they were to ride.

Thaddeus Invers was with them, watching with greedy eyes as the picnic hampers were stowed by the servants in a vehicle ahead of the carriage, ready to depart ahead of the others for the picnic site.

Francis, hovering behind them all, had the strong intention of staying out of Lady Rothwell's sight. Out of sight, out of mind, he hoped.

Standing two steps above the others, he was in a better position to see the approaching Julian Stoddard, and he was struck to the heart. His jaw dropped open and his eyes glazed over, for disaster was now approaching on the second front.

Julian's arrival, perforce, changed the arrangements of the picnic party. It seemed as though Lady Rothwell was ready to go, but the party was waiting for Lady Partridge and Emma to drive over and join them.

After greeting Julian Stoddard with a minimum of civility, the party waited. Lady Partridge's carriage turned in at the gateposts, and the wheels crunched on the gravel drive heralding her approach long before she was in sight.

Julian, making no effort to leave, must of necessity be invited to join them. He took pains to join Chloe, saying something he considered flattering. Chloe answered him with words she could not remember, and moved away. She had no interest in Stoddard, and could hardly hide her dislike. In moving away, unfortunately, she moved closer to Thaddeus Invers.

Invers for his part was angry with Stoddard, considering him an interloper. The two eyed each other warily, and without a word the gauntlet was thrown down. The sound of wheels grew closer, and Lady Partridge and her daughter arrived.

Emma leaped from the coach, greeting Sophy as though they were travelers on a desert, and Sophy hugged her friend with abandon.

It sorted out at last. Lady Rothwell and Lady Partridge rode together in the Rothwell carriage, and it fell out that Lady Rothwell, aware of the situation for once, instructed Chloe to join her in the carriage. Thus she neatly removed the heiress from both Stoddard and Invers. Lady Rothwell promised herself to keep a close eye on Chloe, and an even closer eye on the two strangers from London.

As they swept down the drive, they met Richard arriving in his phaeton. Edward, averse to spending the afternoon on a picnic he didn't expect to enjoy, with his cousin Francis, who was worse than a cipher as a conversationalist, and two others for whom he cherished a secret dislike, hailed Richard with great relief.

He explained briefly the purpose of the cavalcade, and said, earnestly, "You must join us, Davenant. I won't take no for an answer."

14

The object of the cavalcade's progress was a ruined abbey on a hilltop. The abbey, like so many famous sights, was ignored by the locals and only rarely visited by travelers from London. It was picturesque, in a way, but its history was nearly forgotten, and the building had been allowed to fall into disrepair.

The abbey lay at the far end of Richard's land, although the others paid little heed to the actual ownership. It was a matter of public domain, being an historical site.

It was the better part of an hour's drive from Rothwell Manor. The servants would be there well before the others arrived, and it was questionable whether they considered the day as a diversion.

Richard, accepting Edward's invitation, and turning to follow the gentlemen riders, noted the gathering-in. He noticed that Stoddard and Invers, having little in common, eyed each other as warily as stray dogs spoiling for a fight.

The cavalcade turned, just before it reached the village, onto a narrow, rutted lane, and climbed up toward the picturesque ruins. The procession, consisting of Lady Rothwell's carriage, the gig with Sophy and Emma, and Richard's phaeton behind, along with Thaddeus and Julian and Francis, was most impressive. As they turned the corner before the village, small boys ran to watch them go

by, and dogs barked. furiously until quieted by their owners.

Richard longed for a sight of Chloe, and was speculating, as he found himself doing more and more, about what Chloe was thinking. She was immured in that mammoth old-fashioned coach, undoubtedly a paragon of comfort, but the company was undoubtedly lacking in intellectual stimulation. Had he been able by some magic to read her mind, he would have been gratified.

For Chloe, facing two comfortably padded women whose conversation was as predictable today as it had been last week and probably would be next week, retreated into the habit she had formed of abstracting herself from the current conversation. Her thoughts, originally quite dark, had taken on a rosier hue when she had seen Richard driving up the drive, and her mood turned quite cheerful at the thought that he was accompanying them. She longed to look through the walls of the coach and watch him driving somewhere behind them, far enough back to avoid the dust. She would miss him, as one missed one's right arm, she guessed, when he was no longer a bachelor. Chloe had no illusions about a new Lady Davenant making demands upon Richard. And Richard was the kind of man who would do his duty to the utmost.

Lady Partridge, almost as though she could read Chloe's mind, remarked calmly, "It is all settled, you know. Sir Richard is retiring to live here at the Hall."

Lady Rothwell, whose vanity extended to her own superior sources of gossip, said, "Yes, I understand he has offered for Penelope Salton. I have it on the best authority."

Lady Partridge said, with a wise glint in her eye, "Many think that he has."

Lady Rothwell, nettled, retorted, "I know that he went up last week to make his offer."

While the two wrangled amiably over Sir Richard Davenant's marriage as though it were a succulent bone, Chloe found that her head was beginning to ache again.

Chloe laid her head back on the squabs, aware of the faint smell of dust rising from the velvet, and fell into a drowse. She was in that state between waking and sleeping where the most vivid dreams came. It was perhaps her own wish that came to the fore, but she was not conscious of summoning it. She found, in her dreaming, a place of quiet, where someone brought her a dish of tea and some buttered scones hot from the oven, and mercifully left her alone. In her dream her headache was gone, and she felt marvelously restored. Just as she came from her dream into a state of wakefulness, she caught a glimpse of the gates of her dream place. The name on the gates was Highmoor.

The carriage slowed, turned, and then stopped. They had arrived at the ruins. Thaddeus Invers managed to reach the step of the carriage a half pace ahead of Stoddard to help the ladies down. As Chloe alighted on the ground, her eyes rose to catch her first glimpse of the ruins. She saw only a tall tower of stone, broken and jagged at the top. She knew that still to be seen was the moat where the monks of the abbey kept carp swimming until they were removed to grace the table. Henry the Eighth had wreaked havoc with the peaceful existence of those monks, and seized the land and all the treasures of the abbey. The building itself was allowed to fall into ruin.

The land, with a Tudor blessing, had gone to the first Davenant. Being of a practical race, the Davenants had since that time augmented their land, brought the fields to prosperity, filled in the moat, and left the ruined abbey, which was of no practical use, to the ravages of time and weather.

Thaddeus Invers, with a proprietary air, said, "We will postpone our inspection of the abbey until after our luncheon."

The luncheon, which was the best that Mrs. Field could provide on such short notice, complaining all the while that her tooth had come in the way of her devoted service to Miss Chloe, was truly a very tasty meal. Besides, the outdoor air and the long journey had given them all fine appetites.

Only Julian Stoddard had reservations, and gave voice to them. "This is very good chicken," he said, "almost as tasty as was served at the Prince Regent's dinner last week." Inwardly Chloe groaned, for she had had a sufficiency of the Regent's whims, tastes, and activities.

Chloe had learned the trick of turning her mind off, leaving only a portion of her thoughts as sentry, to warn her if someone addressed her, or to provide a clue as to the proper response. Julian prosed on, while Thaddeus Invers, who considered the outing his own idea and therefore his own property, glared at Julian. Who invited Stoddard anyway? Invers, despite his connection with a well enough bred family, had yet been brought up in a middle-class fashion. Without the money and the family reputation to uphold, his family had lapsed into middle-class ways, and Thaddeus tried to bury his past every day. He was uneasy enough in his aspirations to marry Chloe Rothwell, without Julian Stoddard pointing out with every name he dropped his own affiliation with the higher reaches of the fashionable world.

With an anxious eye Thaddeus watched Chloe, the object of his ambition. It was a quiet enough scene, Sir Richard handing Chloe a bunch of grapes, her eyes flickering upward to thank him, and the two older ladies comfortably gossiping and paying no heed to Julian Stoddard. All was not yet lost. Thaddeus could even begin to expand, surveying the entire picnic party. It was all his idea, and he felt gratified that his guests were enjoying themselves. He ignored the fact that the carriages and the repast itself were furnished by Lord Rothwell.

Julian and Lydia were having a comfortable conversation. Sophy and Emma had wandered off by themselves, exchanging secrets that were significant only to each other. By an evil chance, all conversation fell silent at the moment. Lydia, intent upon charming Julian Stoddard, mostly as an exercise in the flirtations that she expected to indulge in later, was oblivious to the others of the party. In the sudden silence, her clear voice rang out, "I'm going to London soon. My sister——" Her voice trailed away as she became conscious that all eyes were fixed upon her.

She subsided, with a sheepish glance out of the corner of her eyes at Chloe. Lady Rothwell, uneasy at what might be the reaction of Edward, leaped ponderously into the breach. "Now, Lydia," she said. "I never saw such a girl for speaking out of turn."

Lady Partridge, mildly curious, said, "Then it is true. I have heard that Chloe is going to take you to London." Unaware of the flush creeping up Lady Rothwell's cheeks, Lady Partridge continued, "How nice of Chloe! A truly dutiful daughter, isn't she? I only hope my own Emma would behave as well, and think of her family first. But at that age—it's hard to see what they will do. Sometimes I quite despair of Emma's future."

Chloe, her heart sinking into her stomach, looked down

at her folded hands. She felt suddenly as though she were in a room in a nightmare, with the walls closing inexorably in on her and no escape. The road to London, paved as it was by Lydia and Lady Rothwell, was no escape. It was the trap itself.

Suddenly, with the uneasiness of an ill-assorted party conscious of undercurrents swirling about their ankles, they all leaped into conversation. Under cover of the ensuing babble, Richard helped Chloe to her feet. Imperceptibly he drew her aside from the others so their words were not overheard. He looked down at her with great concern.

"Are you not well?"

"I had the headache a little while ago," she said, "but it is gone now. I simply need something to eat."

Richard was not satisfied with her evasive answer. "There is something the trouble," he said, "for you have too many headaches. Can't you tell me what it is?"

Of a sudden, her words came in a rush. "Francis has offered for me."

Richard's heart sank into his boots. Had he waited too long to declare himself? Yet it was Chloe's own wish that he refrain, and he was fairly caught on the horns of the dilemma. But Chloe, without noticing, said quite calmly, "I refused him, of course."

Richard felt that he could breathe again. "You are going to London, then?"

Quite sadly she said, "I suppose I shall."

"You wish not to go?" asked Richard.

Chloe said, "I was there once, you know, five years ago, but I was called home almost at once when my father died."

Richard said, "Yes, I was in Europe at that time. I heard the news of your father's passing, in Cairo. I was sorry I could not be here. But why do you go to London, if you don't wish to?"

Chloe did not answer for so long a time he feared he had offended her. But then finally came her wee voice, "My stepmama wishes it. This legacy, you know. . . ." Her voice trailed away in silence.

Richard said, almost brusquely, "What would you rather do, travel?"

He touched her elbow, and they began to stroll slowly toward the object of the outing. The ruined abbey rose on the eminence ahead, dark and foreboding, and Chloe shuddered. "No, I think I would not like to travel. Mr. Stoddard speaks of such terrible mishaps with bandits and other unfortunate things. I am not one for being alone."

Richard said, "You wouldn't be going alone, you know."

Suddenly he quite longed to be able to tell Chloe about all the things he had seen in Europe, and even show them to her. He could picture her eyes widening at the deep gorges in Switzerland, her eyes twinkling when she shared with him some minor enjoyment at the foibles of the Continentals, but he noticed that Chloe was not cheered by the prospect of travel. She said, "Lady Rothwell would not like the inns, and Lydia would pine for London." She smiled, but he noticed that her mischievous dimple was still hidden. Her amusement was only on the surface. Beneath her outer civility, he was sure, lay a deep well of sadness. They were now more than halfway to the ruins.

Richard found suddenly that his fists were clenched, and very carefully he relaxed his fingers. Within, he was seething with emotion. Couldn't his beloved girl see that the harpies were bent upon plucking away everything she held dear?

It was perfectly clear to him, as it truly must be to Chloe, or would be some day, that she was being forced into supporting her sister's ill-advised stay in London, and was not even being protected from unwelcome suitors.

He wondered at Edward. If Richard were Chloe's brother, these suitors would have been sent packing before they entered the house.

Chloe, her thoughts, as often, marching along with his, must have felt something of his anger, for she said, lifting her eyes in an appeal for understanding, "They are all I have, you know. And they do love me."

Richard, not as convinced as Chloe, said almost roughly, "What would you truly want to do?"

She said, very slowly, "I don't think I could put it into words. I know sometimes what I want, and yet when I think about it I don't truly want it."

They had stopped in their slow amble, and she looked up at him and saw in his eyes the tenderness that he did not try to hide. He was her Great Friend, after all, the one who had known her the longest. She finally said, "I shall tell you the small dream I just had in the carriage."

Because it was fresh in her mind, it took on vividness

all too clearly. She considered it a dream, but Richard saw more in it than she did. A small retreat at Highmoor, someone else to run the house and bring in her tea and cakes to her. Richard saw that it was the blessed rest, and someone caring for her, that was a deep-seated longing in her.

She finished her meager confession by saying, "I should, I think, like to live at Highmoor. Edward says it is totally ineligible, so I must not think of it. Besides, how would I go on without my family?"

Richard, overwhelmed by the mixture of emotions that he felt when Chloe was near, opened his mouth, ready to answer. He was on the verge of recklessly declaring himself when he heard the flat voice of Sophy, who was approaching them.

She was awkward as a colt, and laboring under some strong emotion. Without ceremony, she clutched Chloe's arm. "Do you know what has happened?"

Chloe said, "I cannot imagine, but you had best tell me, for I see you will whether I suggest it or not."

"Lady Partridge is taking Emma to Bath, and she will be gone for a month or so."

Chloe said, "We already know that."

Sophy rushed on. "I've been invited to go. There's no reason why I can't go. I want to go, and they want me to go."

Chloe, knowing the answer, said, "Then what is the question?"

Sophy, her pudding face blotchy red, cried out with high indignation, "Edward says no. Without even *reflecting* on it!"

Sophy dealt exhaustively with Edward's iniquity and her grave disappointment.

Richard dismissed her reactions as being only disappointment. She would get over it, he thought comfortably, and forget it.

But Chloe, knowing Sophy better, recognized the unmistakable signs of ungovernable fury, and her heart sank. When Sophy was in this mood, someone would pay.

Richard, for once lost in his own indignation, was not aware of Chloe's expression. Chloe's little dream, to his surprise, worked powerfully in him. He wanted to marry Chloe for himself, but most of all he wanted to extract her from her family. He blamed himself for staying away too long, depriving Chloe of the support that she must have to stand up against them. They had twined themselves around her thoughts and her habits until she could not picture life without them. She was like a tree engulfed by ivy, so that the ivy stuck its roots into the very bark, overwhelming the tree. At this point, if the ivy were killed, then the tree itself might fall. The tree had learned too well to lean against the ivy for support.

The Rothwells had sapped her strength, taken advantage of her sweetness, and her real need for love.

By the time he returned to the present, Chloe was no longer at his side. Stoddard and Edward had left the picnic site and come up to them. They had gathered Chloe in and the three of them were strolling toward the ruined abbey.

Richard, again too late, followed them. He saw that Emma Partridge had run up to join Sophy, but his true thoughts were all turned inwardly, and most of them were thoughts of blame.

15

"The ruins of the abbey are accounted to be most picturesque," said their lecturer, Thaddeus Invers. He was a well-read man, skimming all the new books, paying heed to the intellectual talk in various salons to which he had entry. He considered himself, therefore, an authority, instead of the reflecting surface that he was.

"The picturesque is becoming fashionable," he said. "There are many novels with this emphasis now being published. A writer would be most fortunate could he come upon a ruin like this."

Lydia proclaimed, "They are such romantic stories. Wicked noblemen peering around the rocks, maidens in dungeons. I don't doubt there is a secret chamber in that abbey."

She looked with great care at the ruin ahead of them,

and cried, in a voice choked with excitement, "I think I see something *moving!*"

Sophy said, with scorn, "You think it's a wicked nobleman?"

Stoddard sneered, "It's more likely bats."

Stoddard was out of charity with them all. He was essentially an urban man, and the country required too much walking. Unfortunately, Stoddard believed himself the soul of wit. For this day, in retaliation for Invers' insistence upon a country outing, Stoddard became clever.

Lydia chastised Stoddard openly. "How bad of you to scoff at such a clearly romantic site!"

Edward, audibly but less noticeably, said, "Lydia, mind your manners."

Thus encouraged by Lord Rothwell himself, Stoddard eyed Chloe. "Never mind, Rothwell. Ladies always notice a man for his wit."

Edward, having little wit himself, objected heavily. "The women in my family are full of common sense, thank God, and listen to those worthy of respect." Edward's eyes turned toward Invers, still lecturing on the subject of the novels that were pouring out of the Minerva Press. Meanwhile, Richard was wondering what family he could mean, for Lydia and Sophy gave no evidence of being full of sense.

Edward continued defending his family. "The novels of which Invers was speaking," he said heavily, "are unknown at Rothwell Manor. For you must know that I censor all the reading of my family. It is too bad that the world has allowed such trash to sully the minds of our young people. My bookman insists on sending me copies, from time to time, even though I expressly inform him not to. His excuse for doing so is a flimsy one, at best. They are popular, he tells me," Edward ended with a sneer. "Popular! All that means is the abandonment of all morals and elevated thought."

Invers, tacking in mid-course as he became aware of a breeze from a different quarter, changed direction to match Lord Rothwell's district bias. Richard, while amused at Invers' transparent toadying, was disquieted.

Feeling sorry for Invers, unarmed in any battle of wits, Chloe gave him her attention. "I have no knowledge of the subject for I have not seen these novels. Lady Rothwell's preference, and you must know that I read to her, lies more along historical lines."

Edward agreed, "Yes, indeed. My mother has become much interested in Dean Milner's *Ecclesiastical History*."

Richard all but shuddered. Fortunately no one saw him, for Edward, finding that his mind and Invers' marched together, became more in sympathy with him. Edward considered the possibility that opened before him. If Chloe did not take his mother's choice, and Edward would be much disturbed if she wed Francis, then he himself would encourage Invers. See how Chloe listens to the man? he told himself. He was sure that Chloe was charmed by the intelligence and education of Thaddeus Invers.

Stoddard, taking on a disgruntled air, found himself left with Lydia and Sophy and Emma—subjects not at all in keeping with his superior deserts.

He wished to continue what he considered his advantage by baiting Invers, and he was well aware of various weaknesses in Invers' discussion. What a field for the slashing thrusts of Stoddard's rapier wit! But suddenly he caught Sir Richard's formidable eye and remained silent.

Chloe flashed Richard a glance that told him her true feelings about Invers. Richard was much comforted.

At length they arrived back at the site of the *al fresco* luncheon. Fat Lady Partridge was struggling to climb out of her chair. "At last you've returned and we can go home. These folding chairs are too small for me, and they made me cross, for I realize I must lose weight. Perhaps I can do that in Bath."

Her voice lacked conviction, for the previous dozen trips to Bath had resulted in no weight loss at all, and there was no reason to suspect that the next one would perform the miracle.

But the mention of Bath struck jangling chords in Sophy and Emma, who embraced each other and clung dramatically in anticipation of their prospective parting. It was a sight to wring the hearts of any spectator, but Edward, toward whom the scene was directed, gave it one glance and turned away.

When he was out of hearing, Lady Rothwell said quietly to Lady Partridge, "I cannot bear to see my dear Sophy unhappy."

Chloe's headache had returned in full force. The tension of the scene between Stoddard and Invers and her brother

Edward, added to her dread of what Sophy might think up to get her own way, brought back the pain over her eyes. She had never before been prey to headaches such as these, but in the last few weeks they had come with more frequency than she could understand.

She stood, pale and shaken, and Richard came to her side. "Headache?" he murmured, and seeing her slight nod, he said to Lady Rothwell, "Chloe is in need of fresh air." He helped her into his phaeton, going ahead to avoid the dust.

Chloe protested faintly. "I must help——" but Richard lifted the reins and they were off. They went down the hill at a spirited pace and turned at the edge of the village.

Richard, seeing Chloe close her eyes against the headache, shifted the reins to his left hand and put his right arm around her. "Lean against me if you wish. I'll hold you steady."

The movement, the fresh air on her face, and Richard's steady arm around her, revived Chloe. Richard, feeling that all Chloe really needed was to be away from all those who wanted something from her, could not say what was in his heart. They rode all the way in near silence.

Drawing up before the door at Rothwell Manor, he helped her down. Behind him the door opened and Field came out to meet them. Surveying the situation, the butler took quick action. In only moments, Mrs. Field was in the hall, wiping her hands on her spotless apron. Richard helped Chloe into the foyer. "I'll keep them all away, Sir Richard," Cook told him bluntly. "The poor lamb, always running for them others and never anything coming her way."

Chloe, rousing, said quietly, "Mrs. Field, don't——"

But Cook, taking up cudgels in defense of her favorite, said to Sir Richard, "She may tell you otherwise, sir, but I've got eyes in my head to see with."

Placing her arm around Chloe, Cook helped her up the stairs. Richard watched until Chloe was out of sight. Field said, "It's good to see you back at the Hall, Sir Richard. I suppose London is full of excitement. I don't wonder at that, but give me the good country life every time."

Richard had allowed his feelings to show in his face. He caught the butler's eye. Suddenly a look of understanding passed between them that spanned the gap between their respective classes and needed no words to be explicit.

Field, encouraged by Sir Richard's speaking look, said slyly, "A new lady at the Hall soon, I suppose?"

Sir Richard, cryptically, said, "Yes, I hope so."

Field said, "A change from London for her, doubtless." It was a barefaced bit of bait, dangling before Sir Richard.

Richard, grateful to Chloe's allies in the house, said, "No London lady."

Field allowed discreet happiness to show on his face, and Richard went off, driving down the gravel drive at a good clip.

He was aware now that Chloe's servants were on his side. He was pleased that he was not leaving her alone, in a household without friends.

Things were rapidly approaching a climax, so Richard believed. He was not willing to see Chloe so beset, but at the moment he was not sure just how to extract her from her situation.

Lost in thought, the butler was forgotten. But the butler at Rothwell Manor had not forgotten Sir Richard. What he now knew, by dint of skillful questioning, would give him an edge on the odds in the servants' hall. If Sir Richard was not going to bring down a London lady, then Field would introduce a dark horse, so to speak, and meaning no disrespect, back an unknown to the limit. He had visions of vast wealth coming his way from a Sure Thing.

Chloe, cosseted by Mrs. Field, felt better already. She was grateful to Richard for bringing her home ahead of the confused cavalcade returning from the abbey. Cook brought Chloe up to her room, closed the draperies, got her into bed under an eiderdown, and shut the door. She waited until Lady Rothwell came home, and told her that Miss Chloe was sleeping. Later, Cook took up a light supper, saw that Chloe ate, and watched her fall immediately to sleep again.

Next morning, Chloe felt ready to face the world again and it was well, for Sophy entered without ceremony. "How do you feel?" Without waiting for an answer she added, "I hope that you're going to be well enough to go to the ball next week."

Chloe, with only mild interest, said. "What ball?"

"Lady Partridge is going to give a ball next week. It's short notice, she said, but she and Mama set it up all on the way home yesterday. A simple country affair, before she takes Emma to Bath."

Lydia entered on the heels of Sophy's excited remarks and quickly put the damper on them. "You're not going to any ball. You're too young," Lydia told her in a matter-of-fact way, only slightly mixed with malice.

Sophy gave a howl of protest. "I'm almost as old as Emma! And Emma is going to be there, it's for Emma she's giving it, and I'm certainly going to go."

The quarrel heated up, and Lydia turned to Chloe with an air of righteousness. "I'm right, Chloe. Tell her so."

Chloe, unmoved by the quarrel, said calmly, "I can't tell you. Ask Mama."

Sophy, a look of shrewdness passing across her plump cheeks, said, "If you say you want me to go, they'll let me."

Chloe, shoving Sophy off the bed and throwing back the covers, said, "That moonshine, Sophy. Nobody ever paid any attention to me before. Why now?"

Sophy said, slyly, "Because you're a great heiress."

Chloe said, "If I were a great heiress, I would have a little more privacy to get dressed in. I don't feel like an heiress. Sophy, you've got moonbeams in your wits."

Sophy, stung by one she thought was her ally, cried, "Chloe, you're doing so much for Lydia! Why can't you do something for me?"

Lydia, a pout of jealousy marring her pretty face, watched Chloe. Chloe, remaining adamant, said calmly, "You know a question of propriety must be settled by Mama."

Still exchanging telling recriminations, the two girls went to seek their mother.

Chloe fell into deep thought. She was much troubled by the girls' seeking equal benefits. It was something like two children in the schoolroom, jealous of each other. She could not help but wonder whether the girls had been like this all the time and she had failed to see it, or whether this foolish legacy had stirred up depths in them that she had not known about.

She told herself that it was the way of families who love each other to quarrel now and then. Of course, her inheritance must be shared with them. She would have it no other way. She had their love and their concern, and what did a legacy weigh in the balance with that?

Highmoor might flit through her dreams as a vision like the Holy Grail, yet it was a lonely goal, and Chloe turned away from it.

Once in a while, it would be natural for her to think about Highmoor, and certainly she would be less than human if she did not wish to live on her own property. But it was out of the question, so Edward said, and certainly there would not be time to make a move before they went to London. A bit wistfully, she wished that Mama had asked her first about her wants before making plans.

Chloe was dressed now, and was tying her ribbon around her dark hair, ready for her descent to the lower floors. But she was still beset by misgivings, for Edward had been so opposed to Lydia's going to London for another two years. Had it been only money? He had not said so until this point, so that it was possible that the legacy had made all the difference and Edward's permission had now been gained. At least Mama, although she had not precisely said so, seemed to believe there was no barrier. This must mean that Edward had capitulated.

Chloe moved to the window to look out upon the day. It was fine, but thank goodness there would be no outing today. Below, movement caught her eye, and she saw Richard crossing the wide expanse of lawn toward the house. He must have come across the rustic bridge, the short way from Davenant Hall to the manor. Conscious of her regard, he looked up and saw her. He was carrying something. With his free hand he beckoned to her to come down. She didn't stop even to reflect on her sudden happiness and its cause—for her heart was singing at the very sight of her Great Friend. She patted her curls into place before the mirror and flew down the back stairs.

Richard's gesture had indicated that he would be waiting for her at the back of the house. She flew like an arrow to the rose arbor and greeted him with a smile.

"How is your headache?"

"It is all gone, Richard! Thank you so much for your care. If I had had to go back in the dust and the noise, I doubt I would be up this morning."

Richard said, "There is too much on your shoulders, and it is no wonder your health is suffering."

She dismissed that airily, and said with a laugh. "Oh, I'm fine this morning. I just needed rest."

The object Richard had been carrying was a wicker bas-

ket. Now, without a word, he handed it to her. She set it
on the ground and lifted the lid, and there was the puppy.
"Nimrod!" she exclaimed in high delight. "My little lop-
eared puppy!"

Lifting the animal carefully out of the basket and setting
him on his unsteady legs on the grass, she petted him,
twisting his lop ear in her fingers gently, and was lost in
her great delight in the small animal.

At length, Richard and Chloe sat together in the arbor.
The puppy staggered about the grass, exploring what he
could see of this new place with its strange smells and its
odd little grasshoppers that leaped before him, which he
could never catch, and Chloe watched Nimrod in pleasant
abstraction.

On the other hand, Richard watched her. It was a com-
panionable silence, comfortable and happy. At length,
Chloe mentioned Lady Partridge's ball. "It must have
come up after we left," she said, "for Sophy brought me
the news this morning."

"Are you going to be there?"

"I suppose so. I have not yet heard whether the invitation includes all of us or not."

Richard said, "If you are there, then I surely will be."

Chloe looked up quickly at him. "You're not going to
London?"

Richard, puzzled, said, "No, I do not expect to go.
Should I?"

She dared not answer lest Richard decide to tell her
about his bethrothal. Richard said, "When you go to town
this autumn, I shall go." She smiled, and he added, "To
keep off undesirables. Like that idiot Invers!"

She laughed. "Isn't he a foolish man? But Edward is so
taken with him. He speaks such *fustian*!"

Richard, gratified by his love's astute assessment of the
man, relaxed. But then, slowly, she said, "It is Julian Stoddard who makes me uneasy."

"Why?"

She shook her head. "I don't know. I just don't like
him."

The conversation, as so many at Rothwell Manor were,
was interrupted. This time it was Francis who came after
her, sent by Lady Rothwell. Richard scooped up the
puppy and set him back in the basket. Putting the lid

down firmly upon the howls from within, he handed her the basket. "I cannot abide that idiot Hensley," he said, and beat a hasty retreat.

16

Lady Rothwell had sent Francis to fetch Chloe because Lady Partridge had arrived. Chloe, lifting up the lid of the wicker basket a crack and sticking her finger inside to quiet the puppy, hurried with Francis to the back of the house. She thrust the basket into the hands of Chubb, the second footman, and said, "Take care of it for me, please. I trust you with his life."

Chubb, startled, took the basket thrust upon him and backed away.

Francis asked. "What is that?" He did not wait for an answer. "Hurry up, Chloe! Aunt was quite anxious."

In the Green Salon, Lady Partridge sat comfortably on a chair, a dish of tea and a plate of cakes beside her. Sophy and Emma sat on a loveseat beyond, their arms around each other's waists, whispering in each other's ears. Lady Partridge had come in person to deliver her invitation to the ball. She welcomed Chloe warmly, for the girl was one of her favorites. She wondered sometimes whether Chloe knew all that was going on around her, for Lady Partridge took a dim view of some of Lady Rothwell's stratagems. But Lady Partridge felt, both from inclination and from conviction, that it was not her place to interfere.

She said, "You're looking better than yesterday. I hope your headache is gone?"

Chloe greeted her and reassured her as to her health.

"I came to be sure that you were coming to my ball, a week tomorrow. It will be the last time I have a chance to entertain before we travel to Bath."

Lady Rothwell said, "There's no question but what we will come, but I do hope—although it is none of my affair—that you will not consider asking Invers, Lady Partridge?"

The lady chuckled. She was more than ordinarily indulgent, but she was also a very shrewd woman. "You're speaking of competition for Francis. You're afraid of Invers? I think Chloe has more sense. She'll not take Invers. In fact, I think I know——" she dissolved in chuckles again, and her words were lost in the rolls of fat. But she added, "If you take her to London, you'll find more competition than Francis, I warrant you."

Lady Rothwell sent Chloe out of the room on an errand, and then said to Lady Partridge, "She'll be riveted to Francis before then."

Lady Partridge lifted an eyebrow. "So soon?"

Lady Rothwell said, "There will be an announcement in the *Gazette* before we go to London. I will not see it any other way. Lydia has her heart set on the Little Season."

Lady Partridge said, "I wonder whether she is not too young for it yet?"

Lady Rothwell reflected that the sooner Lydia was married off, the sooner her dear Sophy could come out into society and dazzle them all. Whatever other faults she may have had, she could not be blamed for a low opinion of her own family.

Her errand accomplished, Chloe returned to the drawing room and sat down. Lady Partridge noted the glow on Chloe's cheek. While she did not know the cause, she had a strong feeling that it had something to do with Sir Richard Davenant.

Lady Partridge had watched the two of them drive off yesterday, and wondered whether the headache was a ruse to get Sir Richard alone. Then, she remembered Chloe's pale face and shaking hands, and she knew that the headache was real enough. Besides, she had every confidence in Chloe's integrity, and was positive the girl would not stoop to a device such as that. It was more the style of Lydia or Sophy.

Lady Partridge tried to let Chloe down easy, and by adroit maneuvering, moved the conversation to Sir Richard. Sir Richard was apt to come to her ball, she told Chloe, if he hasn't gone to London. "I understand that Charlotte Venable is expecting Sir Richard to return to London any moment, and then an interesting announcement is to follow."

Lady Rothwell, feeling left behind at the post, interrupted quickly. "My sister Hensley says it is not Charlotte Venable——" but Lady Partridge interrupted.

"No matter. I shall ask him to my party anyway. The party is to celebrate our going to Bath, and if he doesn't come, there'll be parties when I return. And probably we'll be giving many a party to welcome his bride to the neighborhood."

She began the complicated maneuver of getting to her feet. "Come, Emma, my dear, help me," she said. "We have much to do to get ready for the ball, and besides pack for our trip. Sophy, will you be able to go with us?"

Lady Rothwell said, "We must see what Edward wishes to do."

Lady Partridge glanced shrewdly at her. She had heard that Edward was getting more tyrannical every day. And Lady Rothwell's bowing to his dictum bore out that gossip. But Sophy wailed, "Edward's a tyrant!"

Lady Partridge, as accustomed as she was to the Rothwell family, yet had strict ideas of decorum. Her own Emma, while the apple of Lady Partridge's eye, would never have railed against a member of her family else it would have gone ill with her. "Rothwell is of course within his rights. I should never allow Sophy to come along with my dear Emma without her guardian's approval."

Emma, whose affection for Sophy was strong but not entirely approved by her mother, fixed her mother with tear-drenched eyes. "I don't want to go if Sophy can't go," and would have continued except for the light in her mother's eyes. She thought better of her protest.

Lady Partridge, for her part, was loath to deny her daughter anything, and gave in, a little.

"Well, well, Emma," she said, "perhaps I could speak to Rothwell myself. I'll do that much."

Lady Rothwell, sitting in silence while this exchange took place, was conscious of a growing antagonism toward her only son. Edward, in his position as head of the family, was taking entirely too much upon himself. First, he had been thwarting Lydia's wish to go to London, but Chloe's legacy had taken care of that. While Lady Rothwell had not obtained Edward's permission for Lydia to go to London, if Chloe were to offer to finance Lydia's journey, then Edward would not have the excuse that he had used up to now—that they could not afford it. Lady Rothwell anticipated a struggle with Edward, but she had no doubt that she would win out in the long run. Now, with Sophy about to be unhappy, Lady Rothwell made a silent vow to work it out for Sophy as well.

Lady Partridge got up to leave, and with Emma in her wake swept toward the door. Lady Rothwell, escorting her as far as the door, said, "I will miss my young Sophy. There is so much life to her, you know. But Sophy wants to go to Bath, and I am determined she shall."

Chloe, hardly aware that Lady Partridge was leaving, heard the conversation at the fringe of her mind and gave it no heed. At the center of her thoughts was a certain Miss Charlotte Venable. She had thought that Penelope Salton was going to receive Richard's offer, and now Miss Venable's name had come up. Chloe could not remember the latter, and only vaguely the former. Penelope Salton was more of a threat to Chloe than the unknown Miss Venable. Miss Salton was a tall, jolly woman, clearly made to live in the country, surrounded by horses and dogs and a dozen progeny. Chloe disliked her at first thought, and, even more, she disliked the idea of having her as a close neighbor. At Highmoor, she would be far removed from Richard's wife.

The idea of setting up to live at Highmoor uncurled from its sleep just a little. It had quivered only slightly when she first thought of it. It was as though it were dormant, waiting for its time to rouse. Now, it was stirring. It was more a longing, so far, than anything else, for Edward had said it was an ineligible plan. But Richard's cousin, Lady Theale—Chloe suddenly remembered—lived not far from Highmoor, so Chloe would not be entirely alone. If Lady Theale were within visiting distance, the idea of living at Highmoor was a little more feasible than it had been.

She returned to the present with a thud. She was far from alone at this moment. Lady Partridge had gone, but Edward had arrived. Lady Rothwell and Lydia together gave him the news of Lady Partridge's invitation, as Francis entered.

"A ball, tomorrow a week, and we'll have hardly time to get ready to go."

Edward, after hesitating, to emphasize his authority, agreed that they might go. Lady Rothwell plunged ahead to arrange dresses for them all. Her planning was vocal. "I can wear my green again, if Chloe can put some lace insertions at the neck. I understand this is the latest fashion. The seamstress in town is going to be busy with Lydia's gown and I myself will be perfectly satisfied to wear my old gown again."

Edward, his ears prickling up in alarm at the idea of new gowns for all, listened with a frown between his eyebrows. Lady Rothwell unfortunately ignored Edward's glower. "Miss Sinclair will have Lydia's gown, of course, and Chloe's to do all in a week, and we must get in there before all the rest of the ball guests get to her. And Sophy's gown——"

Chloe protested. "I can wear the one I have. It's not been worn above two times. This is just a country ball, from what Lady Partridge said, and there's no need for me to have a new gown."

Lady Rothwell, intent upon her own daughters, passed this by. Edward, slow in comprehension and unbelieving, bellowed, "*Sophy!*"

His younger sister leaped into the air, startled out of her wits. But Edward was not addressing her directly. He advanced toward his mother. "Sophy is thirteen, ma'am. She is not going to London for at least four years," Edward pointed out carefully. "She is not going even to a country ball. She still belongs in the schoolroom!"

Lady Rothwell's face darkened with anger. But Edward continued, "Miss Addis should never have been dismissed."

Lady Rothwell said, menacingly, "You're giving me a headache."

Edward, bent on his own thoughts, said, "With all due respect, ma'am, that's nothing to what the females of my family are giving *me!*"

Fearful that her mother was losing the battle, Lydia joined the fray. "You're miserly, Edward," she pointed out. "I can't go anywhere without a new dress. I can't wear an old dress, for I have never had one. Edward, can't you see?"

Lady Rothwell backed her up, and Edward, who was not basically a bad fellow, desiring the good opinion of his family and seeing that good opinion departing on the waves of a mere bolt of cloth, relented. "A dress for

Lydia, I'll agree that far, but that's *all*." He glanced at Sophy as he finished, and turned to leave the room.

Sophy was at this point possessed by her native shrewdness. She kept very quiet in her corner, her plump face expressionless. She knew instinctively that this was the best course to pursue. Had a tantrum been called for, she would have obliged the company. But she correctly assessed Edward's mood as one of intransigence, and knew that any opposition would only set him harder in his ways.

Edward said that she was not to attend Lady Partridge's ball. Sophy herself knew that according to all the canons of society she was in fact too young. On the other hand, it was an event that she did not care to miss. If her friend Emma, two years older, was to attend, then Sophy, having no doubts about her own worth, was going to go, too.

Sophy had no fear of Edward. The subject was not closed yet. He had said Lydia was not to have a new gown, but he had relented. The ball was only one incident in Sophy's mind. Her true goal was to travel with Lady Partridge and Emma to Bath. She was prepared to do whatever was necessary to gain Edward's permission. If it meant giving up the ball, then so be it. It was the trip, rather than the immediate entertainment, that motivated her.

Sophy was too much like her mother not to understand the basis of intrigue. She could readily see the principle of giving the appearance of defeat while setting up another ploy. Sophy was equal to her mother in understanding; all she lacked was experience.

Chloe, for her part, would in the ordinary way have dismissed the wrangling as the ordinary give and take among a family. But something had happened to change her feelings, though since the change was at the moment only slight, she did not recognize it as a harbinger of things to come.

Francis, an unwilling spectator, was stirred to his depths. He was usually inarticulate, bringing forth monosyllables as required, but at this point he had some opinions. He did not hesitate to air them.

Like many men of limited intelligence, he clung to convention as to a wave-swept ledge in a storm. Propriety girded him about, for after all, one had to know where one was, didn't one? If the strengthening barriers were broken down, he would have nothing to guide him. He was an honest man, of limited intelligence and few inner resources. Thus he clung to convention, outraged at the attitude of his cousins, who flouted the known rules of society.

"A child at a party?" he cried, outrage in every syllable. "I must say it's unheard of. I can't imagine, Aunt, that you would countenance such a thing. Not heard of. Out of the question."

Lady Rothwell, bending a severe eye on him, said, "It is only a country affair, after all. I see no harm in Sophy's going, and I do not like your implication."

Francis, daunted as usual by his aunt, fell back on the things he knew. "It is simply not done. Word gets out, no matter how secret you think it is. I wouldn't like to be ashamed of the family. My own family, but there it is!"

Lydia, with an eye to her own main chance, joined the protest. "If Francis snubs me in London on account of Sophy, I will just *die*. Francis won't be ashamed of us, unless Sophy spoils it for everybody."

Sophy cried out in outrage, "I'm not going to spoil anything! What difference can it make in London, anyway, if I go to a party in Kent?"

Francis, joining battle, said severely, "Half the county will be there. And if you go to Lady Partridge's ball expecting me to dance with you, I'll tell you this. I'll leave before I'll be shamed by my family."

Sophy cried out, "No one will hear about it!"

Francis said, pale but stubborn, "My mother will hear."

Lady Rothwell, an unaccustomed frown appearing between her eyebrows, said, "I suppose you will tell her."

Francis answered quite simply, "Better me than somebody else."

Chloe, quietly, interposed. "Perhaps we shouldn't go to London this autumn." Her remark was in the nature of a bombshell falling in the midst of a startled group.

Lydia cried out in agony, "Not go to London? That's impossible!"

Lady Rothwell protested. "I never knew, Chloe, you had such a mischancy sense of humor. I know full well you have only your family's interest at heart. But it is not kind to upset Lydia by the mere thought of not going to London."

Chloe faltered, "I—I didn't mean——"

Lady Rothwell, seeing with satisfaction that Chloe's defense was crumbling, continued, "I know that if there is one thing you are, it's unselfish, and loving and generous. You would not take out your own feelings on your sister, for I know you could not live with Lydia's misfortune heavy on your heart."

Chloe, unreasonably daunted, said no more.

Lady Rothwell, seeing she had prevailed once more, began to make plans with Lydia to go to town to Miss Sinclair, to get her gowns made. Chloe scarcely noticed that Lady Rothwell was speaking in the plural.

Chloe said privately to Francis, "Will your mother mind having us in town with her?" Chloe knew well that Lady Rothwell had in mind taking a house of their own. But Chloe, always cautious, thought it would be better to stay, at least at the beginning and for the Little Season, with Mrs. Hensley. If they were to go to London again in the spring, then would be time enough to see about a house of their own.

Francis, with surprising vigor, exploded, "She won't like any hoydenish conduct, that is sure. Got to hold her head up, after all."

Francis glanced gloomily at Lydia and turned his solemn gaze to Sophy. Francis was a man of immense tolerance simply because he knew he was not of the first quality of intellect, and was content with life as he lived it. Yet he was becoming more and more distressed. He had been brought down from London for the express purpose of offering for Chloe, to keep her inheritance in the family. He did not like the assignment, but his ordinary obedience to his mother and his aunt worked against him. He saw now that Lydia and her mother had gotten out a fashion book and were pouring over it in total concentration. He shuddered. He could not help but feel for his cousin Edward—all these females around him, each one, except of course Chloe, bent on thwarting Edward's every wish.

Francis summoned sufficient words to say as much to Chloe, bending toward her lest the others hear.

At that point, Lady Rothwell looked up and saw Francis talking with Chloe. She noted a flush mantling Francis's face, and leaped at once to the wrong interpretation. Francis at that point was saying to Chloe, "I didn't mean to count you among the females." He was anxious lest she misunderstand him, and earnestness turned his cheeks pink.

Lady Rothwell called across the room, "At least Edward will have some good news, won't he? Francis, you had best put the announcement in the *Gazette* at once." Lady Rothwell smoothed her hair back in an odd, preening gesture. She had pulled it off, she thought. Francis had offered for Chloe! "At least, the sooner the announcement gets into the *Gazette*," she added, "we'll get rid of those others—Mr. Invers and that terrible Mr. Stoddard."

Chloe, assessing rightly her stepmother's thoughts, said, very gently, but distinctly, "I am not marrying Francis." She got up without a glance at Francis and left the room.

Lady Rothwell, put in the wrong, was struck by the need to do something. She told Lydia and Sophy to leave the room. "I have something of purpose to say to Francis."

Recognizing the determination and steel will of Lady Rothwell in her tone of voice, Lydia and Sophy, surprisingly with one thought, scuttled from the room. Sophy, characteristically, took a quick glance over her shoulder as she left and closed the door behind her. She had seen Lady Rothwell advancing upon Francis. And Francis, standing bolt upright, his eyes fixed upon his approaching aunt, reminded Sophy of nothing so much as a frightened hare.

17

No one ever knew, except the two participants, what transpired behind the closed door. Lady Rothwell and Francis each kept the secret, but it was clear that Lady Rothwell's grim look abated only slightly, and Francis's look of a cornered rabbit was crossed now by a look of dogged hopelessness.

From that moment on, Chloe seemed to run into Francis at every turn. When she emerged from the kitchen wing, after giving instructions to the servants, Francis waited for her. Were she to go in to borrow a book from the library, Francis would be waiting when she emerged.

Chloe was fond of Francis for the most part, but this grim tracking, coupled with the look of misery in his eyes, began to wear on her. She would have told Francis frankly to leave her alone, but she strongly suspected that Lady Rothwell was behind it all, and Francis was no more fit to stand up against his aunt, than—than she herself was, she finally decided.

There was one place, she had discovered, where he would not follow her. Not that it was a haven for Chloe, for it was Lady Rothwell's sitting room.

Lady Rothwell had long ago formed a habit of being read to by Chloe one hour in the morning and one hour in the afternoon. Lady Rothwell said comfortably, "Having the reading in two sections like this breaks up my day nicely."

She was immensely satisfied with her arrangement, without thinking that it also broke up Chloe's day so that she could count on no stretch of time that was uniquely her own.

This day Chloe took a book from Edward's shelves, Taylor's *Life of Christ*, and carried it into Lady Rothwell's sitting room.

To Chloe's surprise, Lady Rothwell told her to close the door. Chloe did so, and advanced to her usual low stool. Lady Rothwell said, "I wish to talk seriously to you, child. I have noticed some things that I do not quite like." The tone of her speech was chiding, as one would speak to a wayward child.

"I have not thought you ungrateful, Chloe," said Lady Rothwell. "I have brought you up as my own daughter, never showing favoritism—" ignoring totally the fact that Lydia and Sophy had no household duties, and Chloe had the entire running of the house on her shoulders—"and I speak to you now as I would to my own daughters."

Chloe said, submissively, "Yes, ma'am."

"You were allowed your governesses long beyond the normal years, for your father wished it so. I myself do not see the reason for so much education for a female child, but he would have his way. Also you had part of a Season in London, and it certainly is not my fault that the Season was cut short."

Chloe's heart sank within her. She hated every word that Lady Rothwell was saying, and for the first time she could remember she formed little phrases to refute Lady Rothwell's statements. But yet she did not speak.

Lady Rothwell rolled along. "Now, Chloe, it grieves me to see that you are begrudging Lydia a Season in London. Even a small piece of gaiety, the Little Season. You are reluctant to have Lydia enjoy herself."

Stung, Chloe retorted, "But Edward says she must not go."

Lady Rothwell waved Edward aside as though he were so much dust in the air.

Lady Rothwell's voice took on a new tone, speaking in sorrow. "Now, Chloe, you are making me very unhappy by your treatment of Francis. It is the dearest wish of my heart that our families be allied, yours and mine. We have worked as one family since you were small and I came here as your stepmother. Now I wish to see a closer tie. Yet you scorn Francis, my own nephew, when I have made all the arrangements for your marriage."

She spoke further in this vein, and her gently sad tone worked powerfully in Chloe. It was not the first time she had heard this tone from Lady Rothwell, for at every turn as she was growing up, Lady Rothwell had known by instinct how to bring her stepdaughter to her knees. There had been very little waywardness to begin with, and Lady Rothwell was now satisfied that she had successfully routed any trace of that fault out of her stepdaughter.

At length, Lady Rothwell brought up what she considered the ultimate good. "You will be safe with Francis," she said with wild illogic, "for the fortune hunters will no longer pursue you. We will be rid at last of Mr. Invers and Mr. Stoddard, and whoever else comes to you, for you know they must have only your legacy in mind."

Her insensitive assumption that Chloe was without charm except for the money she had fallen heir to was not intentional, but it was typical of Lady Rothwell. By the end of half an hour, Chloe was totally cowed and unfit to speak. Her sense of guilt, for wanting something for herself of her own legacy, flooded her with tears. Lady Rothwell, not coldly but merely as a woman who was used to having her own way, moved on then to the subject of Lydia's gown.

In Chloe's confusion of mind, she thought that Lady

Rothwell was asking Chloe to buy Lydia's ball gown, the one that Edward had given permission to have made for Lady Partridge's ball.

Lady Rothwell, intent on her own pursuits, believed that she had obtained permission from Chloe to purchase Lydia's entire London wardrobe. It was not the first time over the years that Lady Rothwell and Chloe had allowed their minds to march along different tracks.

Lady Rothwell, seeing Chloe still weeping, told her very kindly, "You are a good and dutiful daughter, and I am pleased with you. Now, Chloe, pull yourself together. We have half an hour left on our reading time. I need to settle my mind, for you will not believe how much this conversation has taken out of me. Taylor is just the man to do it. Let us not waste any more time. Open the book."

Chloe thought, this half hour promised to stretch into eternity. Her mind was certainly not on the words she was reading, and Lady Rothwell sighed heavily in obvious resignation at Chloe's failing performance.

But the half hour was over at last, and Chloe fled. She hurried to her room. Nimrod was not there. This was his time for the kitchen, where Cook made much of him. The puppy was growing fat, and it was useless to tell Mrs. Field not to spoil him. Nimrod had a roguish way with him. In his shameless way, he had told Cook that she was the most important person in his universe. He had made a slave of her.

Chloe washed her face, trying to repair the ravages of tears. It was not the first time that Lady Rothwell had reduced Chloe to a shattered sense of worthlessness. It was simply that she was an insensitive woman, set in her own ways and incapable of lavishing affection on Chloe.

Chloe could remember, however, her loneliness after her own mother's death. There were endless days and nights alone, except for her nurse, and then Lady Rothwell had arrived as her father's second wife. To do Lady Rothwell credit, she had mothered the little girl over the bad times, and those days Chloe often suspected were the happiest of her own life.

It was not until Edward's birth that Chloe found herself imperceptibly relegated to the status of stepdaughter. Her father's regard, which was totally affectionate and approving, may have influenced Lady Rothwell's adverse feelings. But by the time Lord Rothwell died, Chloe was sufficiently grown up that Lady Rothwell began to lean more and more heavily on her for running the house.

Richard had not come to call at Rothwell Manor for some time, and Chloe began to feel that Lady Partridge's analysis was correct. He had gone to London. The purposes of his trip to London, Chloe did not wish to think about.

She could not settle down to anything. She moved from window to fireplace to bed to wardrobe, picking up a book and setting it down, picking up her needlework and setting it down, and finally going to the window once more. The reading of Jeremy Taylor's *Life of Christ* may have settled Lady Rothwell's nerves, but it had had a damaging effect on Chloe's.

She looked out across the empty lawn, a view that often gave her much pleasure, but not this day.

At length, she saw from the window Francis heading toward the front of the house. She knew that Francis was caught in the same trap that she was, Lady Rothwell's firm intention of allying them by marriage. She felt sorry for Francis, but she felt even more intent on her own feelings.

If Francis were going toward the front of the house, then she knew where he would be for a short time. She quickly snatched up a shawl and hurried down the back stairs.

Leaving the house by the kitchen door, out of sight of Francis, she slipped toward the herb gardens and then toward a small path that led into the coppice. She did not see the tiny puppy staggering hopefully after her. Her step was slow as she moved cautiously away from the house, lest Francis had changed his mind and retraced his steps.

She had not gone far when she heard whimpering behind her. She turned around and saw the panting puppy, tottering on his stubby legs, desperate to catch up with her. She picked him up and cradled him in her arms, stroking his head and talking in quiet tones. He responded by licking her face and trying acrobatically to get down to the ground. She held him tightly, and hurried away from the house. She saw Edward's factor approaching the house by a path that would have intercepted hers, and she didn't want to see him.

She didn't want to see anybody, as a matter of fact. She slipped through the gate, past the rose garden into the home woods. She hurried along the path until she reached a point that had been a favorite of hers in times past. The same log was there, and she sat on it. The path continued on, and would eventually reach Richard's boundary. It had been at one time a well-traveled path between Rothwell Manor and Davenant Hall, for Richard and Chloe both. Now, it was beginning to be overgrown, for there was no need to use the path any more. She sat on the log and began to relax, letting the cool moist air of the woods calm her. The air rose around her, redolent of moist earth, decaying leaves, and the green smell of growing things.

Stroking the puppy's head, she allowed her thoughts to come out. "You're the first thing that anybody has given me in years. You're the first puppy I've ever owned, and I'll be forever grateful to Richard for his thoughtfulness."

The puppy grew tired of licking her face, of telling her with every fiber of him that she was the idol of his life, and at length she set him down at her feet and watched him.

He was a hunter born, although he had no experience. Yet he knew what he should do, for the echoes of his ancestors rang in his head. A squirrel, flickering across the trail, galvanized Nimrod into action. He set out after the animal, hopelessly outclassed, and yipped. The squirrel, halfway up the tree and safe, turned and loosed a volley of defiant chattering at the small dog that had dared to chase him.

Nimrod, suddenly not so brave, retreated at once and sat on Chloe's slippers. From that safe vantage point he barked furiously at the squirrel.

If Richard had given her the puppy to serve as a diversion, he had succeeded, for now Chloe found the antics of the puppy amusing. Her laugh rang out in the woods, and for a short space she lost her cares.

Now she said to the dog, "Highmoor might be just the thing for us. If we went there, I would take you along. I think I could easily promote you," she said, fancifully, "Chief Dog at Highmoor. How does that sound?"

Nimrod agreed that it was no more than his due, and turned to growl again at the squirrel.

Chloe reflected on Lady Rothwell's recent speech. She was putting inordinate pressure on Chloe and Francis both. "*A marriage has been arranged*"—how often Chloe had read those words in the *Gazette*. The announcement of a marriage was always, in Chloe's mind, a happy event.

Now for the first time she caught a glimpse of what loomed behind those five words.

Were there always such brouhahas? Were there always family drudges to be gotten rid of, or family butterflies to be safely bestowed on a household that could thence take over the responsibility for a girl that her own family could not control? She understood Lady Rothwell's wish to have Lydia make her bow in London society. Lydia was a thoughtless, irresponsible child, and if she were married to someone, then her husband could look out for her and Lady Rothwell could turn her thoughts to Sophy.

It was perfectly clear, and full of common sense. But there was little consideration for the inclinations of those who were to wed.

Was there never such a thing as two persons finding their affinity in each other? The bald words in the *Gazette* gave no hint that love was any part of a marriage, and suddenly she had a pixyish view of the two parties to a marriage as being no more than parcels of land, fields, woods, and mansions allying themselves to each other at the altar. Her downtrodden sense of humor also showed her these two parcels of real estate standing up, bowing to each other, and beginning to waltz at Almack's. The fanciful idea restored her mood, somewhat. It was all very well to laugh, yet she saw no way out of her own dilemma.

Suddenly she noticed that Nimrod was not in sight. Alarmed, she began to look for him. Who knew what kind of a trap he might fall into in the woods? She wondered whether the game warden had been able to keep out poachers. There might be a snare set illegally for rabbits, and she called quickly to Nimrod. She heard his barking and heard a squirrel chattering and then a jay screaming in alarm, and she knew the strong likelihood that Nimrod was at the root of the disturbance. She tried to follow the sounds, but Nimrod had slipped through the underbrush on a track that she could not follow. She scrambled through the bushes, the brush tearing her hair and rending her morning gown.

She stopped to listen, and then pursued the sound further. At last she caught up with the dog. Her alarm vented itself in scolding, and she picked him up. She clutched him to her shoulder and started back toward the path. From the safety of her shoulder, Nimrod barked defiance at these animals that had eluded him, and retired at last, winner of the battle.

When she got back to the path, she knelt on the ground. Her gown was already ruined, and a little more mud would not hurt. She held the dog firmly in both hands and began taking the burrs out of his silky hair. Nimrod, feeling this was a very superior kind of game, wriggled energetically. She laughed, scolding him, and finally, holding him firmly, said, "I always find it useful, Nimrod, to count my blessings, and I commend the practice to you."

His barking stopped, and he licked her face. Her laughter gurgled at last, and the man who was watching at the edge of the path was enchanted. Nimrod, aware of the man before she was, turned his head and barked, and Richard stepped forward into view.

"If you must count your blessings, Chloe, then they must be few indeed," he said.

She hardly knew which way to look. Her hair had escaped from its pins, her dress was muddy and torn, and she could not smooth her hair back for the puppy was still engrossing her attention.

She began to apologize. "I didn't know anyone was around, and he got away, and I had to go after him." Her voice died away.

Richard said, "Do you come here often?"

She said, "Yes, it's quiet here." She did not know that there was a lonely note in her voice, one that wrung at Richard's heart strings.

He said, "Without observers, you can be yourself. Is that it?"

There was a note in his voice that she had not heard before, and she did not quite understand. Fearful of taking Richard too much for granted, she withdrew into herself. He watched the shadow come over her face again and hurried to explain. "Your self is engaging, indeed, and I am privileged to witness this. I especially like that fetching gurgle that escapes you when you're amused."

Unused to compliments, she flushed. She must turn the subject away, lest she reveal too much of her own thoughts. "I thought you had gone up to London," she said quickly. "Lady Partridge had said that you had gone."

Richard, puzzled, said, "Why should I go? The mail service is quite satisfactory."

Richard was just now in a dilemma. He had had a disturbing letter from Aston, his man of affairs in London. The news was worrisome, and in a way crucial. He had come to inform Chloe of the letter's contents, but when the moment came his heart failed him.

The subject that had come to her mind unaware leaped to her lips. "I should like to see Highmoor," she told him, "for that is, after all, one of my blessings, is it not?"

Richard, feeling that she must read the contents of his letter right through his jacket, was startled. Chloe hardly noticed, and continued, "Perhaps I can stop in at Highmoor on my way to London in the autumn. I was only a child when I was at Highmoor, and I don't remember the first thing about how to get there."

Richard said, "Highmoor lies not far from my cousin's place—Lady Theale, you remember her."

Chloe said, "Oh yes. We had such good times when she used to visit here."

Richard, gently, said, "I thought you did not want to go to London?"

She looked away. "I've changed my mind," she said in a remote voice.

Suddenly suspicious, Richard demanded, "Why?"

Her lips trembled and she said, "I cannot tell you. I cannot say even to my Great Friend. But I must go to London."

He watched her, sensing her great distress, and longing to demand that she tell him everything. But he must hold his tongue, lest he say too much.

He took the puppy from her and held him close. He was rewarded by a warm tongue licking his hand. "Enough of that." Surprisingly, the small dog obeyed instantly, and, with a sheepish expression, abandoned his display of affection. Richard said, "You spoke of counting your blessings. The pup, I hope, is one? Or is he a nuisance?"

She cried, "He is a darling, *darling* blessing! He asks for nothing, you see."

Unwittingly she revealed to him more than she knew. His Chloe was beset by people who always wanted something from her. She gave far more than she received, he thought darkly, and especially with Aston's letter in his pocket, the full irony of the position struck him with force. The time had come.

He began, "I have something I must tell you. . . ."

18

Chloe felt her heart sink into her shoes. Here it comes! she thought. He was about to tell her that he was betrothed. While it was kind of him to want her to know before the rest, yet she did not want to hear it.

It meant the end of all her reliance on him, her last, even her only anchor slipping its cable and letting her drift away. She had a sudden forlorn feeling, as though she were alone on a vast ocean and no rescuing sail in sight.

She said, with false brightness, "I hope it is good news?"

Richard, thinking of Mr. Aston's letter, was startled. He said, "You have already heard the bad news?"

She was mystified at his sharp reaction, but she said only, "Sophy tells me that Mr. Invers will offer for me—that's not good news precisely."

Richard said, quizzically, "The good news would be that you are going to refuse him."

Chloe looked away, and Richard was conscious once more of the anger that rode him when he considered the vultures that had descended upon Rothwell Manor. How dare Thaddeus Invers, a man barely on the fringe of society, aspire as high as Chloe Rothwell?

Richard insisted, "You *will* refuse him?"

She was so silent for so long that suddenly he was anxious. Finally she burst out, more to herself than to him, "I long to go to Highmoor."

Richard's resolution, fired by the information he had in his pocket, died away. He wanted to offer his heart and his hand to Chloe this very instant. However, he realized again that she was so overwrought that she would not believe his sincerity. The time was not right, but perhaps, he thought, something could be made of this. "Perhaps you can."

Richard, remembering the purpose of his visit, pulled a fat volume from his pocket and handed it to her. She turned the book over in her hands, and he explained, "This was in a shipment of books that just came. It is not new. As a matter of fact, it has been out a couple of years. But I believe you have not read it?"

She read the title aloud. *"Childe Harold's Pilgrimage.* No, I have not read it."

He said, "I brought it for you, for I have already read it."

She was sorely tempted. "This is one of the books that Edward sent back."

Richard said then, "I probably should not give it to you then." Her face fell. He relented. "I shall not give it to you. I shall *lend* it to you. Then, if Edward finds it, he dare not confiscate it and consign it to the dustbin. I shall insist that he take good care of my property else," he added with drawling fierceness. "I shall call him out!"

She giggled, a sound that was music to his ears. He noticed that her eyes strayed often to the book in her hand. She was clearly anxious to read it. She smiled up at him confidingly, and said, "You know, I have never even read a novel."

Richard nodded. "I have the strongest suspicion that Lydia and Sophy have, for they were too knowledgeable when Invers was discussing the ruined abbey."

"Yes. I fear they are learning deceit, which I cannot help but think is more harmful to them than the novel itself would be."

Edward truly had their best interests at heart, and she told Richard so. "Edward is not malicious, he simply wants us to be protected." Then her gratitude burst forth. "How good you are to me! First my dear little Nimrod, and now this book. What a Great Friend you are. How is it you know what pleases me most?"

Richard said, gently, "You remember I have known you a long time, Chloe. You haven't changed much."

Chloe, remembering the change that she believed was coming in Richard's life, a change that must by necessity exclude her, begged him, "I should like, Richard, above all things to know that whatever alteration you make in your own life I may always call you my Great Friend."

Richard, not quite understanding the wellsprings from which her words had come, promised at least that much. "I hope you will always consider me, above all else, your friend." Aston's letter was still in his mind, but he knew now that the wiser part was not to mention it.

She said, taking back her puppy, "You have something to tell me?"

Richard lied. "It was nothing much."

Satisfied, she left and he watched her out of sight.

It was Edward's duty to tell her, not Richard's. He was not sure that Edward knew as much as Richard's agent had told him, but if he didn't, it was time that he did.

Richard thought savagely, Let's see what Edward makes of this coil! He had things to do. He must write to Aston this very day.

Chloe returned to the manor, leaving Richard in the coppice. She was possessed of Richard's two gifts, one squirming in a desperate attempt to lick her face, the other heavy with promise of delight for her near future. She tucked the book in the pocket of her gown and strolled back to the house with her mood exceptionally lightened.

She reflected upon every word Richard had spoken, every expression that crossed his pleasant, reliable face.

She recalled his steady gaze when she had protested that Edward would not approve of the book. She remembered Richard's conspiratorial smile as he suggested that if he kept ownership of the book, she was safe from Edward's retaliation. It was curious how that level gaze of Richard's put heart in her.

She reflected, for nearly the first time, what her legacy might mean to her. She had a right, at her advanced near-spinster age, to read as she chose, for example.

Childe Harold's Pilgrimage, no matter what was contained in it, could not be as bad as Edward thought, when everyone in London had been talking about it for two years. With her money now, she could even order books, or whatever else she wished. She could live at Highmoor, which would make life easier in some ways. Yet she shrank at the idea of being alone.

She could not leave her family, but she might be able to make changes in the way she lived. It was a daring thought—to live at Highmoor. She could no more leave the loving arms of her family than she could ascend in a balloon. But to think of ordering what she wished from London, and paying for it with her own money, was sufficiently adventurous to make her giddy.

When Chloe reached the manor, she was brought back

to earth with a wicked thud. Edward had been looking for her. Awaiting her in his book room with impatience, he felt greatly daring. He did not wish Chloe to wed his idiot cousin Francis, but he knew full well that Lady Rothwell's formidable pressure would be lowered upon Chloe and Francis both until there was no way they could avoid the match. Edward, in his kind regard for Chloe, and sidestepping his mother's wishes, had thought of a way out for Chloe.

When she entered, he told her, "Have you given Francis his answer yet?"

She said, "I have told him that I will not marry him, if that is what you mean."

Edward said, "Do you *want* to marry him?"

Chloe said, quite calmly, and yet feeling her heart stifling her breath, "Perhaps you weren't listening, Edward I said I would not marry Francis. There is no way I can be forced to, is there?" Her eyes were anxious, for she was not quite sure of the ground on which she stood.

Edward said, "No, you would not have to marry Francis. But it might be very uncomfortable if you did not. I have thought of an alternative for you. I have given Thaddeus Invers permission to pay court to you."

"Invers!" she exclaimed in indignation. "Edward, he is no better——"

Edward interrupted. "He is a man of some intellect, some education, and I vow he is better than Francis. I am sure the two of you would suit."

Chloe said, "But *I* am not at all sure he would suit. I do not know why you did not ask me *my* opinion of him first!"

Edward, his voice raised, said, "You know I have only your own good at heart."

The little dog, on the floor, took exception to Edward's harassing of Chloe. He took no heed of his short stature, his stubby little legs, for within him, he had the heart of a mastiff. He advanced upon Edward, growling.

Edward, suddenly in a temper, took it out on the dog. "Look at that idiotic, lop-eared dog. When Richard was foolish enough to offer you a dog, why couldn't you take one of some value? This pup will never grow into anything at all."

While Edward would never kick an animal or otherwise mistreat him, the small puppy seemed to feel that Edward was his born enemy. Chloe scooped up the puppy and quieted him. He still muttered menaces in his throat, but he felt that he had triumphed over her enemy, and he was well satisfied.

Edward, for his part, realized he had put a wrong foot forward with Chloe. He had told her, much as his mother had, what she should do. He now tried to rectify his mistake.

"Chloe," he said, "I cannot help but worry about what will happen to you. You will be better off as mistress of your own establishment. Invers is respectable, and certainly would not be unkind to you. If you were wed, you could order your life as it suited you. Suppose I would marry, and of course, I must. Too many females in the house would certainly make you unhappy. The dower house would be suitable for my mother, but I feel you would not be happy there."

Chloe, with spirit, said, "I quite agree. I will go to Highmoor." Then, curiosity struck her, and she said, "Edward, whom do you have in mind to marry?"

Edward said, "No one. I am simply looking ahead. You simply must not consider Highmoor."

"Why not? It is mine."

"It is totally ineligible for you to live alone."

She said, "Sooner or later I will be alone, and I might as well get used to it now."

Lurking in her mind was the thought that besides the advantages of living where she chose, she would be away from Richard and the sight of his new wife.

Edward, blustering, said, "How would it look? As though your family had thrown you out! You couldn't do that to my mother, for you have known nothing but kindness at her hands."

Chloe was forced to agree. But she said, "My family insists upon throwing me into the hands of men who wish to marry my inheritance."

Edward, wounded, said, "There is no such thing as throwing you——"

Chloe insisted. "Francis, for example. He is such a constant bore, and he wishes to marry me no more than I wish to wed him."

Edward agreed, and said, "There is no need to tell my mother what I say, but I promise you need not marry Francis if you do not wish to."

Chloe said, with an appearance of innocence, "Then Mr. Invers is your choice?"

Edward had the grace to flush, but he held doggedly to his choice. "We aren't children any more, and we must look at things in a commonsensical way. Invers has some money—enough to set up a modest establishment—and you would do well to consider him."

Chloe, unexpectedly persistent, said, "Then why does he wish to marry me, if he has sufficient?"

Edward, almost under his breath, muttered, "Because no one else would have him."

Chloe said, "Then I too do not wish to have him."

Edward, as palliative, said, "I promise you this. I'll send Francis home after the ball at Lady Partridge's."

Chloe, suddenly tired of the whole conversation, retorted, "Don't bother. Perhaps Francis has his uses." She turned to leave the library with Nimrod in her arms. She addressed the dog, but her words were intended for Edward. "Francis," she said to Nimrod, "is in need of instruction, and perhaps Mr. Invers can provide it."

She had left the room, and Edward remained behind, troubled in his mind. There was something a little altered about Chloe, an obscure difference in her attitude that he could not quite fathom, but he did know one thing—he did not like it.

His eyes fell upon an object on the floor, fallen from Chloe's pocket when she bent to pick up the dog. He crossed the room to pick it up, and saw the title. That foolish book by Lord Byron! He was incensed. Where had it come from? How had Chloe gotten it? He himself distinctly remembered sending the thing back, after glancing through it, and he knew that it had not come from his shelves.

The door opened and she returned. He fixed her with a baleful eye. He gestured toward the fire, when she called out—"Edward! Don't do that!"

He demanded, "Where did you get this book? It's not fit for a lady to read!"

She took it from his unresisting fingers. "Richard would not like his property destroyed. It is a good thing you did not throw it into the fire, for you would have had to answer for it."

She left the room again, and would have been gratified

had she been able to glance through the closed door. Her brother did not move, a look of stupefaction on his face and his jaw dropping in a very unbecoming manner.

19

The day before Lady Partridge's ball, Lady Rothwell, taking Lydia and Sophy, set off in the Rothwell carriage to Miss Sinclair's to pick up Lydia's ball gown.

Miss Sinclair was the most popular seamstress in the area. Last week Lady Rothwell had shamelessly engaged in a genteel kind of blackmail, announcing in a casual fashion that Lydia would be going to London for the Little Season in less than two months. She allowed Miss Sinclair's thoughts to dwell on the vast amount of sewing to be done. Having obtained Miss Sinclair's promise to put Lydia's ball gown at the top of her list, she then proceeded to discuss Lydia's London wardrobe.

Miss Sinclair's efficiency was apparent the moment that Lady Rothwell swept into the tiny house. The ball gown for Lydia was finished, waiting for its new owner. Every flat surface was covered with bolts of cloth that had been sent down from London. Such exquisite colors, such elaborate materials! Damasks and muslins and gossamer gauzes, materials embroidered with gold threads or silver—Lydia was struck into silence.

Miss Sinclair watched her, appreciating the effect that her artfully contrived display had made, and turned to Lady Rothwell. "The London draper," she said, "informs me that these are the most sought-after fabrics in his shop. You see how well they will become Miss Lydia, and I think the patterns we spoke of will make the child some exquisite gowns."

Miss Sinclair, true daughter of her Scottish ancestors, insisted that Lady Rothwell examine each fabric and each pattern. "I should like your approval, Lady Rothwell, before it's cut into, for once the shears touch the fabric the die is cast, as Caesar said on the banks of the Ruby River." No one corrected her.

Two hours passed very pleasantly for Lady Rothwell and Lydia. Sophy had time to brood, and her spirits moved rapidly from envy to jealousy, to disappointment. Finally, toward the end of the two-hour session, Sophy was simply bored.

Lady Rothwell, watching the footman stow the ball gown in the boot, wrapped in tissue paper and carefully spread out to avoid wrinkles, said quietly to Sophy, "Don't get overset. Just trust your mama, pet."

Sophy cried, climbing into the coach behind her mother, "What can you do? Old Edward has spoiled everything. I don't know why he thinks of me as a child yet, for if Emma can attend the ball, and after all it is in her house, why can't I?"

On the way home, they stopped at the Partridge manor. Lady Partridge met them at the door, smiling broadly in welcome. She was in the midst of her party arrangements, and her mind was further distracted by the coming trip to Bath. Even her hair took on some of the excitement, for it stood out from her face in small, uncontrolled tendrils. The house smelled of beeswax and soap, with a faint undertone of cooking and flowery scents from the conservatory. Lady Partridge's house had, in the newest fashion, a conservatory built on instead of greenhouses in the garden. It was enough for Lady Partridge to hear of a new fashion that pleased her, for her to have it as soon as it could be accomplished.

Now she welcomed her guests, and said, "Let's go in here; I think they have not cleaned here yet."

They moved into a large parlor behind the main salon. Emma came dashing down the stairs, folded Sophy in her arms, and took her off upstairs to exchange secrets. They had not seen each other for three days, and there was much to talk about.

Lady Partridge and Lady Rothwell relaxed for a comfortable prose. They had very little in common, except that they understood each other and were allied in the need to circumvent the men who ran their lives.

Lady Partridge said, "What trouble for only a simple country dance. Nothing like the affairs they have in London! After all, we are simple people, and I do not attempt anything more than a quiet gathering of my friends and neighbors." She looked around her at the very luxuriously furnished room with secret pleasure. She was quite sure the Prince Regent had nothing more comfortable than her rooms, no matter how much he spent.

Lady Partridge was simply paying off social obligations before she left the area for her journey to Bath. She turned to Lady Rothwell and said, "I understand from Emma that Sophy can't come? Is this true? Emma will be devastated."

"Rothwell has said that Sophy is too young."

Lady Partridge, remembering certain incidents in Sophy's not uncheckered past, could only agree with Edward, but yet her daughter's wishes ruled her heart, if not her head.

Lady Rothwell, beginning her campaign, said shyly, "But Emma will be at the ball, will she not?"

Lady Partridge said, "Naturally, but I have every hope that Emma will behave unobtrusively, so that no one's attention will be called to her. After all, Emma is almost fifteen, and very shortly she will be in London. I should not like to have any untoward rumor mar her reputation."

After a few more remarks, Lady Rothwell inserted the next step in her plan. "I'm anxious to see Sophy have a little fun, and see how things are managed in the better households. I feel that Edward is wrong in not letting Sophy come."

There was much unsaid between the two ladies, but their understanding was complete. It was arranged in only moments that Sophy would stay, the night before the ball, to spend the night with Emma. Thus the question of Sophy's riding from Rothwell Manor to Lady Partridge's home was avoided. Edward would see nothing to disturb his sense of propriety, and Lady Rothwell gave a few pertinent instructions to Sophy.

Lady Rothwell and Lydia returned home, leaving Sophy behind. Lydia was silent most of the way home, her head filled with fancies triggered by the beautiful fabrics and fashionable patterns she had seen in the hands of Miss Sinclair. Lydia's fancy, often given full sway without regard to the realities of life, now presented her with even more satisfying vistas ahead.

Lydia could even see herself dancing with Sir Richard. She had a clear picture of Sir Richard begging her to waltz with him, and whirling her away in the dance that was only now accepted in London. It was her ineffable beauty, Sir Richard told her, in her fancy, that made him quite ready to forget the London belles that so far had filled his mind. She sighed heavily in complete happiness, and shut her eyes, the better to see Sir Richard's adoring face.

Lady Rothwell's head, on the other hand, was full of the subject that had engaged the major portion of her attention since Chloe, through a stroke of good fortune scarcely deserved, had come into money.

It would be a shame to let Chloe's money, and the country establishment of Highmoor, go out of the family. There was only one way she could secure Chloe's fortune to her family's advantage and that was through Francis Hensley. Lady Rothwell was not afflicted with any sense of modesty or of possible failure. She could influence Chloe herself, and also through Francis. She needed Chloe's help to launch Lydia, and, in a couple of years, Sophy, in London society. Lady Rothwell, as any good mother would, had a strong wish to see both her daughters well married and in their own establishments. It was significant, although she did not recognize it, that she considered Chloe's future as already settled. Chloe was to marry Francis, provide the means for the London adventures, and at the same time stay close at hand to run Lady Rothwell's household and perform the myriad small details of living at Rothwell Manor that Lady Rothwell chose not to do.

The day of the ball dawned, to everyone's satisfaction, clear and fair. It gave promise of being a perfect day, and the moon would be at its brightest around midnight, when the party would expect to return home from Lady Partridge's.

Chloe had, to Cook's dismay, fallen by the wayside in pursuit of her duties in regulating the household.

As soon as Richard had given Chloe Byron's epic, she had begun to dip into it an hour a day, and under the guidance of a stern conscience had put the book aside at times to follow her household schedule. But the day before the ball, while Lady Rothwell and her girls were in town, Chloe had sat over the book for two hours. It was slow reading, for she stopped at every line and allowed herself to visualize the poet's depictions. Now, the morning of the ball, Bess had pressed Chloe's dress and it hung waiting for her in the wardrobe. Her slippers were laid out, her mother's pearls were on the dresser, her gloves, her little slippers to match the dress, her shawl ready to hand, to the accompaniment of comments by Bess.

Chloe, seized at last by an urge stronger than her duty, was engrossed in the wanderings of *Childe Harold*. To all of Bess's remarks, Chloe turned a deaf ear. At length, Mrs. Field, puffing, climbed the back stairs and invaded Chloe's room.

Chloe, her fingers still marking her place in the book, turned blank eyes on Cook. Returning to earth with a thud, Chloe said, "Oh, Mrs. Field. Is there something wrong? Your tooth bad again?"

"No, Miss Chloe, and that's the least of my worries. The tooth is gone and I don't feel where it was any more. But I must ask you, Miss Chloe, to tell me this. How many sandwiches will I need to lay out? Will Miss Sophy be staying on, and will some of the gentlemen be returning here?"

Cook's duty was to keep those who had been regaled at a generous dinner, followed by light refreshments during the dancing, and no doubt a supper before starting home, from starving during the night.

"Cook, I can't tell you. You might ask Lady Rothwell what her plans are."

She was too civil to return to her book until Mrs. Field left the room, but she made no secret of the fact that she was anxious for Cook to leave. Cook stared at her blankly, struggling to believe what she had just heard, and departed.

Chloe, pushing her clear duty out of sight, returned to the pages of George Gordon, Lord Byron.

She wept over some lines, sighed over even more, and the morning fled very pleasurably. The Rothwell Manor party was invited to dinner at Lady Partridge's, and they must leave by two o'clock to arrive in good time.

Chloe had no sense of time. Not until Lady Rothwell's maid Ford, Chloe's own maid Bess, and Lydia herself descended upon her, did she start guiltily and close the book. While Bess and Ford wrangled amiably over getting Chloe dressed, Lydia pirouetted before her half-sister and demanded admiration.

Chloe gave it ungrudgingly, for Lydia did look lovely.

The cut of the blue gown was a little old for Lydia, but it did set off her beauty.

Lydia's words came muffled as Bess dropped the gray gown over Chloe's head and smoothed it around her shoulders. When Chloe emerged and Bess was settling the folds of the skirt, Lydia crossed to the dresser. "What are you going to wear, Chloe? Not your mother's pearls?"

Chloe, her mind still with Lord Byron, said, "I don't know what you mean?"

"I'd like to borrow them, for Mama has said no jewels for a country ball. She hasn't anything that would go with this anyway, and I know that the pearls would be just right. They would give me something——" Lydia made a motion around her throat, which was in fact noticeably unadorned. The dress had been cut low enough to provide for a necklace—and at length, Chloe gave in. It did not matter—so Chloe thought—whether or not she made any kind of impression at the ball on people that she had known for a long time.

She helped Lydia fasten the pearls around her neck and agreed that they were just what the gown needed.

"Remember now, Lydia, these belonged to my mother, and I should not like anything to happen to them."

Lydia said, lightly, "What could happen? They are around my neck, and that's where they'll stay."

She dropped a butterfly kiss on Chloe's cheek, and said, "Thanks, sister," and hurried out.

Chloe looked up to find Bess's disapproving regard on her, and said, "What else could I do?"

Bess said, "You could say you were going to wear them yourself, Miss Chloe, for now you have nothing to set off your own gown."

Chloe said, "It doesn't matter to me," and then, mischievously, added, "As a matter of fact, I don't want to appear too attractive to the gentlemen down from London."

To herself she added, My legacy will provide all the attraction that they need.

The party from Rothwell Manor set out in midafternoon. Francis and Edward rode and the ladies traveled in the coach. There were coachmen and two grooms, all armed, and pistols in the saddles were ready at hand for Francis and Edward. Edward, making haste to dress, did not perfectly understand where Sophy was, but he saw that she was not traveling in the coach and dismissed her from his mind. His orders had been obeyed, and Sophy was not to appear at the ball. This was all that concerned him, and the carriage and its outriders set off down the drive and turned left at the gate. Passing Sir Richard's gates, Lady Rothwell commented that they must beg Sir Richard's company on the way home "lest highway men attack such a small party as we are," she pointed out, and having thoroughly alarmed Lydia and the maid, sank back on the squabs and closed her eyes in sleep.

At length they arrived, and Lady Partridge greeted them warmly. As they entered the wide hall, they saw that other guests were before them. Sir Richard was already there, Squire Oswell and his lady, and Vicar Wakeley and his wife. Lady Partridge announced, "We're going to partake of a joint before the fiddlers come. I suppose you ladies would like to go upstairs and freshen up after the ride, and you all know the way. . . ."

After dinner, and before the fiddlers had set up and the guests for the ball arrived, Francis asked Chloe to show him the conservatory. Chloe eyed him with dismay, and said, "Francis, I will not listen to another offer."

Francis, stiffly, said, "I shall not mention the question."

Smiling sunnily on him, Chloe took his arm and together they moved across the salon into the conservatory.

It was quite a large construction. The thriving plants were newly watered and gave off a pleasant smell of fresh, wet earth. The sun came in at a slant, for it was late in the afternoon. Unfortunately, the rays emphasized the two figures at the far end of the conservatory.

Francis stiffened and and allowed an exclamation of horror to pass his lips. At the far end he saw his young cousin Sophy, who everyone thought was back at the manor, and Emma, the daughter of the house. Chloe of course was not surprised, for she had understood Lady Rothwell's ploy and truly saw no harm in it. Certainly it was not a great matter to have Sophy and Emma watch the ball. Even if Emma did attend, it was in her own house, and Sophy was planning—so Chloe understood—to watch from the first landing of the stairs.

Then, on closer examination, Chloe realized it was not Sophy's presence that upset Francis to the point of rigidity.

Emma and Sophy were rehearsing their dance steps.

Here in the conservatory, far from any watchful eye, they practiced *the waltz*—Francis was horrified.

Feeling his position as a member of the family, Francis strode purposefully toward them. "Stop it at once!" he cried out. "That's indecent—you're too young—never heard of such a thing!"

Francis's usual inarticulateness came over him and his speech dissolved into mumbles. Sophy wailed, "Francis, you are so old-fashioned! The waltz is all the thing, you know!"

But Francis closed his ears. "It's only the most daring that dance it now in London, and to see a child already so lost to propriety that she would sneak away and practice the waltz steps—it's outside of enough!"

"What harm is there?"

Francis said, "All kinds of harm! You don't want to be blackballed in society, do you? You're just a child, and who knows what you'll do by the time you get to London! My mother would have a spasm!"

Francis really looked alarmingly as though he were himself about to indulge in a spasm, for his cheeks were flushed and his eyes bulged.

But to Chloe's surprise, Sophy burst into tears. She ran off, followed by Emma, leaving Francis and Chloe alone. "She's only a child," soothed Chloe, "and it is a childish prank. She is not going to do anything to ruin her chances in London. . . ." Chloe continued in this vein for some time, and finally persuaded him to re-enter the salon. Francis was now much calmer in his mind, and in fact felt that he had upheld the honor of the family. He was gratified at Sophy's immediate capitulation. If Chloe could have read his mind, it would only have pointed out to her that Francis had not the slightest inkling of Sophy's thoughts.

In the salon, she heard someone asking Richard about his recent trip to London. Richard, while perfectly civil, was somewhat evasive. Chloe refused to meet his eyes. She remembered the rumor that he was going to offer for Penelope Salton, and did not wish to hear Richard's reply.

But the squire's wife, Mrs. Oswell, cried, "May we hope to see a mistress at Davenant Hall soon?"

Richard, gravely said, "I shall not rule out that possibility."

Chloe's heart sank, and a pall fell over the evening for her.

The sound of carriage wheels came from without. The other guests were arriving, and soon the sound of fiddles tuning up announced the opening of the festivities. There was an air of excitement, stirring all the guests who had been there for dinner, and, with the arrival of the new-comers, the evening took on a gala air.

Richard, seeing Chloe and Francis return from the con-servatory, eyed her carefully and was satisfied. Apparently Francis had not been a nuisance, or if he had, there was no trace of it on Chloe's serene face.

Richard, as though drawn by a magnet that he could not resist, moved toward Chloe.

The arriving guests came up the stairs, and Thaddeus Invers was in the van. Edward, seeing him with relief, for he had the darkest opinion of Francis, hurried to greet him. After Thaddeus paid his respects to Lady Partridge, Edward, clearly impatient, led him toward Chloe. Richard, already near Chloe, saw her obvious distress. Richard, in Chloe's ear, said, "Since Lady Partridge is not dancing, you are the lady of the first rank here, and therefore you have no choice but to accept me for the first dance."

He smiled, that kind and winning smile that could turn her heart over, and often did, and she smiled gratefully back at him. Thaddeus Invers arrived too late.

20

Chloe's dance with Richard was, she thought, as near heaven as she would ever reach. Their steps matched, and she could give herself up to sheer enjoyment.

Chloe danced well, as she was light on her feet and graceful as a willow.

Richard's hand on her waist, leading her through the in-tricate steps, made her forget all but his nearness. She hardly noticed that she was not speaking until, gently,

Richard teased, "One might think you had retreated in your thoughts to get through this dance."

She smiled, then, but she could not recapture the joy of dancing with him. She recalled his successful trip to London. He had not denied that there would be a new mistress at Davenant Hall before long. The magic had gone out of the dance, and her steps faltered.

Just then, Julian Stoddard appeared in the doorway. He was late. While he looked around for his hostess, he was approached purposefully by Francis. From where Chloe stood she could see Francis arguing with Stoddard. It was clear that Francis's words, however serious, had no effect on Stoddard.

Richard said, "What is the trouble? I did not step on your foot?"

"No, of course not." But Richard had by his own actions put himself out of her reach, even as a Great Friend. She believed that life would never be the same after Richard brought his bride to Davenant Hall.

Richard cudgeled his brain to search out a reason for Chloe's sudden distress, and asked whether or not Invers had been a nuisance. "For I know you have the same opinion of him as I do," Richard commented.

Chloe said, almost snappishly, "At least he is eligible."

Instantly she could have bitten her tongue. She had not intended to let her private feelings spill over.

Richard looked at her gravely, puzzled, and then turned to another partner.

The evening wore on, and she was more than popular. She never lacked for partners, and Edward, looking darkly at his half-sister, believed that the news of his sister's legacy had spread.

Edward had a great affection for his sister and found no flaw in her, but it was clear she was experiencing an undue amount of attention this evening. Edward, intent upon keeping both Stoddard and Francis in their places, was moved reluctantly to sponsor Thaddeus Invers. He was the least of the evils.

Edward's eyes strayed to Lydia. She moved from partner to partner, as fast as Chloe did, and with much apparent enjoyment. This was what life was all about, she thought. She was in a giddy whirl, knowing that she was pretty, and taking the compliments of her partners as only her due.

The music, with its steady rhythms, was intoxicating. The heady aroma of potted plants, brought in from the conservatory, perfumed the air. She paid no heed to any of the others on the floor, only looking at one faceless partner after another. But at length Julian Stoddard claimed her, and she knew the pinnacle of her evening had been reached. He was by far the most sophisticated man in the room, for he was well known in London. Lydia was aware that his reputation was not of the highest, but certainly he knew the best people, and he was wicked enough to be enticing. Lydia did not realize that Julian did nothing without purpose.

When he claimed her hand, her cup of self-esteem ran over. Julian gave her the compliment she demanded, and continued, "You would put all the London ladies to shame, for I vow I have never seen any one quite so enchanting as you."

Lydia smiled upon him in the way that she fancied an acknowledged belle would do.

Julian was an accomplished flirt. "I marvel that any such attractive lady keeps herself hidden down here in Kent."

"Oh, but we're going to London!"

Julian allowed himself to exhibit pleasure. He gave Lydia the impression that she was his particular object in coming to Lady Partridge's ball.

Soon he complimented her dancing and ventured upon a variation of a step, and was pleased to see that she followed him.

After a bit, he ventured, "Do you waltz?"

Lydia said, artlessly, "No, I'm not allowed to. But I long to learn the steps."

Julian, pursuing his advantage, said, "Allow me to present an instructor. Myself."

His eye began to rove, for his purpose went beyond flirting with Lydia. He tried to find the object of his quest, and hoped that he could soon take the next step in his campaign. Perhaps that would retrieve this incredibly dull party.

Lydia was aware that his attention had wandered and resented any diversion on his part. Julian, jerked back to the present, said, "When are you coming to London?"

"We're going up in time for the Little Season. I swear I cannot wait."

Julian smiled, allowing her to think that he too was anxious.

She said, "I so long to see the Prince Regent. You know him well, do you not?" Julian nodded. Feeling herself on the peak of the world, she added, daringly, "Will you dance with me at Almack's?"

Ignoring the fact that he could not set foot inside the Wednesday assemblies at Almack's, for he had been exiled by the sponsoring ladies, Stoddard promised lavishly, "You will not be able to get rid of me in London, I swear." Then, he ventured, "Your sister will come to London, too?"

Lydia agreed that Chloe would in fact be with them.

Julian said, "I rather hoped she would not come."

"Why?"

Julian explained. "She'll keep you out of society until she has her fill of parties. That would be a great shame, for you are destined to be a great success. I had not thought your sister to be a jealous person, but I fear. . . ." he let his voice trail away, and Lydia anxious to reassure him, spoke on a note elevated above the music, "Oh no, Mama will not allow that! Mama says Chloe knows her duty to her family, and we do not need to fear that Chloe will be selfish. That's how we can all go to London you know, because of Chloe's fortune!"

Unfortunately for Lydia, her sense of timing had played her false. She had been enjoying the dance and her flirtation with the London dandy, and the dance was over before she was aware it was coming to a close. She had spoken loud enough for Julian to hear, but the violins fell silent midway in Lydia's remarks. So, by an evil chance, did everyone else in one of those odd silences that occur in company now and then.

Lydia's callous remarks, indeed, as her brother told her later, her *vulgar* words, rang out with the clarion sharpness of a battle trumpet. The effect upon her involuntary listeners was notable.

First came embarrassment, and everyone looked in different directions so as to avoid catching anyone else's eye. Then, as Chloe understood her sister's statement fully, she felt as though the floor beneath her had suddenly given way. Her knees shook, and she was as shamed as though she had suddenly stood without clothing in the midst of an assembly.

She lost her wits. Her eyes mirroring shock, she moved blindly as though in a fog, and turned instinctively to the only help she knew, Richard.

Richard, for his part as appalled as she, but recognizing not only Chloe's need but his own need to protect her, was already threading his way through the crowd to stand by her side. He took her hand and felt it icy within his warm fingers. He pressed her hand reassuringly, and murmured words that neither one of them remembered.

Then suddenly the tableau in Lady Partridge's ballroom came to life. Lydia's *gaffe* was by common consent ignored. Indeed, it was such a shocking event that no one could quite take it in. However, the frenzied search among all the hearers for safe subjects to which to turn the conversation had a two-fold result.

The topic that nobody dared mention—Lydia's heartless remark—was even more clearly etched in the minds of the company. It would be taken out, at leisure, to be turned over, discussed in depth, and torn to shreds, seeking all the titillation that could be gained from it. The second was that, to all intents and purposes, the ball was over. An insistent need arose among all the participants to launch upon their discussion of the topic that was uppermost in their minds, and for satisfactory discussion privacy was needed.

Edward, as soon as his feet could move, bore down upon his mother with ponderous indignation. To do Lady Rothwell credit, she was as horrified as was possible to her, and her heavy features turned grim. She did not carry her dismay to the point of blaming herself for Lydia's casual treatment of the conventions, or even, as Edward would put it strongly to her later, for Lydia's flouting of the standards of common decency.

Chloe was hardly aware that the ball was over. Scant ceremony was afforded their hostess, and in some respects the Rothwell departure took on the nature of headlong flight. Richard, with some disgust, noticed that Julian Stoddard and Thaddeus Invers both had dissociated themselves from the Rothwells. Neither was to be seen, and only Lydia's dull flush told him that she realized the enormity of her behavior.

Richard stayed with Chloe while the carriage was hastily brought to the entry, feeling her hand clinging desperately to his. He was prey to mixed emotions, foremost among which was to hold Chloe close to him and let her sob her heart out, and the second was to take Lydia over his knee and give her the sound spanking she richly deserved.

On second thought, Richard began to wonder whether Chloe could cry, for he mistrusted the look of vague remoteness that lay in her eyes. He was sure she did not know where she was or who stood nearby. He released her hands so that Francis could help Chloe into her cloak and hand her into the coach. Richard watched the carriage go down the drive, in haste, and his heart went with it.

Within the coach, Lydia sat in her corner, subdued for once. Sophy, hastily summoned from upstairs, sat circumspectly silent, aware that something untoward had happened, but since she had been too far away from the scene of action, she did not know exactly what.

Even Lady Rothwell could think of nothing to say. After she had wailed, "Lydia, how could you?" she slumped in the seat. For perhaps the first time within memory the Rothwells returned home from a party in utter silence.

Chloe did not notice. The only sound she could hear, above the rhythmic pounding of hooves and the rattle of harness, was Lydia's remembered voice. *"Because of Chloe's fortune. . . . All go London"*. The horses' hooves set the words to their rhythm. *Chloe's fortune—Chloe's duty to her family—Chloe's fortune.* It was almost a litany in her mind. And in the way of litanies, the words soon lost their meaning, and only the grievous hurt that Lydia had inflicted remained. Chloe was not sure she had not sustained a mortal wound.

At last they got home and dismounted from the coach. Still in that state that was akin to sleepwalking, Chloe walked into the house, climbed up the stairs. She was vaguely aware that Bess fussed over her, got her undressed, and into her nightshift. The maid, although no word had been spoken, was aware that something was amiss. She would find out in due course, but just now, she was alarmed at Chloe's vacant stare. Hastily descending to the kitchen, she warmed up some milk and brought it back. Forcing her mistress to drink it, she got her into bed.

Chloe lay back among the pillows, weary to the point of collapse, but she could not sleep.

21

Lydia's words rang ominously through Chloe's mind,
rather like the tolling of a church bell. Sleep escaped her,
and she stared, unseeing, into the darkness.

But Chloe was not the only inhabitant of Rothwell
Manor that night who could not sleep.

On the ground floor, Edward, in his book room, was
giving vent to his anger. He was already furious because
of Lydia's indiscretion, to call it by a kind name, but he
had that evening had even more unwelcome information
thrust upon him.

Lydia herself had exasperated him. He took his position
as head of the family with great seriousness. He believed
that he alone knew what was best for the women of his
family, for he was in the last analysis responsible for
them. He was worldly enough to know that Lydia seriously damaged the family's reputation. If Julian Stoddard
chose, he could make a shambles of the Rothwells' preten-
tion to breeding, for even if Lydia's remark was not exaggerated, as it could well be, it was bad enough so that
Lydia's thoughtlessness might be remembered and held
against them for a long time.

The responsibility thrust upon Edward when he was
only fifteen had been heavy, but he had discharged his duties well. The need for economy had dictated that the governess for the girls, Lydia and Sophy, must be dismissed,
for Lady Rothwell said that she could take it on herself to
instruct them in the proper ways.

He now was forced to see that he had made a great
mistake. His mother, while well-bred and aware of what
was proper, yet allowed her emotions to rule her head,
and she was foolishly fond of her own girls.

Now he could see how grave was the result of his leaving his younger sisters to his mother.

Lydia had been revealed to be a prattler, a feather-headed peahen, telling the family business to the world. Unjustly, he blamed Lydia for the sudden silence that had framed her ill-guarded remarks. Even so, it would have been a disaster had no one else heard the remarks except the man to whom they were addressed. Edward's heart sank when he remembered that Julian Stoddard had been the recipient of Lydia's confidence. He disliked and mistrusted the man, quite rightly, and he was quite sure that, in Julian Stoddard's hand, Lydia's remarks could be made public to all of London.

Edward's affection for Chloe, while not obvious, was strong, and his conscience told him that not the least harm done by Lydia's wagging tongue was the blow that was struck to Chloe's self-esteem. He climbed the stairs like a man suddenly grown old.

And Sophy! Edward had been given much to think about.

Now, in his dressing gown, facing a dying fire in his room, he turned over in his thoughts the interview with Francis. They had scarcely gotten into the house, and the carriage had barely rumbled away to the stable, when Francis had followed him into the book room. Francis was laboring under strong emotion.

Edward said, "Don't blame me for Lydia's stupidity——"

"Of course not. Hardly know how to tell you."

Edward was bitter. "Nothing you can tell me will make any difference."

Francis continued, doggedly, "It's not good news."

Edward replied, "Whatever news you've got, if it's about Lydia, I've already heard the worst."

Francis stood silent for a moment, and then he burst out, "Not Lydia. Sophy."

Edward, startled, exclaimed, "What can Sophy have done? She was not at the ball."

Francis agreed. "No, but she was at Lady Partridge's." Then, without malice but with rigid righteousness, he told Edward what he knew about Sophy's evening.

"The waltz!"

Francis said, "Hardly respectable at Almack's, you know. Had it not been for the Czar. . . ."

Edward had read about this in the London journals. Czar Alexander of Russia, through his considerable charm, had made the waltz respectable at Almack's. But only a very few dared even yet to venture upon the Continental steps, which were considered indecent by many.

Sophy, at the age of thirteen, was too precocious, so Francis said. Leaving Edward to mull over the iniquities of his women, he added, "Thought you should know. Not the thing at all."

He was gone, shutting the door behind him. Edward, placing his head in his hands, swore. By the time he arrived upstairs, he had made up his mind that he would do his best for Chloe, the only member of his family who showed any sense at all. Now, he removed his dressing gown, placed the screen in front of the fireplace, and crawled into bed. He was not at all sleepy. Was ever a man beset in such fashion? He spared a thought of envy for Richard Davenant. There were no women in his life, unless he was to be leg-shackled soon to his bride from London. Edward, pulling up the covers, pictured to himself Sir Richard Davenant sleeping the sleep of the just and untroubled.

In this he was wrong. Richard was not blessed with the sleep that Edward envied. He sat now in his study before a late fire, burning low. The woebegone look in Chloe's eyes haunted him, and he was sorely troubled. He was gratified beyond words by Chloe's turning to him in her blind need. He could still see her searching eyes, and the way they fixed on his face as he started toward her across the room. This, he believed, told him that she was far from indifferent to him. He was her Great Friend, she told him often, but he was quite sure that her feeling for him went deeper than that. If she turned to him in her despair, then she would turn to him at all other times.

He was aware of certain information that could assure her that he was not a fortune hunter. The letter from Aston, that had burned in his pocket the other day, held certain hints. Now he possessed an additional report from his man of affairs in London, relating certain rumors running through the city like wildfire. The news of Miss Rothwell's legacy was common conversation in London. But, said Aston, he was not satisfied. He had set his agents to seek out the truth. And the last sentence in Aston's letter, while as uncommitted as any attorney's statement, suggested caution in the matter of Miss Rothwell's legacy.

Richard could not warn Chloe against an unknown suspicion. But he also had had enough of seeing his dear

Chloe beset on every hand. The fury he had felt to begin with over Lydia's informing the world that the Rothwells considered Chloe's fortune to be theirs, even though it came from Chloe's mother's family, had stirred him to the depths.

Clearly things were coming to a head. Chloe must be removed from that abominable household—before Lydia's tongue drove Chloe past rescue. Now, spurred by Aston's veiled hints, Richard believed it was time to look further into Chloe's affairs. His cousin Nell, now Lady Theale, lived a short distance from Highmoor. Theale would know the truth, and Richard, abandoning his pose of dear friend, wrote a letter to Lord Theale. Then, feeling he had done all he could, he went to bed.

Chloe, unaware of Edward's resolve to do his best for her, and equally unaware that Richard was taking action on her behalf, still could not sleep. She tossed and turned. The trancelike state that Lydia's indiscretion had induced in her was wearing off. How could Lydia have brazenly counted on Chloe's fortune for herself? Chloe had not refused to go along with Mama's ideas. But to have the outcome so clearly expected, without the formality even of Chloe's offering, was more than Chloe could stand. She realized that she had let Lady Rothwell assume that she would provide Lydia's Season in London for her. But she had not realized that they were taking it for granted as though there were no choice.

It was not that Chloe wanted them to beg her on their knees for her generosity, but still it was a sore trial. Lady Rothwell had made no bones about keeping Chloe's duty before her eyes, but it was not for Chloe's benefit, but for the benefit first of Lydia and Sophy. Lady Rothwell, even in pressing Francis's suit for Chloe's hand, and Edward, backing Thaddeus Invers—all these were still more signs that her family thought first of themselves, and only, when all else failed, thought of Chloe herself.

Chloe had felt guilty over even the thought of ordering books from London, or ordering new clothes for herself, but there was no question in Lady Rothwell's mind that Chloe's fortune could be used to pay for Lydia's wardrobe in London. Chloe had turned down Francis's offer, and if Edward were to press her on Thaddeus Invers, she would tell him that she would not accept Thaddeus Invers either.

But it was Julian Stoddard that Chloe feared the most.

When Stoddard's eyes fell upon her, she felt somehow
soiled in a way that she did not understand. But she believed now, after Lydia's incredible blunder, she would
probably be done with Julian Stoddard.

However, the subject of Chloe's fears, a few miles away
in his bedroom at the inn, was also wakeful.

He regretted Lydia's indiscretion, most particularly because he was with her at that moment, and the harsh light
of public attention thus fell full upon him. He wished it
hadn't. Julian Stoddard had a devious mind, and over the
years had grown to prefer working in an unseen manner
rather than overtly.

He now had Francis under the hatches, by means of a
marked deck in a private residence. If it had not been in
the home of someone whom he trusted, Francis would not
have entered the game. Francis had little enough money,
but he clung to it with all the conservatism of his Tory ancestors. Julian had been able to get Francis into his debt,
and now he had promised to let Francis off if he could get
Julian into the Rothwell circle. Julian's object was to
marry the heiress.

Now Julian was having second thoughts. The public notice at Lady Partridge's ball was too much. There were too
many men who came to Chloe's rescue—Julian had a
strong recollection of Francis and Sir Richard Davenant
and Edward converging on Chloe and getting her out of
the ballroom. It would be surprising if he—Julian Stoddard—were allowed near Chloe again.

Julian particularly disliked the look in Davenant's eye.
He had a healthy respect for the man, and considered him
dangerous.

Yet Julian was loath to let Chloe's fortune slip through
his fingers. There must be another way. He turned his
mind to various devious schemes until he found one that
suited him. He was in a way relieved that all this had happened, when he thought about it, for he did not wish to be
leg-shackled. But the money, if he planned well, could
come to him without the necessity of marrying the lady. If
his luck held, and he had supreme confidence that it
would, he would get out of this even better than he had
thought. He sank, with satisfaction, into restful slumber.

For her part, Chloe drowsed. She woke with a start. Her
dream was disturbing, and as she sat up in bed and reflected on it, it was even more unsettling. She had dreamed of

being all alone. There was no one there, no one to answer when she called, and in her ears she still heard the cry of fear with which she had awakened.

She did not wish to go back to sleep, and got out of bed. She put on her robe, stirred up the fire, and added another small piece of wood to it. She wrapped the eiderdown around her and sat up until daybreak.

The dream was more than disturbing. What did it mean? Did it mean that she must not go to live at Highmoor where she would be all alone, cut off from her family?

What then did she want? Her family had revealed themselves as selfish, but still they were her only kin. She was afraid of the lonely dark, and she determined, eventually, to overlook her troubles. It was not a matter of choosing what was best. It was choosing the lesser evil. Besides, she told herself wearily, Lydia was young and thoughtless and only repeated what she had heard.

Chloe, at last, having made her life less unpalatable, fell asleep in her chair, where Bess found her in the morning.

22

The next morning, when Chloe awakened, stiff and far from rested, to a gray day, threatening rain, she was convinced that she had misread the whole affair. She must overcome her hurt feelings. She could not abide an existence isolated from her family.

Highmoor, nonetheless, hung in her thoughts. It was like a desert mirage, unreal but lingering in the thoughts as the embodiment of hope and peace.

She sent Bess away and was dressing slowly when a knock sounded tentatively at the door. Lydia, waiting until invited, sidled in. She wore an unaccustomed air of diffidence, and she searched Chloe's face for a reflection of her mood.

Lydia had come to apologize. She was truly regretful

about her misbehavior of the night before. She was not so lost to decency that she overlooked the devastating effect that her remark had made on her family. It was not for a small reason that the Rothwell party had hurried home, and she had heard all she needed to hear on the subject the night before. Lydia was truly regretful, although she could not believe her mother's ominous fear that she had ruined her Season in London.

Lydia's affection for Chloe was overshadowed by her intense longing for bright lights and gaiety. Her mind, shallow at best, was stimulated by outside influences rather than by any inner resources. Sunlight and shadow passed over her thoughts with no more than momentary hesitation. She herself would have dismissed her own remarks last night as being a laughable misfortune, and she had no true idea of how badly she had behaved.

However, she knew what she must do.

"I am sorry, Chloe. I had no idea it would all turn out this way. I wouldn't distress you for the world. Please say you forgive me?"

Chloe of course could do nothing else. "Yes, Lydia, of course, I forgive you."

Lydia threw her arms around her sister, and kissed her cheek. "I knew you wouldn't hold a grudge, you never have, and you're the best, dearest sister anyone ever had."

She even remained to help Chloe arrange a scarf around her shoulders and said, "There, you'll be just fine to go with me and Mama to town to Miss Sinclair's."

Chloe, somewhat surprised, said, "Why? You have your ball gown." Then fearing to bring up the memories that she was trying to bury, she added, "Besides, I'm too tired."

The girls descended the stairs, arm in arm, and met Edward in the hall. "There you are, Chloe," he said, "I'm glad to see you. I wanted to say good-bye to you before I leave."

"Leave?"

"Yes I'm going up to London for a sennight. My correspondent in London has written, and what with the ball and everything—" Edward broke off here to glare at Lydia, who promptly found a matter of interest in another direction—"I had not read the letter until this morning."

"So you're going for several days then, in the coach."

Edward raised an eyebrow, and said, "Of course. Look at the weather."

Chloe turned to Lydia and said, "That settles it, then. We can't go to town in an open carriage on a day like this."

Lydia wished that Edward had not overheard Chloe's remarks.

Edward said, in a minatory fashion, "What are you going to town for?"

Lydia, with an offhand air, said, "Ask Mama."

Edward said, "Later I will. But just now Invers is paying a morning call on Mama, and I hesitate to interrupt them."

Lydia, shocked, cried, "Invers?" And incontinently fled.

Edward, left alone with Chloe, apologized. "I can't tell you how sorry I am about last night. I trust the affair will not linger in your mind, for you do not usually carry grudges. Lydia is thoughtless, and says what comes first into her mind." Or, thought Chloe, whatever somebody else has said first.

Edward said, "I only want what is best for you, and Lydia has nothing to say to the point."

Chloe, surprising herself, said, "Do you, Edward? You think Invers and I would suit?"

Edward flushed with embarrassment at having his inner thoughts read so closely. "At least he isn't that idiot Francis. But," Edward added on a quieter note, "I'd hate to see you leave Rothwell. This is always your home, no matter what happens."

Awkwardly patting her shoulder in real affection, he took his leave and mounted into the coach. He did not go at first to London. The letter he mentioned was similar in content to Aston's letter to Richard. It had thrust Edward at last into action.

In the ordinary way, Edward was propelled solely by duty and an unshakable belief that he knew what was best for all under his roof. The letter from his correspondent in London had unsettled him to a large extent. Truly, it was on his half-sister's behalf that he was making this hurried trip. He needed to settle Chloe's affairs, once and for all, for he believed that Thaddeus Invers was going to offer for Chloe. There would be questions of marriage settlements—and Edward needed to have more facts in his hands than he had now.

On the way to London, he stopped first of all in town to settle Miss Sinclair's bill for Lydia's ball gown. The gown was most unsuitable for a girl of Lydia's age, and especially for a country ball, but it was not Miss Sinclair's fault. His mind turned over the events of the ball last night, and he found little therein to satisfy him. He knew his mother was ambitious, and while her thoughts might now lie on getting Lydia "off," her real affection was reserved for Sophy. An unfair arrangement, Edward thought, but there it was, for he himself had no true rebellion in him to make him stand up against his mother's wishes. It was a coil, to say the least.

Edward was not one to look into the future. Today's duty was enough for him, and he considered that he did his best each day. Today, he stopped to see Miss Sinclair, for he was quite sure she would need money. She had made an outlay for the cloth and her work on the dress, and Edward was not like most Londoners, letting bills pile up and having little regard for the financial stringencies of the tradesman.

Bidding the coachman stop, Edward descended and was admitted to Miss Sinclair's house. He was inside for some time before he emerged from the seamstress's door, tight-lipped and flushed with anger. Coachman watched Edward helped into the coach, and waited for further instructions. When none came, for the simple reason that Edward was too furious to speak, the coachman set his vehicle in motion, and they were partly on the way to London before Edward was able to make a decision. Then, although his first wish was to return to the Manor and make his wishes known without possibility of misunderstanding, he realized that it was too late. Satisfied that he had at least dealt effectively with Miss Sinclair, he allowed the motion of the well-sprung coach to lull him, and, thinking of his wakeful night, he dropped off to sleep.

Meanwhile, at Rothwell Manor, Thaddeus Invers emerged without notice from Lady Rothwell's morning room and caught sight of his quarry. Chloe, watching Edward's coach disappear down the drive, had turned to seek Lydia again, and came face to face with him.

"I must go——" she began, but Invers, not to be denied, urged her into the Green Salon. He was clearly going to offer for her, she realized with sinking heart. He approached her, and she retreated. He pursued her, and her instinct was again to move away, until she realized, with faint amusement, that they were performing a very odd dance figure. She stopped short. It would not help to evade him. Best simply to have it out and be done with it.

She settled herself on a small green-and-white striped satin chair, and waited. Invers, unable to say anything directly, said, "I came down from London last week because I had heard reports of a rustic beauty hidden in the countryside. I congratulate myself that I have at last found her."

Chloe turned startled eyes upon him. "Rustic beauty?"

Thaddeus Invers continued. "I myself have long since tired of the sophisticated charm of the ladies of society. Lady Emmaline Parker, for instance. A charming lady, but I weary of being instructed at every turn."

She let him talk, with only half her mind attending, and at the mention of Miss Thalassa Morland—not so beautiful as she was reported to be, so said the ungallant Invers—Chloe's thoughts turned into a new channel. Miss Morland was one of those whom Lady Rothwell's sister, Mrs. Hensley, had mentioned as hoping to become Lady Davenant. It was clear that Richard would not long remain unmarried. Chloe did not wish to think about the changes in her life that would follow upon Richard's marriage, but it was a subject that drew her like a magnet. Tears welled in her eyes when she thought of how very much alone she would be.

Invers, surprisingly, noticed the tears in Chloe's eyes, and felt he was clearly moving her beyond composure. Encouraged, he told her, circling around and coming closer to the point, "I wish to find an unsophisticated lady, of little learning, who would become a partner to me, one who would learn to value the things that I value, who would in fact be a complement to myself."

He continued in this vein. Chloe listened, at first appalled. Then, realizing the exact meaning of Invers' remarks—that he wished to find a bride of little learning and little sense, whom he could shape and educate as he wished, she realized that she was becoming angry. Chloe had often been irked lately, and had not responded with any quickening of her temper. But this time she was tried too sorely. Invers had gone too far, and her temper boiled closer to the surface.

Chloe stood up. "You wish an answer? I'll *give* you an answer."

Thaddeus was privileged to see an angry spark in her

gray eyes that very few people had seen, and no one for the last fifteen years, at least. Her childish temper had been long since brought under such control that it hardly existed any more, but Thaddeus Invers was accomplishing the near impossible. He was rousing it.

Chloe cried, "You believe to ingratiate yourself by telling me I know nothing of society? That I am ill-educated? That may be so, for I make no pretensions along that line."

Thaddeus put out a hand as though to stop her, but she ignored him.

"I suppose one might feel honored at your offer, Mr. Invers. Although I make no pretense at logic, I suppose one might expect a man's most ardent words to come on the occasion of his offering marriage. However, if this is a sample of your regard for me, to turn every word into an insult, then I fear you have nothing to teach me. I do not know a great deal, for I have been involved in running a household and have not had time to pursue the intellectual channels you speak of. But I do know this—I shall not enjoy being educated by a man for whom I feel absolutely no respect."

She was gratified to see that he stared at her in stupefaction, and could not at first find words. His lips moved like a fish's, but then his natural self-love took over. "I did not expect such spirited response," he began, "but I assure you that you need not fear I shall not be a devoted husband."

Chloe said, "You were not listening. I shall not marry you."

Recovering somewhat, he managed a smile, and said, "Perhaps I have made a mistake, and should have approached you with a different emphasis. I had the feeling that you were a woman of good common sense, but now I see that you need affection just as anyone else." He advanced toward her with the clear intention of giving her a first installment on the caresses he thought she demanded. She retreated, but eventually he backed her against the table. She had no escape. He took her in his arms and attempted to plant a kiss on her forehead. Loathing swept over her, and she summoned all her strength. She broke away, ran to the bell, and pulled it. She glared at Invers and tried to arrange her hair into a more orderly appearance.

Field, waiting outside and debating with himself as to whether to interrupt Miss Chloe and her unwelcome suitor, responded immediately. The situation was clear to him. Standing large and firm as Gibraltar, and holding the door wide, the butler fixed Thaddeus Invers with a cold eye.

Chloe said, "Field, Mr. Invers is just leaving."

It was an unnecessary remark. Field stood, the embodiment of respectability and supported by the knowledge that half a dozen strong men were within call. There were two footmen in the kitchen, and a stable boy and two grooms in the servant's dining room, having their morning tea.

Thaddeus, clearly in the wrong, yielded the victory. He turned at the door to sneer at her. "I understand why you haven't wed until now. Your fugitive charms, out of sight to the ordinary, had to be brought to light by the reflection of silver." Then he gathered his strength and hurled the one epithet that he thought would wound the most. "Vinegar-tongue!"

Chloe closed her eyes and stood with one hand on the table to support herself. Her knees shook, and she felt that if one more person spoke to her she would fall into screaming hysterics. Part of her was aware that Thaddeus was crossing the hall with urgent step, and she was sure that Field was right behind him. Invers, full of his own injuries, did not look where he was going and plunged out the front entrance directly into the arms of Sir Richard.

Richard, staggered by Invers' impact, set the man aside and continued up the steps. Richard entered the door held wide open by Field, and said softly, "Trouble?"

Field, gratified at Sir Richard's appearance, nodded with his head toward the Green Salon. The two men understood each other.

Sir Richard said, quietly, "I see no need to inform Lady Rothwell that I have called."

Field, feeling that Sir Richard was a man who knew what he was about, nodded wisely. Richard entered the Salon. He was dismayed to see Chloe with both hands to her face, in tears.

Richard crossed to her, speaking softly as he came. The butler, ears at the strain, did not hear. The door closed softly behind them. Field, turning to the newly arrived footman, said, "You didn't hear nothing, did you?"

The footman, startled, could only nod agreement. Field continued, "Our Miss Chloe didn't ought to have to put up with the likes of *him!*" Field jerked his head toward the departed Invers, who was now no doubt halfway to town.

Within the Green Salon, Sir Richard, greatly distressed by Chloe's misery, did not need to speculate far to understand what had happened. He led her gently to the settee and let her weep. Eventually, a frown between his eyebrows, he sat beside her. He pulled one hand away from her face and folded it together within his own fingers.

"Don't tell me you had to listen to that foolish man," sympathized Richard. He was unaware that he was echoing the butler's less polished sentiments in the hall.

She managed to say over the lump in her throat, "Oh, Richard, he was dreadful!"

Richard said, in a matter-of-fact voice, "Of course he was. But I would not at all wonder that he left here with worse than he gave. I saw his face, you know, and he didn't have things all his way." It was clear to Richard that she was beginning to recover somewhat, for she had stopped her sobbing and only gulped now and again.

"I can't quite believe that my old playfellow remembered that she had a temper?" he rallied her gently, and was rewarded by a watery smile.

Chloe said, "I did rather lose my temper. He was dreadful, but then—" she finished with a rush—"so was I. I do not wish to think of the things I said!"

Richard said, "Some day you will tell me, and we will both laugh at the idiot's pretensions." Finally, judging the time was right, he said quizzically, "My dear, shall I challenge him to a duel?"

She gurgled appreciatively, and he judged the storm was over.

He was becoming weary of coming and finding Chloe beset by one trial after another. Each time, the trial was of such a nature that Richard felt he could not speak his heart to her. Richard, never a patient man, found the waiting intolerable until the time was right to speak to Chloe. He still had not heard from his cousin Nell, and while not a prudent man, Richard was a thorough one and wished to have all the threads in his hands before he made his next move.

He resolved to keep a closer eye on Rothwell Manor, even to the point of interfering. He wondered where Edward was, why had he not thrown Invers out in the first place, and when he left Chloe, restored to good humor, Richard returned home more troubled than ever before.

23

Richard had come and gone, and Chloe was alone. It was true that around her moved the various activities of the household. Cook, fully recovered from the removal of her painful tooth, was planning an especially intricate dinner, Sophy and Lydia were following pursuits of their own, and Lady Rothwell was rousing from her long day's nap.

Edward, before he left for London, had had a strenuous interview with his mother. Lydia's behavior at the ball had been the subject of his strong representations to his parent, and while Lady Rothwell took exception to some of the terms her son had dared to use, yet since he was out of sight, he was also to some degree out of mind.

She had not the slightest doubt that she could bring Edward around to her way of thinking. While Lydia's outburst at Lady Partridge's ball was regrettable, yet it changed nothing in the long run.

But, feeling a strong need to settle her nerves, she sent for Chloe.

Chloe had busied herself with small, routine, everyday things in order to erase the memory of Thaddeus Invers. Bess stored Chloe's gown in the wardrobe and put away her slippers. Chloe thought, I won't wear them again, and was conscious of a feeling of wistfulness.

She had enjoyed the affair until that dreadful moment when Lydia's voice rang out across the room.

The thought of Lydia moved her to check and find that Lydia had not yet returned Chloe's mother's pearls. Just then came the summons from Lady Rothwell, so Chloe stopped on her way and rapped lightly at Lydia's door. If she had expected Lydia to become overcome by embarrassment and regret for the evening before, she was wrong. Lydia had spread out around her on the floor old copies of the *Ladies' Magazine* and she scarcely looked up when Chloe entered the room.

Chloe said, "Lydia . . ."

Lydia looked up then, and said, "Oh, it's you."

Chloe, somewhat nettled, said, "Whom did you expect? I just stopped by to ask you to be sure to return my pearls, before you forget."

Lydia looked up at her then, a veiled look crossing her face. "All right," she said, "but did you see this new magazine?"

Chloe said, "Later, Lydia. I don't have time now. Mama has sent for me. Don't forget the necklace." Lydia's mind, once fixed on fashion, could not be easily distracted.

Lady Rothwell was waiting impatiently for Chloe. "Ah, there you are, Chloe," said Lady Rothwell. "I feared that you must have fallen asleep. After such a late night, it is only understandable. But Edward seemed not to need as much sleep as the rest of us. I do not understand where he gets the energy that he exhibited this morning."

Lady Rothwell, some of Edward's remarks still lingering in her mind, thought it wise to test Chloe's present mood. Lady Rothwell now realized that Chloe had become someone to be reckoned with—for any heiress could upon the wink of an eye become capricious, even the gentle Chloe. Lady Rothwell had much to gain by Chloe's good humor, and much to lose if Edward's prophecy—that Lydia would have turned Chloe against them all—came true.

So now, when she suggested that Chloe read to her—"to settle my nerves"—she was more than ordinarily civil.

A copy of *The Pilgrim's Progress* on her lap, Chloe found that her mind was not on her reading. Whenever her voice faltered, Lady Rothwell opened her eyes and said, "Are you too tired, Chloe, to go on?"

Chloe, brought up sharply to a sense of duty, protested and took up the book again.

Chloe had much to think about, none of it pleasant. She had told no one, after all, about Thaddeus Invers' offer. Edward had gone to London and she must wait until his return to tell him that she had refused his entry in the Chloe sweepstakes. The thought was frivolous, and owed much to her mischievous sense of humor. Richard had settled her back on an even keel, and she was now, or would soon be, able to regard Invers in the light which he deserved.

She was safe from a renewed assault on her marriageable status from Invers, but the words that he had spoken still rankled. There was no way she could forget them, for they had etched themselves already into her mind.

It was more than lowering to realize that even someone whom she respected as little as she respected Thaddeus Invers could tell her that her only charm lay in her inheritance. The obvious corollary to that was that there were many women more deserving of attention than she. This led naturally to the thought that Sir Richard had had a "successful" visit to London, and therefore was more than certain to have come home with arrangements already made for his marriage.

Chloe was turned back upon herself. She feared everyone now, for her self-esteem was at its lowest ebb. No one but her family valued her—and Edward had said she always had a place here at Rothwell Manor. Chloe realized that her family was her life, and whatever they said to her, or did, meant nothing as opposed to their steadfast affection for her.

Pilgrim had long since begun to pall, and Chloe almost welcomed Sophy's interruption.

No matter what Edward said about her reprehensible laxness in bringing up her girls, yet when Sophy pleaded, as she did now, Lady Rothwell was not proof against her.

Sophy cried out, "I promised to let Lady Partridge know whether or not I could go with them to Bath, and, Mama, please say I may. I must go, for Emma will be gone above a month, and I cannot abide the thought!"

Lady Rothwell hesitated. "Your brother has said you may not go——"

But Sophy interrupted. "He said I couldn't go to the ball either, but you arranged it after all," Sophy reminded her mother astutely. It took a long time, and Sophy almost despaired of getting her own way, but at the end Lady Rothwell gave in.

"You know how angry Edward will be," she said, "and I do not know how to see this through. Chloe?"

Chloe said, quietly, "I would not know how to go on, either."

Lady Rothwell fell back upon her previous gambit. She could get Sophy out of sight before Edward ever came back. She said, musingly, "Your brother won't be back for a week—I shall try to see what we can do."

Lady Rothwell's own conscience in the matter was not clear. She had a lowering feeling that Edward was right, that she was too lax with her girls. She had had so little trouble bringing up Chloe that she had felt the same tactics would prevail with her own girls. But they were of a different mettle and it was quite too late to change. Besides, Lady Rothwell had the underlying feeling that Chloe, not being her own daughter, was therefore in some way inferior. Lady Rothwell might even have been made to admit that she felt that Chloe's legacy was totally unjust—that the legacy should have come to Lydia and Sophy. Logic told her that she was foolish, but her heart said that her girls should have the best.

For peace in the family, she explained to Chloe, "I do not feel that I can abide Sophy's being unhappy for six weeks."

There was no time to get gowns made for Sophy, and Sophy, to her credit, did not ask for any.

It was enough for Sophy that she would be able to go with her dear friend Emma, and she bounced out of the room, her mother's fond gaze following her as far as she could see her.

It was expected that Edward would not return until the following week. He would, of course, stay with Lady Rothwell's sister in London, but his patience was sometimes uncertain and he might tire of them before the week's end.

The women of his family had no idea why he had gone to London. They did not even ask. Edward ran all the business of the family and told them nothing, and it did not occur to any of them to ask what business could have taken him so abruptly to London.

Lady Rothwell, talking privately with Chloe, said, "Lady Partridge and her party will be leaving in three days. That's time enough."

The unspoken word between them lay quivering in the air. In good time to avoid Edward, was Lady Rothwell's thought. Chloe, with only part of her mind, heard Lady Rothwell's request for a few new ribbons for Sophy, and it was decided that the next day they would go to town, for, "you must know," said Lady Rothwell, "I am longing to see how Miss Sinclair is getting on with Lydia's gowns."

The next day dawned clear and pleasant. Lady Rothwell ordered the open carriage and they all began the hour's trip to town.

They were all in unaccustomed good humor—the more surprising since they were embarking on what was after all a conspiracy to balk Edward's wishes.

Even Chloe, although she had slept badly and had lost her appetite, felt her spirits rising, for they had claimed they could not do without her on their trip to town, and she felt needed once more.

Try as she might, she could not dismiss Thaddeus Invers' last remarks to her. She did not wish to think of the excoriating accusations he had laid at her feet, but neither could she erase them. They had cut too deeply.

Lady Rothwell did not travel as Chloe had, behind a green groom. She traveled at a spanking pace behind a pair, the assistant coachman, a groom, and a footman— the latter to carry parcels—and the trip was made safely. The sun was warm, June was toward its end, and the trip was enjoyable. They passed the church. Lady Rothwell bowed and spoke kindly to passersby, in her role as gracious lady of Rothwell Manor. But many more friendly looks came Chloe's way, for she was well known for her kindness, her sweet disposition, and as much generosity as she could manage.

At length they pulled up before Miss Sinclair's house, where Edward's coach had stood only yesterday.

Miss Sinclair, looking out the window, felt what could only be described as intense dismay. She must let them in, but she dreaded the next moments with all the intensity of her spirit.

She was quite correct. The next half hour turned out to be even worse than she feared.

Lady Rothwell came in, followed by Lydia and Sophy, Chloe lagging behind.

"Lady Rothwell—I did not know you were going to come today—may I offer you tea—I fear I have no small cakes," stammered the seamstress.

Lady Rothwell, as gracious as usual, looked around her with hard eyes. "I confess, Miss Sinclair, I had expected to see you hard at work. There is not much time, you know."

Lydia, impatient as always, wandered around the edge of the room, picking up various fabrics and setting them down again. She recognized none of the work in progress.

Lady Rothwell, refusing tea, sat in the one comfortable chair and fixed Miss Sinclair with a firm eye. Lady Rothwell often said that she knew well how to treat her inferiors, and was prepared to demonstrate.

"Now, Miss Sinclair, let us see what you've done."

Miss Sinclair, taking her courage in both hands and unobtrusively edging toward the door to the interior apartment, said, "I've done nothing."

Lady Rothwell seemed to swell in size, and Miss Sinclair, casting about for any excuse, whether or not it be the truth, said, unfortunately, "Luckily I had a headache——"

Lady Rothwell seized upon the word. *"Luckily!"*

"So I didn't start—so there is no harm done—no harm at all—I will simply——"

Lady Rothwell demanded an explanation. "You haven't started? I think you need to explain a little further, Miss Sinclair. I had not thought you so lost to duty as to let a headache interfere with your work. If I let a headache interfere with my affairs every time I felt like it, nothing would get done."

Chloe shot a sidelong glance at her stepmother. It was true—Lady Rothwell never allowed a headache to interfere with the running of the household. Whether it were Lady Rothwell's headache or Chloe's made no difference to Lady Rothwell.

Miss Sinclair, finally resenting Lady Rothwell's overbearing manner and remembering that she had Lord Rothwell himself on her side, decided to stand up against tyranny.

"Lord Rothwell was here yesterday—he's not like many a man, to let a person run up a bill and not know how to meet their own expenses—Lord Rothwell is always one to pay his bills promptly, and I must say——" She realized she was not getting anywhere, and started over again. "Lord Rothwell cancelled it all."

There it was, the bald statement, out in the open at last. They learned, by dint of questioning by Chloe, for Lady Rothwell was so angry she seemed about to burst and dared not speak, that Edward had come in to pay for Lydia's gown and learned about the other orders for Lydia's trip to London. "He turned white," said Miss Sinclair. "I've often heard of people turning white with anger, but I never saw it before."

"Cancelled——"

"Cancelled everything!" Miss Sinclair, appalled at the various family emotions laid out barely before her, faltered once more. "He said, plans had been changed, Miss Lydia was not going to London." Her voice trailed away, for she had no longer the power of speech.

Chloe fished the smelling salts out of her reticule. She had never needed them before, but at Lady Rothwell's instructions she always carried them.

Now they came into their own, for Lady Rothwell was near collapse. Miss Sinclair, now that the die had been cast and the word passed to Lady Rothwell, simply washed her hands of the whole matter. She knew that her customers would not return, but if only Lady Rothwell did not blame her and spread the news that Miss Sinclair was unreliable. Lady Rothwell couldn't be so unjust! Could she?

Miss Sinclair, having had dreams of her gowns making a great splash in London, scrapped her ambition without a backward glance. Now she was simply hoping that she did not lose more clients than Lady Rothwell.

At length they were all back in the open carriage and starting along the road to the Manor. Lady Rothwell, no longer attempting to play gracious lady, glowered at all whom she met. Chloe, for her part, strove for a little deportment, but even her smile lacked force.

They were so intent upon their own troubles, Lydia sobbing in her corner, Lady Rothwell frowning forbiddingly into space, that no one saw Julian Stoddard leaving the inn, and struck by the attitude of the Rothwell party, saying to himself, Something is sadly amiss there!

Lydia wept all the way home. Lady Rothwell gave the impression of a fireworks display mistakenly set alight and about to explode.

Sophy, without her new ribbons, began to have second thoughts about deceiving her brother. If Edward were so high-handed as to cancel their order to Miss Sinclair without a word to anyone, then Sophy thought quite simply there was *nothing* he wouldn't do. If she could get to Bath, then she might be safe—but now she began to wonder if Edward would in fact come to Bath and drag her home in disgrace.

Chloe, judging the time was not right to set forth her ideas, nonetheless sympathized entirely with Edward. It was not miserliness, it was not high-handedness—it was simply that Edward was trying to keep the family living within the bounds of propriety, and finding it uphill all the way. The journey home was endless, and it seemed that even nature sympathized with Lady Rothwell, for a thin veil of cloud moved across the sun, darkening the day.

Once home, they all retreated to their various rooms to recover. Chloe decided to set her dresser drawers in order. It was while she was engaged in this commendable activity that she noticed that the pearl box was still empty. She went to Lydia's room and found Lady Rothwell trying to console Lydia, being much in need of consolation herself. Chloe said, "Lydia, if you'd just give me my pearls——"

Lydia, to whom Chloe's natural request was simply the last straw, cried out, "I've lost them!"

Chloe, her knees shaking, cried, "Lost! How could you?"

Lady Rothwell, as an indication of the seriousness of the matter, joined in the search. Lydia's room was turned inside out. But there were still no pearls. "Did you lose them at Lady Partridge's?"

Lydia said, "I don't know where I lost them. Does it matter?"

Chloe was shocked to her toes. "I'll send to Lady Partridge and ask her to make a search for them." Chloe's voice tightened. "When did you see them last? Were they in the dress? Are they caught in the coach cushions? In that case, they are in London."

Suddenly Sophy became very quiet. If anyone had noticed, there was an arrested look of realization on Sophy's plump face.

The house was turned upside down, but there were no pearls. At last, late in the afternoon, Lydia gave up the search. She cried out, "What difference does it make to you, Chloe? You're rich enough to buy half a dozen strands of pearls!"

Chloe, shocked and hurt, turned instinctively to Lady Rothwell for support, but to her great dismay, Lady Rothwell said nothing. Lydia was not even scolded for losing the pearls, nor for her very *common* remark.

24

The third day after the ball arrived, and there was still no sign of Richard. That first day, she had cried on his shoulder when Thaddeus Invers had left her in such an emotional state. Now she feared that she had turned Richard away, with her constant clinging to him as though he were the only rock on the shore. For her, he was.

Chloe was, as her stepmother pointed out critically, in the mopes. "I hope that Lady Partridge finds my pearls, for I am heartbroken at losing them," she explained.

The habit of sharing was deeply ingrained in her. All her life, she had been told that she must share with her younger sisters and her brother, and she could not now change, even though she saw now how little she was valued! Like sand on the shore, her generosity was taken for granted, with no suspicion that there might come an end to it. Chloe herself felt fairly caught, trapped in unhappiness of her own making. Even her Great Friend Richard was avoiding her.

But Richard, had she only known it, was absenting himself for good reason. After he had seen her real distress at Invers' offer, even though he did not know what accusations Invers had hurled at her, Richard traveled again to London. He spent some hours with Aston, and satisfied at last, if not pleased, accomplished his purpose. He had stopped at Lady Theale's on the way, and had received certain information from his cousin-in-law that had put wings to his feet. As soon as he was finished with Aston, he returned, anxious to be at Davenant Hall as soon as possible.

While Richard was in London, Julian Stoddard brooded over his own scheme. The inn he stayed at was not luxurious, but at least there were no bailiffs banging on the door. He needed money. He wished once and for all to be put beyond the reach of clamoring tradesmen, of the uncertainties of life, even, if his luck turned bad, of being evicted from his modest lodgings. His luck had not been overly generous recently, and he had a fear for the future.

Chloe, a shy nullity, was not to his taste, but her fortune certainly was.

Julian did not wish to approach Rothwell Manor as boldly as he had the first time. His welcome then had been cool, and he feared that now, after dancing with Lydia and prompting her outburst, he would be turned away. But Julian, a man with a devious mind well honed by circumstance, was in the process of working out a scheme which would bring him everything he wanted.

Francis, at last, arrived in the inn, and Julian greeted him impatiently. "I've been waiting for you to come—so I can tell you that I've given up on your cousin."

Francis was manifestly relieved. "I can pay you what I owe you, I think."

Julian, with an expansive gesture, said, "You did what I asked you to, so we'll consider the debt paid off."

Francis, as a matter of honor, promised Julian, "I'll pay you. It won't be today, but soon."

Now on much easier terms with each other, Julian called for drinks, and he and Francis sat further in conversation. Francis, for lack of anything else to say, explained that Chloe's pearls were missing.

Julian said, "Was your sister wearing them?"

Francis said, "Yes, Lydia was, and now the fat's in the fire for sure. For she has lost them, and no one knows where they are. I am going back to London, for there's no reason to stay any longer." In Francis's mind were mingled gratitude that Chloe had refused him and relief that he would no longer have to meet his aunt's accusing gaze at every meal.

Julian, pursuing his own scheme, told Francis that he was going on to Brighton. "For the Prince Regent is much more amusing than Rothwell Manor, I'll tell you."

Francis, when he left, thought he had seen the last of Julian Stoddard. He made a vow to himself never again to gamble in a private house, or in fact—and this was a hard decision for Francis to make—to gamble anywhere. He had a strong suspicion that the cards had been marked, and while he had thought that his host was a man of honor, clearly he was mistaken.

Julian, on his part, brooded over the new information

that Francis had unwittingly given him. Dare he try? Stoddard weighed all the facts, and finally decided that at worst he could only be shown up as a gambler—and the world already knew that.

Poring long over the form that his plan was to take, he at last penned an equivocal letter to Miss Lydia Rothwell. Reading it over, he was satisfied. It said enough, not too much. If, on the basis of the letter, Lydia thought he had the missing pearls, so much the better. He had not said so, but he banked heavily on Lydia's shallow intellect to fill in the missing blanks in the letter.

Julian's plan was simple in the extreme. He knew that Chloe, being as honest and clear as a fresh spring of water, would not pay to get her pearls back. And Julian did not have them to return. It would become a question of being able to produce the goods, and there could be a nasty aftermath.

But if Julian Stoddard had Lydia's person, and her reputation, in his hands to do with as he would, then Chloe certainly would pay for the girl's release. He was delighted at his own astuteness, for he would get the fortune without the girl.

How to get the note to Lydia? He could not go to Rothwell Manor himself, but he was not without resources. He stepped into the taproom and studied the idlers who were there in the middle of the day. One in particular caught his fancy. He was a little better dressed than the others, and he looked at Julian Stoddard with a frank curiosity that boded well for his intelligence.

Julian, had he only known it, had made a mistake. The idler was Grimes, one of the footmen at Davenant Hall. The gambling fever had struck all the servants of Sir Richard, and the footman, rightly considered by Julian as more intelligent than the average, had become suspicious of the actions of Sir Richard's butler. Dall knew something, that was certain. So the idler had come to town to hedge on his bets on the London ladies.

In the taproom he had found other gamblers of a like mind, and he was much satisfied at his cleverness in making his wagers so that he could not lose no matter which way Sir Richard's choice fell.

When Julian Stoddard gave Grimes the letter addressed to Miss Lydia Rothwell and enjoined him privately not to give it to anyone else, he accepted with alacrity. It was the easiest half crown he had ever earned.

But he had kept his eyes and ears open on other subjects than Sir Richard's approaching choice of a bride, and he knew he did not like Julian Stoddard. The man was a mischiefmaker; his eyes were set too close together, which proved—at least to Grimes—dishonesty. The footman, on his way out of town, reflected that it was not at all likely that Miss Lydia, barely out of the schoolroom, would have legitimate business with the likes of yon fancy man.

On his way home, Grimes pondered. What would be best to do? Should he deliver the message, as he had been given it, to Miss Lydia, which would in fact make him much later home than he wanted, or should he tell somebody in authority what he thought? Part of his reasoning lay along the lines of the question, Could I get in trouble with this and lose my job? The answer came clearly—Yes.

It was the right thing to do, then, to allow Sir Richard to decide what to do with this missive which burned inside his jacket pocket. Having made up his mind, eased his conscience, and thrust the responsibility onto someone else, the footman quickened his pace and was soon at home.

Julian Stoddard, lolling at his ease in the private parlor at the inn, planned the most persuasive conversation of his life, to be carried on with Lydia.

In his mind he followed the rude fellow whom he had entrusted with the note. He did not stop to think that his judgment might be mistaken—that his letter might have gone astray.

A knock came on the door, and without waiting for an answer the door opened. So soon! Julian's eyes lit up, and the name *Lydia* trembled on his lips.

The newcomer was not Lydia. Instead, the caller was a man above the average height, somewhat stocky in his build, and dressed with quiet elegance. Stoddard gibbered. In spite of himself, his weakness overcame him. It took a supreme effort to pull himself together.

Stoddard cried out, "Sir Richard! You're in London."

Richard, calmly, said, "Fortunately for you I have returned. In time."

Stoddard's wits scattered. "In time?"

Davenant said, "In time, yes. To save you from a grave error."

Stoddard said, "I don't understand."

Sir Richard said, "I think you understand me only too well. I have here a note to Lydia. I confess I should have thought better of you. You must be under the hatches indeed, to resort to such a foolish stratagem."

Stoddard eyed the folded slip of paper in Richard's hand. "How did you get the note?"

Richard said, with a hint of a smile, "Your choice of a messenger played you false. He was one of my own men."

Julian, seeing his hopes lying in pieces around his feet, yet struggled. "Save me? You said, to save me?"

Davenant, checking to see that the door was closed behind him, explained. "You would not wish to be horse-whipped like a common fellow, I am persuaded."

Stoddard said, "You? Why you?"

Davenant said, "Not I. I would not soil my hands with you. But Rothwell——"

Stoddard said, "No! He wouldn't dare!"

Davenant added persuasively, "Rothwell is very old-fashioned. Even gothic. He has a strong sense of his family's honor, and you would have been well advised to avoid him like the plague."

At length, seeing Julian sitting with his head in his hands, Richard provided him with a solution. "I suggest that you leave town at once. Brighton or London, your destination is immaterial to me. But I must tell you this, any further word to the Rothwell ladies—even a note of farewell—will have dire consequences for you."

Stoddard, not trusting his voice to reply and longing to find an occasion to throttle Sir Richard, at a time when there would be no chance of harm coming to himself, nodded agreement. Sir Richard turned and opened the door, and then giving Julian one last look and dusting his fingers lightly as though to remove dirt, vanished from Julian Stoddard's ken.

Chloe, at Rothwell Manor, did not know that Richard had returned from London. Her attention was still centered on the lost pearls. Lady Partridge had sent word that she had turned her house upside down and there was no sign of the necklace. She was leaving in a couple of days, and told Chloe kindly that she had left word for the servants to continue the search and to let Chloe know if the pearls were discovered.

Chloe avoided the company of her family, for she could

think only of Lydia's thoughtlessness and her very cruel remark. Nimrod, sensing that his mistress was distressed, did his best to divert her. She watched his antics with an absent air, and at length he gave up and crawled into her lap to sleep. Chloe, trying to shake off her brooding thoughts, reached for the book that Richard had lent her. Opening it at random, she expected to become lost in the story—but it was to no avail.

The sound of carriage wheels in the drive roused her, and carefully picking the puppy up from her lap and carrying him with her to the window, she looked out. She could not see the front drive from here, but she could see the carriage when it was brought into the stable yard beyond. It was the Rothwell closed carriage. Edward must be home! He had planned to stay a week, but something must have happened to bring him back so soon. She hurried downstairs. Edward scarcely noticed her, going at once into his book room. She looked at Lady Rothwell in the foyer, and Lydia, and both wore expressions that matched her own feelings. Whatever was in Edward's mind, whatever had happened to him in London, it had brought him home in a foul mood.

Lydia and Lady Rothwell, who had separately decided to plead with Edward for a reversal of his decision on Lydia's trip to London, kept their silence and realized the time was not right. Sophy, pursuing her own strategy, remained out of sight. If Edward did not see her, then he would not miss her.

Upon returning to the bosom of his family, Edward was gratified to find that Francis had left. "Now," he said, "we have our own family group. I have had enough of outsiders."

Lydia, having tasted the heady air of excitement, with visitors from London falling over each other in the entry, took exception to Edward's calm pronouncement. She had not recovered from her disappointment at having her perspective gowns cancelled. Still in her mind lay the rose brocade, the gauzes embroidered with silver thread, not to speak of the most fetching bonnets!

Edward, a somber mood upon him, said, "There are going to be some changes made around here. I will want to talk to you, Mama, about Lydia and Sophy."

Lydia, still smarting from her sense of injustice and her great humiliation by Miss Sinclair, worked on the theory that misery loved company. "You may not have a chance to work on Sophy very long," she said, spitefully.

Edward, more alert than usual to nuances around him, inquired, "And why is that, pray?"

"You'll have to put it off for a month or two, until Sophy gets back from Bath with Lady Partridge." Lydia, watching Edward's face grow pink, wished that she had not spoken.

Edward turned to his mother. "Pray tell me that this is not true, for you know my wishes in the matter."

Lady Rothwell, almost afraid of the alteration in her only son, said, "I saw no harm in a little diversion for the child."

"Child!" cried Edward. "That's the point. She is no more than a child, and I will not have her away from the house. There is much to be done before either of my sisters is fit to come out into society. I take it amiss that you, Mama, have abetted this mad scheme. I shall not wish to have the family name disgraced, and if Sophy's behavior is anything like Lydia's, then we are in for it."

Lady Rothwell bridled, but even she was no match for Edward. She gave him a quelling look, and was dismayed to see that it had no effect whatever.

Edward was strangely exercised. "There will be no Little Season for Lydia, and I am not at all sure that her faults can be mended even in two years."

Lady Rothwell cried out, "But you cannot keep Lydia from town forever!"

Edward agreed. "I have no wish to keep Lydia in this house forever, nor Sophy either. My peace of mind will be assured if both the girls are out and safely wed. But I cannot countenance turning them loose on society until they have learned a little decorum."

Lady Rothwell allowed her jaw to drop unbecomingly. This son was like no son she had known before, and for the first time it began to cross her mind to wonder why he had gone to London.

Edward, in no mood to enlighten her, said simply, "Let me have no more of this. I am the head of the family—all the family—and I do what I consider best for us all."

Chloe, in an unaccountably low mood, had gone upstairs to her own room. She had had her fill of the family, even though she would not admit it to herself. It was quite likely that Richard's absence had given her some dismal

thoughts, but even if Chloe had realized that it was his de-
fection that had set her into a depression, she would have
fought that idea as well, for she had no claim on Richard.

Even Nimrod, digging furiously in the wood basket next
to the fireplace, failed to divert her.

Her mood, while dark, was also reflective and tending
toward decision. She could not live the rest of her life in
the mopes. She must get out and make some change, or
she would have no one but herself to blame for her continued low mood.

There seemed nothing to do, no decision she could
make, that was satisfactory. Byron's hero, in the book that
Richard had lent her, moved on when his affairs became
unmanageable. He had a goal, of course, and that was the
difference. Chloe had none. She did not want to be away
from her family, she could not wish to be alone, and yet
her choices were greatly limited.

All the stirrings of the past weeks, the unsettling news
that she had inherited Highmoor, seemed to be the beginning of her depression. And yet she would not wish to give
away Highmoor, for it represented at the same time both
cause and escape. Inheriting Highmoor was the event that
had set all of this in motion—her unwelcome suitors, even
her foolish cousin Francis joining their ranks—and yet the
only thing she could think of doing was going to live in
her own home.

And yet it was not home, for her family was around her
here at Rothwell Manor and Edward had said this was her
home as long as she wanted. Her fearful self told her, You
need your family. But the unexpected stirrings echoed,
Why?

It took a long time, but she finally threw out the idea of
removing to Highmoor. She would simply have to make
the best of it here, and she told herself she was simply
sickening for something. Her head began to ache, and she
remembered she had not eaten most of the day.

But at last she was back on an even keel, she told herself, and moving to Highmoor was out of the question.

While Chloe thought her mood had been settled, yet
beneath the surface lay fuel and tinder invitingly ready for
a spark. Into this mood of uncertainty and dissatisfaction
came Sophy, unwittingly carrying the spark.

Sophy, having carefully avoided Edward in the hall below, was nonetheless quite aware of his new-found sentiments.

There was very little that escaped Sophy, and almost everything she did was for the direct benefit of Sophy herself. She was oblivious to other people's feelings, and was totally insensitive to others' moods. This moment was no exception. She burst into Chloe's room, without ceremony, intent upon her own feelings.

"Edward is unjust," she said without ceremony. "He has no feelings for anybody else."

Chloe cocked an eyebrow, since Sophy could have been describing herself.

"How dare Edward tell me that I may not go to Bath with Lady Partridge! There is no harm in it—Edward simply wants to show his authority. That's what he said, you know, 'I am the head of the family.'"

Nimrod ceased his digging in the wood basket. There was very little in there, after he had finished, to excite his attention, and he now turned to the protection of his mistress. Nimrod had a strong recollection of tweaked ears and pulled tail, and he held Sophy in abhorrence. Just now he watched her with suspicion, and a certain amount of distrust. Sophy, in the exercise of her strong feelings, paced the floor. Nimrod retreated to shelter himself behind Chloe's skirts. Sophy narrated a quick overview of the scene in the hall below. She had not been there, but she was not far away.

Chloe said, "Too bad, but there will be other times."

Chloe's own "other times" never came, she reflected silently. Even Highmoor had come too late, drawing only rickety flies to the honeypot of her legacy.

"Besides," added Chloe, "if Lydia can't go to London—then her disappointment is hard indeed."

Sophy dismissed her sister's unhappiness with a wave of her hand. "Other times are fine," she added, with an air of sweet reasonableness that sat oddly on her, "but I want to go now."

Chloe was unutterably weary of the tug-of-war constantly going on between the different members of her family. She leaned back in her chair and closed her eyes.

Sophy came to stand before her and repeated, "I want to go now. And you can help me."

Chloe said, without interest, "How?"

"You could stand up to Edward."

"Why should I?"

Sophy said, "You are independent. He'll listen to you because of your fortune. Mama said so."

" I doubt that very much, for Mama often says exaggerated things. Besides, why should I?"

Sophy came to kneel beside her. "For something you want back."

There was an altered tone in Sophy's voice that struck Chloe. She opened her eyes to stare steadfastly into her half-sister's pale blue eyes. "What do you mean?"

Nimrod, at Chloe's ankle, decided things were not going to his taste, and growled. Sophy said, "Don't you want your pearls back?"

The reaction that Sophy received was beyond her wildest expectations. Blood drained from Chloe's face, leaving it white as a sheet, as Chloe took in the enormity of Sophy's monstrous blackmail. She could get her pearls back—at a price!

In a strangled voice, she said, "Do you know where my pearls are?"

And Sophy, still not as astute as she would have liked to be, nodded wordlessly.

Chloe stood up, ashen, shaking, but a blaze in her gray eyes that Sophy had never seen. Always before, her half-sister had been calm, tolerant, and totally to be trusted in secrets that Sophy would just as soon did not reach the ears of her mother or brother.

Now Chloe blazed at her, and Sophy scrambled to her feet. Chloe could hardly speak. Sophy could barely understand the words, but even the ones she could understand she had never heard before from Chloe.

Never before had Sophy been called a grasping, selfish monster!

25

If Sophy had never seen her half-sister in such a rage, neither had the other Rothwells.

Chloe stormed out of her room, followed by a stunned and belatedly contrite Sophy. To do her justice, Sophy was not maliciously inclined. She was possessed of a juvenile wish to seek her own advantage, and she had her heart set on the trip with her dear friend Emma. To her all means to attain that end were feasible.

Sophy hastened after Chloe. She had clearly made a mistake, and while she had little hope of retrieving her error, at least until Chloe calmed down, yet she dared not leave Chloe's side. She hurried along in her half-sister's wake, feeling the very air churned by Chloe's angry passing.

Chloe's mind, as she moved swiftly to the head of the main stairs, was a jumble. Everyone knew how much store Chloe set by her mother's pearls. She wore them only rarely herself, and she had lent them with great reluctance to Lydia. But Lydia had paid so little heed to Chloe's wishes that she had lost the pearls. The house had been turned upside down trying to find them, and Lady Partridge had joined in the search at her home.

To think that Sophy had known all the time where the pearls were—Chloe could not think of words strong enough to use. There was only one thought that emerged from this jumble in her mind—she had been betrayed. Driven by resolutions she did not yet know she had made, she swept down the stairs. She was still holding Nimrod, and she did not remember picking him up. As she reached the foyer below, Field and the footman sprang to attention and stared at Chloe. There was scarcely time for them to think. Certainly they too had never seen Miss Rothwell in such a regal rage, and they were struck dumb. Chloe said in an icy voice, "My brother?"

189

Field, still mute from shock, nodded, and the footman sprang to open the door into the Green Salon. Chloe crossed the tiled entry and left both Field and the footman bobbing in her wake. The butler's remark, "Lord Rothwell is in company," died a natural death on his lips. Chloe would not have heeded him had he been able to find his voice.

Chloe paused on the threshold, and looked upon her assembled family like one returned from twenty years at sea. It seemed as though she had not seen these faces in a true light in all her life. She was somewhat feverish as she scanned the faces. Her morbid fancy told her, These faces were once loved, but are now disclosed by the harsh and blinding light of disillusion.

As Chloe stopped in the doorway, Sophy, hurrying after her, was brought up abruptly. Sophy could not see beyond her half-sister, and the expressions on the faces of those who were already in the room were lost to her.

Startled by Chloe's unheralded entrance, all faces looked toward her—Lady Rothwell, her jaw dropping at the unexpected apparition of her stepdaughter, Edward and Lydia turned toward her as though they were puppets on a string. The fourth person in the room, whom she did not notice at first, was Sir Richard Davenant. An alert spectator might have noticed that Sir Richard, as startled as the others at Chloe's entrance, tensed his muscles. He was alert, fearing what would happen next, and his sudden anxiety brought him politely to his feet.

Lady Rothwell was the first to recover. "Chloe," she cried, "what can you be thinking of to appear before me in such a state of undress?"

Lady Rothwell's remarks, characteristically, avoided the emotion on Chloe's ashen face and addressed only her shawl awry and her curls in disarray. "And that foolish dog," continued Lady Rothwell. "I beg your pardon, Sir Richard, but the dog is forbidden the lower floors. I will not tolerate dogs having the run of my drawing room.

"The subject has never come up before," she informed Sir Richard, "but I certainly did not think it necessary to tell Chloe the basics of civilized behavior. . . ."

No one heeded Lady Rothwell, all eyes being fixed on Chloe, her breast heaving and her eyes glittering. Belatedly, Lady Rothwell's voice trailed away.

Eventually, but more quickly than his mother, Edward

became aware that something was sadly amiss with his sister.

"What is it, Chloe—what has gone wrong? I don't believe you've spoken to Sir Richard," he ended in a weak attempt at civility, indicating their guest with a gesture.

Chloe had eyes only for one person. Stalking across the room, oblivious to the others, she stopped before Lydia. "Where are my pearls?"

Lydia, cowering in her chair, protested, "I lost them. You know I lost them, and I *said* I was sorry!"

Chloe did not accept this. She continued to glare at Lydia. Nimrod, tired of being confined without a voice in the proceedings, growled in his throat.

Chloe said, "How much do *you* want to return my pearls?"

The reactions on the faces of those others in the room would, on a happier occasion, have been amusing to Chloe. Just now she was hardly aware that she and Lydia were not alone in the world.

Edward and Lady Rothwell sat as though stunned. Richard, by now knowing there was something dreadfully awry, frowned. Lydia leaped to her feet to protest. "I don't know what you mean, Chloe," she exclaimed. "I lost the pearls. I've hunted for them—and I don't know why you are so upset now."

Chloe said, "I'll tell you why——"

But by now Lady Rothwell had found her voice. Speaking sharply, she cried, "Chloe, have you gone mad?"

Sophy, desperate to stop the revelation to the family, had followed Chloe. The footman held the door, hoping to hear what went on. Miss Chloe was certainly up in the air, he thought, and stood hesitantly in the doorway.

Now Sophy, recognizing trouble when she saw it, edged toward the door. However, she met Sir Richard's gaze and found a cold warning in his blue eyes that she dared not ignore. She stopped, and although reason told her that Sir Richard could do nothing to her, yet such was the state of her unsteady conscience that she dared not risk it.

Richard, thinking furiously, decided that Chloe's disturbance was due to the young lady in the doorway. Young Sophy was up to something, he was positive, and his fingers itched to implement his next thought—a sound thrashing might elicit the facts of the matter.

Chloe, realizing that Lady Rothwell had spoken to her,

at last responded. "No," she said with angry sadness, "I have been blind. I saw what I wanted to see, believed that my family was generous and happy for me."

Her emotion was more than she could contain in her small figure, and she began to pace the floor. "I saw what I wanted to see—I believed that my family loved me——"

Her pacing took her toward Richard, but she apparently did not recognize his presence. As she went past, he reached out and deftly extracted the puppy from her arms. Chloe did not even notice.

The direction her thoughts took as she spoke to her stepmother was too emotional, and she shied away from the lump in her throat. She could not speak further of her sense of betrayal—instead she whirled and faced Edward. She had thought upstairs that she had successfully quieted the stirring of rebellion within her. There were many reasons why she must stay at Rothwell Manor, and her mind had been made up. But Sophy had released the gates that barred the flood, and her resolution vaulted over it. Chloe announced in a firm voice, "I am going to live at Highmoor!"

The words hung in the air, almost as though they were fringed with fire. Edward's jaw, hanging open, echoed his mother's astounded expression, and Sophy, her round eyes wide with excitement and dismay, was rooted to the floor. Lydia, her conscience about the pearls clear, was merely bewildered. Something was going on that was not her fault, and she did not understand it. She allowed a sound like the bleat of a lost lamb to escape from her.

Only Sir Richard was not shocked. He noticed that his dear love Chloe seemed as stunned by the words as the others. She could hardly believe she had said them. But Edward's expression, even to Chloe, was unreadable.

Somehow the spoken words brought her to a modicum of control. She had not meant it, so she told herself, and yet rebellion, once loosed, could not be fought back.

Her long habit of looking to her stepmother for approval was strong, and she glanced now at Lady Rothwell.

Lady Rothwell herself could not have said whether her disapproval was for Chloe's lack of decorum or her announced plans.

Chloe did not pause to consider. She knew Lady Rothwell disapproved—and in the ordinary way she would have retreated. She did hesitate, almost faltering, and one might have expected her to awaken from a bad dream and apologize. But she did not.

The dam of repression, having sprung small leaks along the way since Chloe had been informed of her legacy, was swept away, and the spate of rebellion raged unopposed.

Still, even rebellion could not sour Chloe's naturally sweet disposition. She brought up no past injuries, and applied herself to deal, however shakily, with her present wrongs.

She buried her sense of injustice at her stepmother's pressing Francis's suit upon her, of Edward's favoring Thaddeus Invers, but her listeners were not so generous.

Lady Rothwell cut across Chloe's remarks and said, "Edward, I told you you should not bring Invers into this."

Richard, mentally, added Julian Stoddard to the list of wrongs that Chloe had suffered, but he checked Stoddard off, for reasons of his own.

But Lady Rothwell did not take Chloe's rebellion silently. She had long accustomed to ruling her household, and said as much.

"I am not accustomed to being spoken to by my children, even by Chloe, in this fashion."

Edward interrupted in vain. "Mother——"

Lady Rothwell swept on. "I hope I know my duty to my son, who is the head of the house, but in my family I still claim to be mistress. Chloe, you are overwrought over a small thing like an insignificant string of pearls——"

She had made a mistake. Instead of damping the fires of Chloe's anger, she merely stirred the embers. The flames leaped up again. "Those were *my mother's* pearls—the only thing I have left from her—and they are far from insignificant to me."

Lady Rothwell paused only briefly. "And the pearls will turn up——"

"Sophy has them."

Lady Rothwell was shocked. "I am persuaded not."

Chloe, taking on a curiously remote air, an air that bothered Sir Richard mightily, said, turning her smoldering gray eyes on her stepmother, "Ask Sophy. Ask Lydia how she came to lose them. I myself am no longer interested." She waved a hand recklessly, and Richard was glad he was holding the puppy. The puppy, seeing his mistress distressed and speaking more loudly than he was accustomed to, gave vent to a protesting bark.

Chloe added, "Edward, I beg you send word to Highmoor to have all in readiness for me in a week."

Edward, faced with a mixture of guilt and social outrage—feeling that his world, placid as it had been, had unaccountably been turned upside down—tackled the minor problem first. "How will it look? You leave my house——"

Chloe eyed him coldly. "I leave for my own house."

Edward said, "My mother, who's given you nothing but kindness, and my sisters, you are leaving them to set up for yourself to live *alone*! I will not allow it."

Richard judged it time to intervene. He said mildly, a voice of sanity in this melee, "Rothwell, she is of age."

It was as though his voice had broken the spell that kept them immobile. Lydia cried out, "I truly lost the pearls." She turned to her sister and said cryptically, "Little sneak!"

Sophy, clearly lying and knowing she fooled nobody, took refuge in denying everything. "I did not tell Chloe I had her pearls. You lost them, how could I?" Even her denial proclaimed her guilt.

Chloe, calmer now, and hearing her determination to go to Highmoor set forth unequivocally, paused for breath and caught Richard's eye. In his steady blue gaze she read warmth, comfort, support, and even encouragement—whatever she wanted, or needed, at that moment he seemed to promise it.

The exchange of glances lasted only seconds, but it was enough to put the seal on Chloe's fate, to tell her what she had hidden but now must acknowledge at least to herself.

She had long been conscious of a *tendre* for him, a sense of missing him when he was not nearby, a feeling of total trust in him, and a dismal sense of loss when she thought about his approaching marriage.

Now, this glance that took only seconds was a thunderclap that shook her to her core. No matter what happened to Richard, she herself knew there would be never another man for her.

Belatedly she remembered that her face was quite often an open book, and she turned away, afraid to reveal in her face the realization that had come to her. She turned back to her family, not realizing that Richard had read in her face the exact truth that he had longed to make sure of.

Chloe turned back to her family, who were in the throes of mutual recriminations. Although what they said only touched the surface, yet at bottom was the thought of Chloe's fortune receding from their grasp. Only Edward did not agree. In fact, he had fallen into a studied silence. He turned his pale eyes toward Chloe, apparently on the verge of saying something, but he did not speak.

Chloe realized that she had said words that could not be taken back, and she must go ahead. It must be the right thing to do, to leave her unattractive family, to be miserable over Richard by herself, unobserved, and go to Highmoor.

Slowly she said, "Edward, I have a little income from my mother's trust. Add that to my income from Uncle Bradford and I believe I can do very nicely. In a week I shall be at Highmoor."

Edward, with the air of a man who has been forced into a corner and sees no escape, said, in a strangled voice, "You can't. I've sold Highmoor!"

26

The room swung in erratic circles around Chloe, and failed to right itself. Blindly, she stretched her hand out in a piteous gesture.

There was no support, anywhere in the room, until Richard, one-handed because of Nimrod, provided a chair. It was just in time, for Chloe's knees refused to hold her any longer.

A tiny voice was all she could manage. "Sold?"

Edward, not trusting his own voice, nodded. His face was alarmingly flushed.

Richard murmured, "Rothwell, are you prone to apoplexy?"

"S-sold?" Chloe shook her head as though to clear it of

cobwebs. "Sold? But I thought it was mine. It *is* mine! I'm going to live there." She rose from her chair, in a sudden frenzy. "I'm going there now. You're mistaken! Edward, you can't sell it. It's mine!"

Richard, judging that the time had come for intervention, set Nimrod on the floor. He seized Chloe's hands in his and held them fast. His fingers were warm and strong and steady. His grasp calmed her enough so that she could turn to Edward with a semblance of reason and say, "How? How could you sell my house? You had no right!"

Edward returned to his dogged manner. Frowning, he took on an air of aggrieved righteousness. He had learned nothing in the last half hour.

He pointed out with force, "You gave me your power of attorney. Chloe, I've always dealt fairly with you." She nodded, for he spoke only the truth. "I showed you the books on your mother's trust. You remember that, and you were satisfied with my accounting. Believe me, Chloe, I have always dealt honestly——"

She broke in. "You've stolen it. First, my sisters and now my brother have played me false. I had not thought it possible."

Lydia, still smarting under the accusation that she knew where the pearls were, began to protest. Her mother put out a hand to stop her.

Edward said, stubbornly, "I didn't *steal* it. I *sold* it."

Chloe said, her voice stony, "Get it back."

Edward, surprised, said, "What do you mean—get it back?"

Chloe, with an air of explaining something to a small child, said clearly and distinctly, "You have sold my house. I said, Get it back."

"I can't."

Chloe said, half rising from her chair, "Why not?"

"It's gone. I don't even know who bought it. An agent bought it for a third party. I can't get it back. I have the price already in hand."

She pulled her hands free of Richard's grasp and covered her face. She did not sob. No one could detect her shoulders shuddering with weeping, but she was the very embodiment of despair, a desolate figure hiding her face from her beloved family.

Edward, conscious of Richard's eyes weighing him, explained, "It was a white elephant. It would take a fortune to keep it up."

Chloe interrupted bitterly. "Fortune! And that's what I thought I had."

Edward explained, in far more detail than anybody cared to hear, that all the lands were sold off, all that Bradford could sell before he died. "He came to the close of his life owning only the house and grounds, which were sadly neglected. You could not have lived there, for your income would not run to taking heed of the repairs that were needed."

Chloe's thoughts circled and came back to the main point. "You had no right to sell it without telling me!"

Edward added heavily, "The sale brought very little, besides."

Words, words, words! They were like a swarm of bees buzzing around her and driving her quite frantic.

Although she was not aware of her cry, she shouted out, "Edward, be quiet!"

It was an outburst totally unlike her. All but Richard were shocked. He, with a vital interest in this scene, was remarkably unmoved. His love had become furious, had lashed out in unheard-of rebellion, and he smiled.

Lady Rothwell, not for years having been constrained to react swiftly, found she had not forgotten her old ways. She did not understand Edward's business, nor whether he was in the right of it. Did he in fact have the right to sell Chloe's land?

Lady Rothwell cared little about the fact. She herself was used to allowing men in her family to take care of all business, and she did not even try to understand it. But there were some things she did know, and one was that her stepdaughter was behaving outrageously. "Chloe!" she said sharply. "Your language is uncivil. It's not befitting my daughter." She continued in this vein, battering Chloe with words. "I had not thought you selfish——"

Chloe, with more insight than tact, said, "I truly doubt you ever thought of *me* at all!"

The exchange between Lady Rothwell and her step-daughter was overlooked totally by Lydia and Sophy. Sophy, still smarting from Chloe's accusation of stealing the pearls, flung her contribution to the row in a voice that carried more than ordinary blame. "You're no better than a thief yourself, Chloe," she said, unjustly, "passing yourself off as an heiress when you're not at all, and playing the great lady at Emma's ball."

"Emma's ball!" cried Lydia. "She had little enough to do with it."

Sophy, once in stride, could not be easily halted. She cried out, "And besides that, Chloe, you tattled to Edward that Emma and I practiced the waltz, when the Czar himself danced it only last month at Almack's, and everybody knows that."

Chloe brushed Sophy aside as though brushing off a fly.

But Sophy continued. "And we weren't dancing it in company either, but you had to tell Edward——"

Edward weighed into the running battle in a ponderous fashion. "I am not, I thank God, responsible for the Czar, but I am——"

Lady Rothwell, seeing control of the situation fading from her grasp, cried, "You'd think her father would have provided for her, but now she's *penniless!*"

Richard was reminded of nothing so much as a fox brought to earth. The hounds were yapping around her, and if he did not prevent them, there would be real danger of Chloe's total collapse.

Richard spared a thought to the late Lord Rothwell's improvidence, but that could not be mended now. Chloe turned blindly toward Richard, instinctively seeking support where she trusted.

Events were moving faster than Richard would like, or indeed had anticipated. He heard Edward saying, interminably, but in an effort to be fair, "Chloe said not a word to me about you and Emma, Sophy. It was Francis who was outraged, and rightly so. He was right to tell me."

To Chloe's pitiful, unspoken plea, Richard responded. His voice was quiet, yet it cut across the babble of the mutually recriminatory Rothwells, stopping the flow of justification and accusation. "Enough! Miss Rothwell is not penniless, and I can't think why you said so, Edward, unless you have managed to do away with the late Lady Rothwell's dowry?"

Chloe murmured, "Oh no, oh no."

Richard, dropping his hand to rest on Chloe's shoulder, and feeling the trembling lessen within her, continued, "Edward?"

Edward, wounded by the accusation, and knowing his own honesty, blustered, "Of course not!"

Richard, to Edward's surprise, said, "Just so. My informants have assured me of this. So Chloe has as great a fortune as she ever had."

Lady Rothwell, turning an inward eye upon her own endorsement of Francis's offer of marriage, said indignantly, "She almost married Francis!"

Richard, sadly hampered by the need to be civil, fixed Lady Rothwell with an exceedingly cold blue eye and said, "I should not have allowed that."

It was clear to all that a new element had been added to the Green Salon—the steel of Sir Richard Davenant. They reacted as though someone had set down a man-eating lion in their midst.

Lady Rothwell and Edward were caught up short, and intangibly joined forces against the intruder. While Sir Richard Davenant, as Lady Rothwell would have told anyone, was a man of the utmost gentility and impeccable breeding, yet he was interfering in a fashion that could only be considered vulgar.

Lady Rothwell said as much. "I do not understand, Sir Richard, why you see fit to meddle in our family's affairs."

Lydia, intent on her own loss, mourned, "Now I'll never get to London! Not for *two years!*"

Sophy fell silent, for her conscience regarding the pearls was troubling her badly. If she had not hinted that she knew where the pearls were—and she did—then Chloe would not have turned angry and this whole very uncomfortable afternoon would have not happened. Sophy had no doubts but what she herself would come out of it well, but her thoughts ran seriously along the line of returning the pearls before anyone knew where they had gone.

Chloe herself had spent her fury. Richard remembered, irresistibly, that once as a child, Chloe had impetuously poked a hornet's nest and he had been hard put to preserve her from the consequences of her own indiscretion.

This incident today was much like that. Chloe had stirred up more than she had engaged for. A move to Highmoor had seemed at the time to require all her resolution. And that had been thwarted, not only by her family's wish that she stay at Rothwell Manor, but by the fact that she no longer had Highmoor as a last resort.

Now, in retrospect, how simple a move to Highmoor seemed in comparison with the unpleasant days that were certain to lie ahead! She had accused her family of every crime in her book, and the words could not be taken back. Her courage, of a high order, was of a kind which endured rather than led a charge through a breach in the wall. Her head ached, her thoughts thrummed within her brain, and she knew only that matters of some moment were being discussed over her head. But she faltered, and most of what was said now was going past her.

Lady Rothwell echoed Richard's words, in high indignation. "*You* should not have allowed?"

Richard said, glancing sidelong at Chloe, "Chloe is going to marry me. So you see, I should not have allowed her to marry anyone else."

There was dead silence. For a long enough space so that the silence caught Chloe's attention, no one said anything. Then there was tumult.

Edward, predictably, was angry and hurt. "You should have asked me. I'm the head of the family. I don't recall that you said anything to me about pressing your suit with Chloe."

Lady Rothwell for once was totally silent. It was something she could not take in—the dashing Sir Richard had actually offered for Chloe, and been accepted, and Chloe, that sly minx, had said not a word!

Lydia, participating in the general feeling of anger and hurt feelings, cried out, "Chloe said you had offered for someone else. She should have told me the truth!"

There was nothing anyone could answer to that, for logic had vanished from the scene. As logic had disappeared, so did Sophy. Seizing the moment of great tumult, of Chloe's betrothal to Sir Richard, Sophy quietly slipped out of the room.

She climbed the stairs, low in her mind. Everything she had tried had gone awry. She had wanted to go with Emma to Bath. She had thought that Chloe's influence was irresistible, for after all they all said she had a great fortune and Edward would listen to her. If Chloe had taken her part, Sophy was sure she would now be on her way to Bath with Lady Partridge. Evertyhing had gone awry, and there was only one thing to do.

If it were discovered that she had indeed secreted the pearls away, and not told Chloe, then the expected retribution would be tenfold. Sophy opened a secret hiding place that she had devised for herself. She fished out the pearls and held them in her hand. Just so had she fished out of the cushions in the coach on their way home from Lady Partridge's that night, when they had come undone from around Lydia's throat and slipped behind the squabs. To be truthful, Sophy had had no intention at first of using the pearls for her own advantage, but things had gone wrong even at the beginning. Sophy was quite sure that Edward would keep her from going with Emma, for he had summarily dismissed Lady Rothwell's order for gowns for Lydia. There had been so much going on that in truth Sophy had forgotten the pearls. It was only when Edward came home from London in such a somber mood that she remembered. She had only wanted to look at them, and put them away until a later time.

He reminded her of her adventure with the hornets' nest, and received for his trouble a watery smile. Then, convinced she had not listened to the announcement he had made to her family, informed her, "I have announced that you and I will be wed." Her reaction to the news, clearly the first she had heard of it, astounded him.

Now, sooner or later, the subject of the pearls would be reopened and she would face consequences. However, there was one way—if the pearls were where they belonged, then Sophy would be safe. In moments the pearls were restored to Chloe's drawer. She hurried back to the stairs, intending to rejoin the family before inquiry was raised.

From the top of the stairs she saw Richard holding Chloe firmly by the wrist and pulling her across the hall into the book room and closing the door firmly behind them. Sophy spared a thought to listening at the door, but Field and the footman were both still in the hall, and there was no opportunity.

Inside the library, Chloe found her voice. "I've made such a mess of things."

Richard, amused, was deeply touched. His poor Chloe! But she had turned to him in her need, and the future looked rosy indeed for Richard.

The longer the search continued, the more difficult it was to produce them. And she had a sure instinct that counseled her to keep her secret until it could serve her.

Chloe, for reasons of her own, and very conscious of the fact that Richard was presenting her with all she longed for in life, cried out, "Oh no, *no!*" and burst into tears.

27

A disinterested spectator, were he watching the interview between Richard and Chloe, would have noticed that Richard's knuckles had turned white. He clutched the back of a small chair and felt rather than heard it creak beneath his strong grip. He had neglected many a time when he could have told Chloe what was in his heart, and he had now left it too late. He had not intended to declare himself in the midst of a quarreling family, but he had had no choice.

Now, as he looked at his intended bride, his dismay was carefully hidden. She was sobbing as though her heart would break. He watched her gravely, feeling even the air around him turn gray and black. Had he misread her feelings? Did she regard him as only her Great Friend? He did not realize how greatly he had staked his future upon the reaction that he had read in her eyes. And now, from all appearances, he had made the worst mistake of his life.

He had precipitated this spate of tears, and although he regretted the result, there had seemed to be little choice. But what did she mean—No?

He guided her, unresisting, to a small love seat and sat beside her. She cried into his shoulder. He waited—indeed, all his recent life seemed to have been *waiting*—for what he thought was the right moment. Finally he said, in a gentle rallying voice, "It is a good thing I am not a Corinthian, else I would regret my coat's being ruined. Weston, you must know, looks dimly upon a wet jacket."

She moved to pull away, but he held her tight. Still cradling her head on his shoulder, he murmured in her ear, "I'm sorry to make my offer in such a public way, but I was sincere, you know. I truly was serious. Chloe—look at me." She looked up at him. He thought she was even more beautiful with her eyes drowned in tears and her lips trembling. "Now, Chloe, believe me. I should like you to share my life. I'm throwing myself at your feet." Then, lifting an eyebrow when he saw that she still was not amused, he said, "Shall I go down on one knee?"

In spite of herself, she gurgled in amusement and said, "Of course not." But she wondered, had he gone down on his knee to Penelope Salton, or whoever?

Chloe could not bring herself to accept him. At length, he pointed out that her family thought them already betrothed. "And are you going out and say that I was mistaken?" She shook her head mutely. "Then what will you do, if you don't marry me?"

At length she asked him, in a weak voice, "Can I get Highmoor back?"

Richard took a long time to answer. Finally he said, "If Edward has sold it, and does not know to whom he's sold it, then I see no way to do it." He took her hands in his, and said, "Does Highmoor mean so much to you?"

She said, "It is only that I don't know what I should do."

"Well," he said, "you know you may not be comfortable here after all this."

"I know," she said, "and I do not know what possessed me to say all the awful things I said." Forlornly, she said to him, "I have no fortune. You have forgotten that, I think?"

Richard, sturdily, said, "It's good that I have kept beforehand with the world then."

Richard was head over heels in love, but even so he was on the verge of exasperation with his beloved. Chloe remained silent, and he could not know what lay behind her sad eyes.

Her thoughts were a mixture of shadow and sunlight, as a March day. She had long dreamed of Richard, and had come to know that her future, if it did not contain him, was not worth the living. But yet, having happiness handed to her on a platter, so to speak, she feared it. She did not wish to reach for it, lest it vanish and leave her to desolation. But what else could she do?

Finally, she placed her hand in his, and said, "Richard, I am so grateful."

Richard was suddenly savagely furious. "Don't say that to me! Never again tell me you're grateful!"

She had an uneasy feeling that she must throw a sop to Providence. She feared lest she wake up and find it all a dream. She said, to ease her superstitious fear, "What else can I do? I can't stay here, and I've lost Highmoor."

His disappointment was keen, for he had thought she had a regard for him. If she were taking him as only a last resort, as an alternative to staying at Rothwell Manor and being ground into bits by her unappreciative family, then so be it. He had to trust that after this shock was over and she grew used to the idea, she would once again look at him as she had less than an hour ago across the hall in the Green Salon.

He rallied, and said, "I agree—you may not stay here very long. Our wedding must take place as soon as is convenient." Seeing her nod agreement, he pursued the matter a little farther. "Did you really want Highmoor that much?"

She said, tremulously, "Just owning something gratified me. And it seemed to me the beginning of a life that was all my own."

Richard, at sea on an outgoing tide, hardly knew what to say. He murmured, "You will have a free hand at Davenant Hall."

Chloe, having lived through an experience that was devastating to her, was equally at sea. The words came from her without her thinking, for she had no known landmarks to guide her. She had lashed out at her family, told Edward to be quiet, accused the others of being selfish. To cap it all off, she was now, so it seemed, truly betrothed to Richard.

This was the thought that was uppermost. She was engaged to Richard, and he had arranged this only because she was so desolate.

She fumbled an explanation. "I really want you to be happy, Richard, and I will try my best. Indeed, I shall not object," she added in charity, but not in fact, "if you keep your other interests."

She thought, but later could not be sure, that she had told him point-blank that she knew his heart was elsewhere even though his honor was now bound to her. She was confused now so that she did not remember what thoughts had found vocal expression and what still lay too deep in her heart for speech.

Richard, for his part, was as thunderstruck as she. He had thought she was in love with him, and he still believed so. But he had thought all he had to do was fix his interest with her, that she was waiting eagerly for his offer, and all would be well. All he had had to do, he had told himself, was at the proper time to sweep away the other suitors and offer Chloe his heart and hand. He had had no doubt that she would accept with joy.

Now, if his understanding of her words was correct, she was taking him as a last resort, for she had nothing else that she could do. She did not care even enough to hope that he would not keep what she called his other interests—she didn't even want his whole self. Now, he was wounded where he never thought to be vulnerable.

He took her hand and said, "Let us return to your family."

They crossed back to the Green Salon, Chloe clinging to Richard's hand as though it were the only block of flotsam in the ocean.

Lady Rothwell, still seething with anger but having had time to recollect the advantages that a marriage to Sir Richard Davenant might give, and swiftly altering her plans for Lydia and Sophy to march with her "stepdaughter Lady Davenant in London," had begun to be reconciled.

Lady Rothwell insisted that Chloe stay at Rothwell Manor until the wedding. She must preserve the appearances of decency, "even though," said Lady Rothwell, "this whole hubble-bubble is not to my liking. In my day, this kind of behavior would not have been countenanced."

Richard said, in his quiet way, "I quite agree. However, I am anxious for the wedding—and I hope that two months will be sufficient time. I should like to take Chloe to my cousin, Lady Theale's, for a visit, and I shall write to her at once to find out a convenient time."

On his way out, he caught Edward's eye, and the two of them left together. At the door, Richard said, "I know there will be details—Chloe's mother's dowry will, of course, be tranferred to her as Lady Davenant. But my man Aston in London will handle the details."

Edward nodded, and said, "I'm sure you will find the accounts in good order."

Richard, sensing Edward's downcast mood, reassured him. "I never thought otherwise."

Edward, laboring under a strong sense of injustice and

disappointment, said simply, "I thought it was all for the best."

Richard, speaking from the depths of his recent interview with Chloe, "That's all either of us thought to do—what was best, in our limited view."

Edward said in a burst of confidence, "I'm glad she's marrying you. This whole business of flies around the honeypot was not to my taste."

Richard spared a thought to Edward's short memory. He certainly had advocated Thaddeus Invers with all his strength.

Edward continued, "I just wanted to see her settled. Now, as near neighbors, all will be well. We will not truly have lost Chloe."

Richard nodded, feeling a growing regard for Edward, beset as he was by such scatter-brained females. "Her family," said Richard, "took Chloe for granted, but she is a pearl of great price. Too bad you learned it too late."

But Richard was speaking more truly for himself. He left Edward and returned to Davenant Hall. His thoughts—it seemed that his thoughts always were in turmoil when he left Rothwell Manor—were busy. Even observing Chloe with more sensitivity than the Rothwells could manage, yet he failed to understand.

He had considered Chloe as a country lady, without experience, and with dreams in her head of marrying and setting up a household. But he was wrong.

Chloe had the beginnings of a search for something more—a search for independence, and even, so Richard was beginning to understand, for a certain integrity. It was the only word he could think of—for independence was not the answer. No one was independent. Even he himself was not independent without a staff of servants, a number of tenant farmers, a man of affairs, and others who ministered to him. Integrity was the word. Chloe Rothwell was to be herself—she was not Lady Rothwell's stepdaughter, she would not be Richard's wife—she would be simply Chloe.

Richard was learning more than suited his palate. But whatever Chloe wanted—he vowed to himself—she would have. Even though Richard's own wishes might fall by the wayside.

He informed his butler as he came in the entrance of

Davenant Hall, "You may wish me happy, for I am marrying Miss Rothwell."

Dall was delighted, and allowed his happiness to show in his eyes. Not the least of all reasons was, because, reading the signs in the wind, he had quietly placed bets against long odds and stood by this marriage to win a year's wages.

Richard, for a bridegroom, was not happy. Dall watched him shut himself away in the book room, and the butler felt uneasily that his winnings might be fading away. If Sir Richard did not make it to the altar, then all bets were off.

Over the next week, Richard's fears unwittingly paralleled his butler's. He visited Chloe daily, and found Chloe civil but very quiet.

Trying to rouse her to a display of interest, he mentioned changes that she might wish to make at Davenant Hall. "For you must know," he told her, "that you will have full rein over the house."

Chloe, clearly evasive, said, "Your mother's taste was impeccable, Richard. I do not think I should change anything."

To one subject after another broached by Richard, Chloe turned a deaf ear or returned an evasive answer. Once, Richard said, seeing the puppy frolicking at their feet, "At least Nimrod will be happy, rejoining his littermates." It was clear that Chloe was sunk in misery and when Chloe was miserable, Richard himself could not be happy.

The pearls had miraculously reappeared, and the other members of the household had regained their good humor. The wedding plans were going on apace, and Richard told Chloe that his cousin Nell was asking for them to come next week. Chloe apathetically agreed.

The Rothwells were planning the wedding. Lady Rothwell had given an order to Miss Sinclair, with Edward's full approval, for Chloe's wedding dress. There were guests to be invited, and plans for the reception to be made. Lady Rothwell found herself at sea without Chloe's competent management. She spoke quietly to Edward. "Tell me about money—how much will I have to spend?"

Edward could hardly believe that his mother was so chastened. Clearly this summer had changed them all in one way or another. He said, "We're out of debt, and I should say we couldn't have done it without Chloe's income to help us. We owe her a fine wedding."

Lady Rothwell, revealing her innermost thoughts, said, "We must make her proud of us, so she'll be glad to have Lydia to stay in town. In due course, naturally."

Edward, flaring up unjustly, spoke harshly. "Haven't you done enough to Chloe already?"

For Chloe herself, all the wedding plans went ahead as though on another continent. As it had taken a long time to build up to the explosion, so it took a long time wandering among the shards of her life, before she could begin to pick up a piece or two and try to fit them together again.

She was deprived of the moral support of her family, as though the foundations of her life had been swept away. She still resented their taking her for granted, yet being a kind person, she was shamed by her very resentment. But she had nothing to put in the place of the foundations which were gone.

She had Richard, of course. He had always been her Great Friend, but now he was that no longer. Even her relationship with him had changed, and she did not think it for the better. He had almost married, so she believed, someone else, and now he was betrothed to Chloe. Her own need had swerved Richard's course. Though she herself had always loved Richard, she knew in her heart the truth—having all she ever wanted within her grasp, she was the most miserable of creatures!

28

Having gained his heart's desire, Sir Richard Davenant should have been a happy man. He had routed Chloe's suitors, as Odysseus home from his years of wandering had cleared his own hall of Penelope's harassers.

He had found that he was, more than he believed he

ever could be, deeply in love. It was a passion strengthened by long acquaintance, and a steady friendship, and such a love would last his lifetime.

But his unwilling bride did not share his happiness, and thus, inevitably, Richard sank into a blue-deviled mood so low that even his worst enemy could not have faulted it.

He had thought Chloe returned his regard. She turned to him at the slightest excuse, just as she had when they were play fellows in the sunlit days of their childhood. By no stretch of fancy could he believe that their regard at that time was love—or was that the beginning of his own love for her? Perhaps it was.

The question was—had that early regard deepened in Chloe as it had in him?

Her refusal to look at him, her sudden loss of speech when he was near, her retreat into inarticulateness as complete as that idiot Hensley's, spoke volumes for her. She did not want to talk to her betrothed. If propriety had not ruled her, he was sure she would have bolted when he entered the room.

Once more he began the walk to the Manor. This time he would try to penetrate Chloe's reserve, to make her confide in him. If she only would tell him what he had done to distress her, or what he could alter in himself to please her, he would try. Better that than a life bereft of all happiness and the comfort of a congenial marriage.

Deep in his own thoughts, he shied like a highly bred steed when an apparition bolted out of the shrubbery beside the road and stood in his path.

It took a moment, but he recognized her. "Sophy! It's a good thing for me I wasn't riding! If you shot out in front of my Thunder, he would have me in the nearest tree!"

"For heaven's sake, Richard, I know better than to scare your horse. You're not riding, are you? Then there's no harm."

He shook his head slightly, as though to clear the cobwebs out. "I had not thought a strain of eccentricity ran through Chloe's family. I see I should have investigated her background."

"Don't talk fustian!" directed Sophy. "You know I want to talk to you, and there's no way I can get you alone back there." She jerked her head in the direction of Rothwell Manor.

"I should hope not," murmured Richard. "You want to talk to me? Then here I am."

"It's Chloe," said Sophy succinctly.

Intrigued, Richard encouraged her. "What about Chloe?"

"She's not happy. She doesn't want to marry you, Richard. It's like all of us—she wants what she can't have." Her adult wisdom sat oddly on her plumpish adolescent figure. How much of what she said was truth, Richard could not know. But what she told him marched only too well with his own thoughts.

"What *does* she want?" said Richard, a queer feeling in his chest.

"Highmoor," Sophy informed. "It's all she talks about. When she talks. I myself think she is going mad."

Richard wished to be alone with his thoughts, fearing that his face might reveal more of them than he wished, especially to this precocious child. "What's that noise?" he said sharply. "Someone watching——"

Sophy sped up the drive toward the Manor like a startled doe, but without grace. Richard watched her pounding retreat until she reached the end of the plantings and emerged on the lawn in sight of the Manor. Then he turned toward home. He could not face Chloe today.

Once again, he was faced with decision. The measure of his regard for her was his wish that she be happy, even at the cost of his own happiness. She wanted to be free—she had said—and if that meant free both of the Rothwells and of Richard, then he was in a position to grant her wish.

Dall, opening the door for Sir Richard as he strode purposefully into the house, saw in his mind's eye his gambling winnings winging their way into oblivion. Sir Richard had made the right decision, but Dall feared that they would never get as far as the altar.

She wants Highmoor, thought Richard, closing the door to his book room behind him and crossing to the big chair behind the mammoth desk. A place of her own, she had said—with someone bringing her tea. The beginning of a life that was all her own.

"I've meddled," he told his desk, "to no purpose. She had no choice but to accept me." A long time later, he added, "Well, I'll meddle once more, to set things right."

His thoughts moved on to the future. The rooms at Davenant Hall were no longer full of Chloe. His rigid self-discipline told him he must be forever separated from her quiet wit, her common sense, her kindly tolerance. He would never again contrive to amuse her in order to catch sight of the dimple on her left cheek. Her steadfast gaze, her clear integrity—all these he had lost because he had thought he knew best.

"I'm no better than Edward!" he muttered, slamming his fist into his open palm.

The invitation from Richard's cousin Nell came, almost as promptly as Richard could have wished, to Rothwell Manor. Chloe opened it at breakfast—one boon she had earned now was to open her own mail!—and read it through welling tears.

Nell Theale welcomed Chloe into the family with open arms. "I cannot wait—simply *cannot*—for your wedding to see you. Please come for a visit, *now*, and if you arrive tomorrow it will not be a moment too soon. Tell Richard to bring you. . . ."

Lady Rothwell asked, "What have you got there, Chloe? An answer to my wedding invitation? I wonder they sent it to you and not to me, but then, manners are sadly declining in this day."

Chloe dutifully read the letter aloud, to her stepmother's gratification. "I knew all along that Sir Richard was the one for you, Chloe. Lady Theale is a lady of impeccable breeding, and had the wit to marry Lord Theale, who has a prodigious fortune. I am sure you will be very comfortable in her house."

"But I'm not going," said Chloe remotely.

"I insist that you go," said Lady Rothwell, oppressively. "I cannot endure your mopes much longer, Chloe. I tell you for your own good, and I should not be surprised if Davenant doesn't have a second thought about his offer. You must go, Chloe. It is your duty, both to me and to him. Go and put as good a face on it as you can. Many a maid has made a worse marriage than yours, and I cannot help but wonder at the strong strain of ungratefulness in you . . ."

In two days, Chloe set off with Richard for the day's drive to Theale. "Be sure to bring her back in two weeks, for I do not permit Chloe to be wed from any place other than her home," called Lady Rothwell.

Richard answered tightly, "I'll bring her back, you may depend on it."

The ride passed as though in a dream to Chloe. Even seeing Nell again failed to raise her spirits, although her hostess made much of her. But Nell looked past Chloe at her cousin, and was dismayed to see the grim lines bracketing his mouth—lines that had not been there a month before.

Richard lost no time in putting his plan into motion. The second day after their arrival, having given Chloe a chance to rest from the journey, he insisted that she go with him on a drive.

"Now that we're betrothed," he said, "we do not need my groom to accompany us."

A picnic hamper was bound to the boot at the rear, and they set off down the drive, as Nell and Theale waved them on their way.

"Something badly wrong there," pronounced Theale.

"Never mind, Richard will fix it. He always does," said his optimistic cousin brightly. She wished she believed it.

The drive took turns Chloe did not notice. The land folded into small valleys, and the road they followed rose even higher. At last they turned onto a small road, hardly more than a wagon track. They drove along hedges that had not been pruned in this century, until finally they reached a pair of crumbling gates. The letters on the pillars had eroded until the name could not be made out. All she could see, before they turned between the gates was "H———OR." It couldn't be—but it was!

At last she was entering the grounds of Highmoor! Her heart thudded painfully. But it was too late. Highmoor was forever out of her reach.

She asked timidly, "Won't the new owner object?"

He covered her hand with his. "No."

She fell silent. Events had moved beyond her, she realized, and she was borne on the surface of a current she could not resist.

They drove up the graveled drive, overgrown with grass, until they reached the sweep before the door. She stared at the house that had been hers, for a little while.

It was not precisely a ruin, she decided, but before long it could be. There was a general aura of decay emanating from the house, manifest in small things like a shutter

missing a fastening and hanging loose, a crack in the front step—items a careful owner would set right at once.

To her surprise, they stopped before the door and Richard helped her down. She stood on the porch while he tethered the horse, and waited for him to join her. He tried the latch, and the door opened at once.

"Richard——" she protested, but he waved her in before him.

"Don't worry," he said, "I know the owner."

Thus reassured, she moved, tentatively at first and then with more assurance, through the rooms of Highmoor. She had fancied them so long in her mind, but the reality bore no resemblance to her dreams. Here, in the small salon, she had thought of her afternoon tea. But the window was too small to permit a chair to be placed to admire the view.

The dining room seemed oddly bare, until she realized that the marks on the wall indicated an enormous sideboard for serving—a piece of furniture no longer in place.

"Probably sold," said Richard, "for I have heard that Bradford was sorely pressed for funds toward the end."

She moved from the dining room to another, and then another room. All were small, she found, and sadly ill-arranged. The wallpaper was stained, and in places torn. She moved to the doors to the terrace.

As Lady Rothwell had informed her family, the terrace commanded a fine prospect. She could not see the grape planting from here, but she had no doubt it did exist, probably reverted to a wilderness by now.

But she was caught up in a spell of what-might-have-been. "I could have been happy here, I thought, with dear Bess and a cook," she said to Richard. "But it's out of the question now."

Richard, his features grim and tight, went out to the phaeton. She could see him through the riotous vine that covered the tiny window looking onto the drive, making the room dusky as twilight. He took the basket out of the boot. She had no appetite for lunch, but she began to realize how much Richard was trying to cheer her. She saw him crossing the drive, and saw—as Nell had seen—the lines in his face that spoke emphatically of misery. Full of compunction, Chloe moved toward a decision she must make. She knew she could not wed Richard, not when he

was pining for the woman he wanted. She could not become his wife knowing he still held another in the core of his heart.

He came into the room with the basket, and she managed a smile. "Lunch?" she asked, with an attempt at brightness.

Richard opened the basket. But instead of boxes of sandwiches, ham, bottles of wine, clusters of grapes—he brought forth a paper, rolled into a tight shape like a waterpipe. Looking steadily at her, he said, "I had hoped to give this to you as your wedding present. But since it is most unlikely that there will be a wedding, I wish you to have it now. As a belated betrothal gift."

Automatically she took the proffered document. But her heart sank into her slippers. He could not stomach the idea of marrying her. Perversely, while she had vowed to give him his freedom, the idea that he was repelled by her was distressing in the extreme.

The roll, as she glanced through it and then read it more carefully, was the deed to Highmoor. "Highmoor is yours," said Richard harshly. "To do with as you wish."

"You b-bought Highmoor?" she stammered, unbelieving. "*You?*"

"Your idiot brother," pronounced Richard, "wanted to sell, so since I knew what Highmoor meant to you, I thought you should have it."

She had her life in her hands, in this apparently insignificant roll of official paper. Highmoor was hers, to live in with her maid and her cook, to exist in peace away from people she had lately learned to mistrust. She could make the house over, she could spend her day refurbishing, restoring, mending linen—all by herself in perfect solitary peace.

The silence lengthened and she knew she must say something to him, for he had done so much for her. By ill chance, she burst out, "What a Great Friend you are!"

Her eyes misted over, and she did not see the dreadful, desperate expression that crossed his face.

I've bungled all the way, he thought. I misread the signs from the beginning. At first it was only what I wanted, he analyzed his motives—now I've turned to look at what *she* wants. A new Richard—but too late. She deserves better than me!

She held the deed in her hand, her eyes full of unshed tears. Like an anchor, he thought. "How can I pay you for this?"

His voice rasped, on a note she had never heard. "Now you won't have to marry anyone, not even me!"

Her emotions gave up the battle and joined forces in one mighty surge of anger. "Then Miss Venable, or is it Miss Morland or Miss Salton—*whoever!*—will be greatly relieved at your eligibility once more!"

He gazed at her speechlessly, before stalking out, stiff-legged with anger and hurt.

He moved out onto the terrace, but the fine prospect did not exist for him. His hopes lay in shards around his feet. He had been cast down before, but now he was as one shut out from the warmth of the hearthfire, into the cold, cold night, to wander fitfully for the rest of his life.

The breeze came up the slope and, without his knowing it, beguiled the anger in him until it began to cool, and he remembered hearing once—Where there is no love, then there is no reason for anger. He was well aware of the cause of his own anger, but was it possible? In Chloe's outburst, there was a tinge—the very slightest tinge, he thought—of *jealous woman*. Could she have been so blind as to think he wanted to marry someone else, and was forced by circumstance to offer for her?

If so, he thought confusedly—but on the other hand, she had clutched the deed to Highmoor as though she were clinging to a lifeline in heavy surf, her only hope. . . .

A wave of tenderness swept over him. His dear Chloe! Perhaps there was yet a chance. He turned to go in to her.

She stood in the doorway. Her face was pale and her eyes shone with her tears, but there was a different look about her, a sense of awakening hope. "Richard, why did you buy Highmoor?"

Very gently, he answered her. "Because I love you."

Softly, she cried, "Oh Richard!" She dropped the deed as though she didn't know she held it. She ran to him, and he opened his arms and folded them around her, holding her tightly against the world.

They stood so for a long time, on the terrace of Highmoor, unaware of the fine prospect below the terrace, oblivious to all but each other.

The wind drove the rolled-up deed hither and yon on the terrace as though it were no longer a thing of any importance.

And it wasn't.

ABOUT THE AUTHOR

Vanessa Gray grew up in Oak Park, Illinois, and graduated from the University of Chicago. She currently lives in the farm country of northeastern Indiana, where she pursues her interest in the history of Georgian England and the Middle Ages. She is the author of a number of best-selling Regencies. THE MASKED HEIRESS, THE LONELY EARL, THE WICKED GUARDIAN, and THE WAYWARD GOVERNESS, available in Signet editions.

Big Bestsellers from SIGNET

- ☐ **THE ENIGMA** by Michael Barak. (#E8920—$1.95)*
- ☐ **GOING ALL THE WAY** by Susan Hufford. (#E9014—$2.25)*
- ☐ **HEIR TO KURAGIN** by Constance Heaven. (#E9015—$1.95)†
- ☐ **PACIFIC HOSPITAL** by Robert H. Curtis. (#J9018—$1.95)*
- ☐ **SAVAGE SNOW** by Will Holt. (#E9019—$2.25)*
- ☐ **THE ETRUSCAN SMILE** by Velda Johnston. (#E9020—$2.25)
- ☐ **CALENDAR OF SINNERS** by Moira Lord. (#J9021—$1.95)*
- ☐ **THE NIGHT LETTER** by Paul Spike. (#E8947—$2.50)*
- ☐ **SUNSET** by Christopher Nicole. (#E8948—$2.25)*
- ☐ **HARVEST OF DESTINY** by Erica Lindley. (#J8919—$1.95)*
- ☐ **MADAM TUDOR** by Constance Gluyas. (#J8953—$1.95)*
- ☐ **TIMES OF TRIUMPH** by Charlotte Vale Allen.

  (#E8955—$2.50)*
- ☐ **THE FUR PERSON** by May Sarton. (#W8942—$1.50)
- ☐ **FOOLS DIE** by Mario Puzo. (#E8881—$3.50)
- ☐ **THE GODFATHER** by Mario Puzo. (#E8970—$2.75)

  * Price slightly higher in Canada

  † Not available in Canada

Buy them at your local bookstore or use this convenient coupon for ordering.

THE NEW AMERICAN LIBRARY, INC.,
P.O. Box 999, Bergenfield, New Jersey 07621

Please send me the SIGNET BOOKS I have checked above. I am enclosing
$_____ (please add 50¢ to this order to cover postage and handling).
Send check or money order—no cash or C.O.D.'s. Prices and numbers are
subject to change without notice.

Name _____

Address _____

City_____ State_____ Zip Code_____
Allow 4-6 weeks for delivery.
This offer is subject to withdrawal without notice.